$\mathcal{S}$hadows *of*
BRIERLEY

In the Valley of the Mountains

VOLUME FOUR

Shadows of BRIERLEY

In the Valley of the Mountains

VOLUME FOUR

a novel

ANITA STANSFIELD

Covenant Communications, Inc.

To my new and dear friend in Scotland, Liz Bear.

And a special thank you to Kathryn Anderson,
for once again offering her expertise in history.

Chapter One
Gillian's Wish

Salt Lake City, Utah—1862

Gillian Brierley stepped out of the house and paused on the back porch to lift her face to the summer sun and enjoy its warmth. She knew that in a few hours the July heat would become unbearable. But at this early hour its rays felt pleasant, and she basked in it as she descended the back steps and headed across the neatly manicured grass toward the immense garden at the edge of the yard. She quickly set to work pulling weeds from the long rows of vegetables that were thriving brilliantly from the irrigation water that was guided painstakingly into the valley on a regular basis. Normally Gillian's father joined her in the garden at this early hour to keep the weeds under control before the sun got too hot, but today he was keeping a close eye on Gillian's mother, who was about to give birth. He was also making certain Gillian's younger siblings each did their chores and pitched in to help prepare breakfast. Those who weren't assigned to help cook would be on the cleanup crew, the entire family working together to keep the household running while Wren Brierley was confined to bed until after this child was born. Wren never seemed to mind the sacrifices and suffering she endured when it came to the opportunity to bring another child into this world. She loved her large family, and she was an excellent mother. But each birth jeopardized her health a little more, and Gillian's father, Ian, worried each time his wife faced the uncertainty of childbirth, especially now that Wren was getting older and her body was not as resilient as it used to be.

Gillian had always shared a close relationship with her mother, and since she'd become an adult, she had assumed a significant role in helping Wren through the process of childbirth and the weeks of recovery that followed. There were aspects of bringing a child into the world that were frightening to Gillian, and these made her wonder if she had it in her to actually endure the suffering required. But the results always appeared to be worth any pain her mother endured. Wren would declare boldly that every bit of the pain and discomfort were hugely compensated for when that infant took its first breath. Gillian had been a close observer of the joy her younger siblings had brought to her parents and to the rest of the family. Each new addition made them all wonder how they'd ever managed minus the most recent member arriving to make the family complete. But the birth of the youngest, little Gavin, who had just turned two, had been especially difficult on Wren, and Ian had declared that Gavin would be the last. This most recent pregnancy had come as a surprise, since the doctor had said that Wren had shown signs of being past that stage in life when conception was possible. But apparently it still was, and so another baby was due to arrive soon. Wren had been confined to bed for more than a month now, and Ian had been tense with nervousness, even though he did well at concealing it most of the time, especially around the younger children.

Gillian did her best to be supportive to her parents, since she had the maturity and sensitivity to see how difficult this was on them. But there were certain things that only a parent could do in the way of comforting a child and spending the time with the children that they needed in order to feel loved and secure. Weeding the garden, however, was something that Gillian *could* do, and it did ease some strain for her father. The other children who were old enough were each required to spend a certain amount of time each week pulling weeds, but Gillian enjoyed being out here on her own without the noisy chatter or complaints of her siblings to distract her from her daydreaming. She hummed quietly as she made her knees comfortable in the recently watered soil, not caring that her dress would come away with muddy spots that would give away where she'd been spending her time. She loved the feel of the soil on her hands, and she admired the beauty of the thriving vegetable plants in contrast to the growing piles of weeds that were being removed. She felt almost powerful in her ability to stop the lives of the nuisance plants whose only purpose was to inhibit the growth of the fruit-bearing plants that needed to thrive in order to contribute to the needs of a growing family.

Gillian became aware of a familiar sensation while she worked. She stopped humming in order to pay closer attention. She had known since she was very young that it was rare for people to be able to see and hear the things that she saw and heard. A few years earlier she'd had the opportunity to visit with one of the Apostles concerning her gift, and he had verified himself that it was indeed a God-given gift, and he'd quoted Moroni chapter 10, verse 14, from the Book of Mormon—which was the very verse that her mother had been led to by the Spirit early in Gillian's childhood when this issue had first come up. Gillian didn't need an Apostle to personally tell her that her gift was from God, and that her intentions and actions related to it were righteous. She had known from many, many experiences over the course of her life that it was true and real and right. But some people were put off by it if they became aware of it, and while it was a remarkable gift, it was also accompanied by intense opposition at times—as are all good things in this life. *The gift of the beholding of angels and ministering spirits.* That's what it said in the Book of Mormon, and Gillian had that gift.

Over the years she had deeply pondered the gift and its implications. She had prayerfully sought to understand its purpose, and she had learned very clearly how to discern light from darkness. She had found great confidence in her gift, knowing that Satan could not deceive her as long as she earnestly and righteously sought the guidance of the Spirit. Satan and his evil followers could not mimic or counterfeit the peaceful joy of the Holy Ghost—no matter how hard they tried.

While Gillian quietly pulled weeds, surrounded by a stillness that was broken only by the singing of birds in nearby trees, she had a subtle sense of not being alone. The feeling was familiar, but she often had to prayerfully ask questions in the quiet of her mind and listen carefully for the answers to know who it was that had been allowed by the Savior to ease a little farther through the veil and make his or her presence known.

The garden is lovely, Gillian heard more as an impression in her mind than an actual voice. Sometimes it was the other way around. It was common for her to turn at the sound of a voice and find no one there. But today, it was simply a quiet whisper inside her head.

It is lovely, isn't it, Gillian responded with her thoughts and smiled. *Who are you?* she added, not even certain yet if the spirit was male or female, but she sensed a strong connection and felt certain her visitor had a family connection.

"Good morning, Miss Brierley," a mortal, male voice said and startled Gillian from her sweet reverie. She turned and saw the younger Brother Skimpole leaning over the fence that separated their yards. The height of the fence was a perfect fit for him to lean his arms there, and he was resting his chin on his arm very comfortably. She wondered how long he'd been there watching her, and she felt mildly unnerved. It wasn't that she felt afraid of Brother Skimpole, and she certainly wasn't intimidated by him. He was just . . . strange. She reminded herself—as she always did in their encounters—that he too was a child of God and she needed to be kind and appropriate. But that didn't change her opinion of him. And she found him . . . strange.

"Good morning," she said and turned her attention back to her weeding, determined not to let his interference deter her from accomplishing as much as she could before the sun became too hot.

"You're looking lovely, as usual," he added. Gillian glanced at him to try to assess his possible motives in making such a comment. His reddish blond hair—what little there was of it—was slicked down over his head with a distinct part on one side that always seemed oddly off balance, as if he had guided the comb to create a line where God had never intended hair to be parted. His complexion was ruddy and pale, and his eyes reminded her of a relaxed puppy who couldn't make eye contact with any human for more than a second or two.

The younger Brother Skimpole lived with his aged father. His mother was dead, and his siblings had long ago left the Salt Lake Valley to pursue their own lives in marriage and distinguished careers. But the younger Brother Skimpole seemed to love the fact that his father needed to be cared for. His apparent lack of motivation to do anything more than see to his father's needs was unimpressive to Gillian. She knew that the older Brother Skimpole had received a significant inheritance some years back, and they were therefore self-sufficient. Such a situation was rare around here, and ironically Gillian's own family shared the same blessing. Her father had come from a *very* wealthy family in the Highlands of Scotland, and they were living quite comfortably on his inheritance. But that didn't keep her father from working hard to personally help run the household, care for the animals, grow food for the family, and keep the yard in good order. Of course, he enlisted the help of the children in order to teach them the importance of work each and every day. Ian Brierley also contributed many hours each week to the building of the temple. Gillian considered the possibility that it wasn't fair to compare Brother Skimpole to her father. But Ian was a fine man with the characteristics that Gillian wanted to find in her own husband. How could she not compare his strong work ethic, his humility, his spirituality, and his tenderness to every man she met who showed any interest in her? And frankly, Brother Skimpole couldn't measure up to even a small degree. He hired someone to clean the house and cook, and he hired someone else to keep the yard in good repair. He didn't grow a garden or spend any time working on the temple, due to his "dreadfully inconvenient health matters." She'd heard him use the phrase many times, but her attempts to kindly inquire over what *exactly* that meant were always met with vague answers and downright avoidance. She'd never personally seen evidence of him struggling physically, except perhaps with the fact that he didn't get enough exercise or enough sun. He only seemed to come outdoors when he had an opportunity to annoy Gillian and disrupt a rarely peaceful moment.

Gillian ignored his compliment and said, "How is your father today, Brother Skimpole?"

"Not awake yet," he said with an unfavorable chuckle, as if it were somehow funny. "Can't say how he is until he's awake."

"Perhaps he's awake now," Gillian said, hoping he would leave to go and check.

"Not for a long while yet," Brother Skimpole said, and Gillian sighed. "Wait just a moment," he added and she sighed more loudly, wishing he could have heard it. She knew what *that* meant, and sure enough a minute later he was actually standing beside her in the garden, having come around the fence. Gillian kept weeding while he rambled about his father's gout and his wish that the woman who cooked for them could come up with a little more variety.

Gillian attempted to defend the cook and still remain polite. "With our limited resources here in the valley, I would think it's difficult to come up with too much variety."

Brother Skimpole ignored her comment and went on with his complaints. Feeling ignored was something that didn't settle well with Gillian at all. She came to her feet and attempted to brush the dirt from her hands, determined to remove herself from the conversation—whatever it took. She was formulating an excuse in her head when Brother Skimpole surprised her by taking her hand in an awkward handshake, saying, "You *do* look lovely today, Miss Brierley," as if the words were deeply significant.

Gillian felt a little nauseated, her instincts confirming what she had only suspected previously: Brother Skimpole was showing a romantic interest in her, likely with the hope that she would marry him, move into the house on the other side of the fence, and allow him to fire the woman who cooked and kept house. Gillian felt startled by his clammy and limply passive handshake. The very idea of being married to such a man inspired a deep desire in her to remain a spinster until the next life. Perhaps the right man for her was a long-deceased Nephite warrior who had fought diligently and died young on the battlefield, and he was even now watching over her as an angel. Perhaps the right match would not present itself in this life. As disappointing as such a thought felt to her, looking into the sheep-like eyes of Brother Skimpole made the idea much more appealing.

Gillian removed her hand as politely as she could and again focused on finding an excuse to remove herself from the present situation. At that very moment she heard the approach of a horse. She and Brother Skimpole both turned at the same time to see a rider coming up the long drive that stretched out along the fence connecting the street to the large barn behind the house, curving around the garden where Gillian had been enjoying a pleasant reprieve until Brother Skimpole had intruded on it.

Gillian immediately recognized Hugh Montgomery and felt deeply relieved by *his* intrusion. He was a very good friend to the entire family, and Gillian felt very comfortable with him. Even though he was near her father's age, the two of them had shared many stimulating conversations over the years. They shared a great deal of history, and he was much like an uncle to her, or perhaps more an older brother, even though their age difference made such a relationship unlikely. Hugh had been baptized nearly twenty years earlier in London by Ian Brierley when he'd been serving a mission there. Hugh had then come to live in Nauvoo, where Gillian had been living with her mother and two younger siblings while Ian had been away serving the Lord. Gillian's first encounter with Hugh had been the day she'd been lost in the woods and he had been the one to find her. Of all the people that had been in the search party, scouring every part of the city of Nauvoo, it was ironic that Hugh Montgomery had been the one to rescue her. Gillian clearly remembered the feeling of being lifted into his arms and carried back to the safety of her mother's embrace. She'd never lost that secure feeling with Hugh. In spite of their age difference, he was a dear friend and she was always glad to see him.

"Hello," Gillian said eagerly as Hugh dismounted his horse and looped the reins around the fence. She wondered if Brother Skimpole would detect her enthusiasm in contrast to the distinct lack of it she had displayed toward him.

"Hello," Hugh said. He nodded toward Brother Skimpole with a polite smile, but Gillian knew him well enough to know that he too was displeased with this man's presence.

Brother Skimpole nodded in return and scurried away like a mouse at the appearance of a cat, mumbling something over his shoulder about needing to check on his father. For some reason, he was apparently intimidated by Brother Montgomery.

"My knight in shining armor," Gillian said to Hugh. "If you'd not shown up to rescue me, I would have needed to come up with some other means of escape, which would have required going back into the house where the noise is just getting started."

"It's always a pleasure to be your rescuer," Hugh said and smiled. Gillian smiled in return, and their eyes met for a moment while they silently shared the memory of him carrying her to safety when she was a child.

Hugh was a fine-looking man, with broad shoulders, dark hair combed back off his face, and a gentle countenance that was almost contradicted by his distinctive masculinity. He had much in common with Ian Brierley by way of personality and spirituality, and even in his background prior to leaving his former life behind to come to America and embrace the gospel. Hugh's accent was a continual reminder that he had grown up in England, just as Gillian's parents could not open their mouths without being known as natives of Scotland. Gillian had been raised in America and spoke American English, much like most of the people around them. Of course, there were many immigrants from the British Isles and other countries as well here in the great valley where the Saints resided, so accents were not uncommon. But Gillian liked the way that Hugh spoke. There was a melodic quality to his voice that made their conversations all the more pleasant.

Wondering over the purpose of Hugh's visit, Gillian said, "Father is probably in the kitchen with the children if you would like to—"

"I came to see you," he said, which made her smile. "I had a suspicion you might be out here before the sun got too hot."

"How well you know me," she said and went back to her knees to continue pulling weeds. She was pleasantly surprised when Hugh knelt nearby and began to do the same. She felt certain that Brother Skimpole never would have gotten his hands dirty to assist her in any way.

After a few minutes of working in comfortable silence, Gillian pointed out the obvious. "It's very kind of you to come and help me pull weeds, Hugh, but I suspect there's more purpose to your visit than this."

"You know me too well," he said, focused on the work his hands were doing.

"As you do me," she replied and kept working. "Are you missing Felicity?" she asked.

Hugh had been betrothed to a wonderful woman whom he'd met at Winter Quarters in 1847. They had bonded strongly during the journey to Salt Lake City, and he'd proposed marriage to her during the course of the westward exodus. However, they'd not wanted to be married on the trail, traveling every day, while everyone was generally miserable from the heat and the bugs, and where the entire focus was on arriving safely in the valley where they would find peace. Hugh had wanted Felicity to wear a pretty dress for the wedding, and he'd wanted to provide some kind of home for her beyond a covered wagon. But Felicity had died of illness before they ever reached the final mountain pass that led into Salt Lake Valley. She was buried somewhere in Wyoming, and a part of Hugh's heart had remained there with her. He'd many times told Gillian—when he was in an especially sentimental mood—that he believed if they'd been married they would at least be together in eternity. But since no ceremony had taken place, he wondered if that would be the case. Gillian assured him that God's plan of happiness was called that for a reason, and that surely he and Felicity would be perfectly happy in eternity, and if that meant being together, then God would surely work it out.

You always have a way of making everything seem right, he'd said to her dozens of times, but she had said the same to him in regard to her own struggles in life when she'd confided in him.

"You haven't been talking to her, have you?" Hugh asked and tossed a handful of weeds into a growing pile at the edge of the garden. He asked it in a matter-of-fact, straightforward manner that had a way of reassuring and validating Gillian every time he spoke of her gift that way. She had shared her experiences with him, and he had never doubted that they were true. She *had* felt Felicity close more than once, and it had been a great comfort to Hugh. Gillian suspected it was one of the reasons he enjoyed her company so much, simply because she had a closeness to the woman he loved, a closeness that no one else could know or understand.

"Not recently," Gillian said, and they exchanged a comfortable smile. "Nothing new, if that's what you're wondering. Does that mean you *are* missing her?"

"Always," he said. "You would think with this many years passing, it would not be so difficult, but it is."

"I understand," Gillian said, and she did. Hugh had long ago found peace over Felicity's death. He was a man who fully allowed the Atonement into his life and his heart, and he was in no way angry or damaged in regard to the heartbreak of losing her. He simply missed her, and Gillian was one of the few people he could talk to about it. Others were kind about the loss, but it had been so long ago that people would only encourage him to move on and get past it. He'd certainly tried. Gillian had heard firsthand of his many adventures in being matched up with a number of suitable single women of varying ages. But nothing had ever worked for Hugh. He wasn't overly fussy or unwilling to compromise. He'd simply known in each case that marriage was not the right course for him. He was a man who relied on the guidance of the Spirit when it came to significant decisions, and he'd never felt approval to move forward. And so he continued to miss Felicity, but he also went about doing much good everywhere he went. He worked hard keeping track of the accounts for a number of small businesses, and he served others continually; he put hours in each week on the building of the temple, and he lived the gospel to its fullest.

"I know you understand," he said, "and I want you to know that I'm grateful for that. Your company means a great deal to me."

"And to me," she said, and they exchanged another smile.

Silence accompanied their ongoing weed pulling and Gillian wondered if Hugh had come here simply because he'd been feeling more lonely than usual and he'd wanted some company. It wasn't unusual for him to spend a great amount of time with the family. He came and went casually and frequently. He sat with them at church meetings and was involved in practically every family gathering or event, no matter how large or small.

"Would you take a drive with me later today?" he asked.

Gillian stopped working and turned to look at him. A number of times Hugh had offered to take some of the children on an outing to get them out of the house, and she had usually gone along to offer assistance. Occasionally she had accompanied him on an errand simply to be helpful. But she couldn't recall ever actually going anywhere with him unless it had a practical purpose. She tried to think of the right words to ask what the purpose of this outing might entail, but before she could he said, "Just the two of us; just to talk. Would you?"

Gillian couldn't think of a single reason to decline. She sensed something different about his purpose, but the possible reasons intrigued her more than they put her off. The expectancy in his eyes implied that whatever he wanted to talk about was very important. She liked knowing she was such an important confidant in his life. There was no truer friend than Hugh Montgomery, and she felt privileged to have that role.

"As long as I'm not needed here," she said, "then I would like that very much."

"Good," he said and smiled.

"I know it will be hot," he said, "but perhaps we can find a shady spot somewhere to visit and—"

"I can bring a picnic along," she offered.

"That would be nice," he said, smiling again. He had such a nice smile. "But I don't want you to go to any trouble."

"It's no trouble," she said. "I can just pack up something we have on hand."

"It's settled, then," he said and stood, brushing off his hands.

He held out a hand to help her to her feet, and she asked, "Where are we going now?"

"I'm going to help you make certain all the chores are done so that you can leave and not be missed."

Gillian laughed softly. "Are you up to hanging laundry and making sure the little rascals do what they're supposed to do?"

"Oh, I'm up to it," he said, and they walked toward the house. They stopped at the water pump to clean their hands, wiping them dry on the parts of their clothes that weren't dirty from the garden.

They were almost to the back door when Gillian's brothers, Alfred and Harry—ages fifteen and seventeen respectively—came out, responding pleasantly to seeing Hugh, but ignoring Gillian completely. Hugh comfortably teased the boys for a couple of minutes, and even got into some semblance of a lighthearted boxing match with both of them at the same time. He finally laughed and roughed up their hair as if they were toddlers before the boys moved on to the barn to milk the cows, gather eggs, and feed the animals.

Hugh held the door for Gillian, then followed her into the kitchen where Ian was teaching nine-year-old Sarah how to flip a griddle cake. Twelve-year-old Mont was busy keeping little Gavin from climbing into the flour bin, and five-year-old Rachel was setting the table.

"Oh, hello," Ian said to Hugh. His curly black hair, barely showing signs of gray here and there, looked a mess, as if he'd been needed by the children before he'd actually had a chance to comb it. The dark shadow on his face verified the theory; he'd not had time to shave yet, either.

"Hello," Hugh said.

"Looks like you'll need to set a place for Uncle Hugh," Ian said to Rachel just as she hurtled herself into Hugh's arms with a giggle.

"Hello there, little lady," Hugh said and twirled around with her before he set her down then got a similar greeting from Sarah. Hugh greeted Mont much as he had the other boys with boxing motions going back and forth that never actually connected. But Gillian knew that Hugh had a special bond with Mont that had nothing to do with the fact that the boy's name was actually Montgomery, which made him Hugh's namesake. While Hugh played with Mont, Gillian picked up little Gavin to keep him from getting into the flour bin, but Hugh took the toddler from her and said, "I'll keep track of this one for a few minutes."

"It *is* the toughest job in the house," Ian said.

"I think the toughest job is making griddle cakes," Sarah said while she struggled to flip one over without damaging it.

"You're doing brilliantly," Ian said. "It takes some practice."

"I've never been very good at it myself," Hugh said, but Gillian knew that wasn't true. She remembered even as a child watching Hugh make griddle cakes. In fact, she had a specific memory of being on the trail when they were all in the same wagon company coming west, and Hugh would sit by the fire for a ridiculous amount of time, making griddle cakes for a number of hungry people.

Hugh sat down with Gavin on his lap. Gavin was squirming, but Hugh quickly had him engaged in a dramatic game of peek-a-boo that made the other children laugh, including Gillian.

"How is Wren?" Hugh asked Ian in between his histrionic expressions aimed toward Gavin.

"The same," Ian said. "We're just counting days until it's over, even though we don't know how many days that will be."

"She's in my prayers," Hugh said. "You all are."

"I know," Ian said. "And we're grateful."

Gillian fixed a breakfast tray for her mother and took it toward the stairs, declaring that she'd be back to eat with the family before the boys got back in from the barn. She stepped into her parents' bedroom to find her mother partially reclined against several pillows, her long hair scattered, her eyes closed. She looked the same way she'd looked for weeks: bored, and weary, and a little too pale. Wren looked young for her age, in spite of how the years of childbearing had worn her down. Her dark hair, which was a vivid contrast to

Gillian's blonde tresses, didn't show even a hint of gray, and her skin was pleasingly unwrinkled. When Wren was up and about, it wasn't uncommon for strangers to ask if she and Gillian were sisters. Their coloring was entirely different, but they did have a similar look about their faces—something that Gillian was deeply proud of. Ironically, the resemblance came through the fact that Wren's sister was the woman who had given birth to Gillian. Since she'd become an orphan within days of her birth, Ian and Wren Brierley had taken her on as their own, and she'd never felt any evidence of having a status any different in the family from her eight younger siblings.

"Here's your breakfast," Gillian announced.

Wren's eyes came open, and she smiled. "Oh, thank ye, dear," she said. Wren had lived in America for more than twenty years, but her accent still betrayed that she'd been raised in the lower classes of Scotland. But the son of an earl marrying the tailor's daughter was of little consequence here in the American West. They were a family, and nothing else mattered.

Gillian set the tray over Wren's lap, then helped her sit up a little more so that she could comfortably eat. She then curled up on the bed close to her mother, folding her dress so that the residue of dirt from the garden wouldn't come in contact with the bedding. Gillian listened while Wren blessed her food, and she added her own amen. While Wren began eating, Gillian told her about Brother Skimpole's apparent growing romantic interest.

"If ye marry a man like that, I'll have t' disown ye," Wren said facetiously. Gillian knew there was nothing she could do that would *ever* make her parents disown her, but the statement expressed how strongly Wren felt about Gillian marrying a man who could be everything she wanted and deserved. Gillian knew what she wanted in a man and she was not willing to settle for less. But she was beginning to wonder if such a man would ever come into her life. She'd had many long conversations with her mother about all of the important characteristics to look for in a man, but they'd also talked a great deal about feeling the kind of love that could take a person's breath away. Gillian had never felt such a thing, but her parents felt that way about each other, and they had talked about it a great deal. Gillian was determined to find a man of great character who could also take her breath away. It was her greatest wish! Until she did, she would remain single and do her best to make her life of value to God and to those around her.

When she quickly became bored talking about Brother Skimpole, Gillian said, "Hugh is here. He helped me in the garden, and he wants to take me for a drive this afternoon. I'm going to pack a picnic."

Wren looked surprised. "Just the two of ye?"

"Yes," Gillian said. "Do you think that's a problem?"

"No, not at all," Wren said and smiled. "I'm sure ye'll have a lovely time."

Gillian heard a commotion from down the stairs that indicated the boys had come in from the barn and breakfast was being put on the table. She kissed her mother's cheek and made certain she had all she needed before she went down to take her place at the table amidst the rest of the family—and Hugh, who smiled at her across the table just before the blessing was given by Alfred at his father's request. Once the amen was spoken, the chattering and mild chaos of a typical meal began. But Gillian liked the noise and busyness of her family, and she was glad to be here. She had two younger siblings— her brother Donnan and her sister Anya—who had both married fine people and had moved to different settlements south of Salt Lake City. They weren't too far away to visit, but they didn't see each other very often. Gillian hoped when the time came for her to marry that she would be able to remain near her family.

Partway through the meal, Gillian found herself preoccupied with observing her father and his kind interaction with the children. Their different ages and personalities required a great deal of patience, but Ian Brierley had it mastered. Gillian admired and loved her father so deeply that she had difficulty comprehending the importance of his place in her life. She could not have been blessed to have better parents, and it was something she thanked God for every day. And every day she asked God to send her a man who could be the same. She wanted and needed someone who could be everything that Ian Brierley was to his wife and children. Having recently passed her twenty-third birthday, she couldn't help being aware that she had passed the age when the majority of women around here were married and having children. Having two younger siblings who had already entered that season of life didn't help. Gillian had become very good at putting forth the proper attitude and allowing everyone around her to believe that she wasn't worried, that she found joy in her life, and she was content to allow time to take its course. It was partly true. She certainly *did* find joy in her life. But in the deepest part of her heart, she ached for the kind of companionship that she could find only in a good marriage. Sometimes at night when she was alone she couldn't hold back her tears. Only God knew her sorrow, but then, only God could bring the right man into her life. She prayed every day that it might happen soon. She thought of Hugh and wondered how he had dealt with such loneliness for so many years. Her attention turned to his comfortable interaction with her siblings. He had a way of gently teasing them that seemed to magically ease their tension and differences and allowed them to focus instead on laughter. Hugh had a gift for keeping life from getting too serious. Gillian was grateful for the distraction he offered that kept her from her own self-indulgent thoughts, and she turned her focus to her love for her younger siblings, keeping a prayer in her heart that her mother would come through the delivery of this next baby without any complications—for her *or* the baby.

After breakfast, Hugh remained true to his word. He helped Gillian with the laundry in between bouts of supervising the younger children with their chores while Ian and the older boys took the wagon into town in order to purchase supplies. Gillian and Hugh both laughed a great deal as he helped her hang the freshly laundered sheets and the younger children began running in and out of them, playing hide-and-seek. Hugh started chasing them and playing tickle games when he caught them. He made them giggle uncontrollably while Gillian observed and laughed almost as much as the children.

Following a fair amount of fun, Hugh got the children engaged once again in doing their chores, and he kept an eye on little Gavin to keep him out of trouble. Hugh continued his vigil with the children while Gillian helped her mother get cleaned up and made certain she had everything she needed. They chatted comfortably throughout the process, and Gillian was ever grateful that her mother was also her best friend. It occurred to her, however, that even Wren didn't fully know the loneliness pressing on Gillian's heart. Or perhaps she did, and Gillian was naive in thinking that her mother couldn't see through her efforts to put up a good facade. It seemed illogical to Gillian that she could live in such a noisy household and feel lonely, but she did. A part of her wanted to verbalize it with her mother, but now wasn't the right time. Not when Hugh was left in charge of the younger children and Ian was not around to make certain the women could have some uninterrupted time for conversation. Perhaps another day, Gillian concluded, and left her mother to rest, first making sure that everything she might want or need was within easy reach.

Gillian packed a simple picnic while she put lunch out for the family. Her father and the boys returned just as the little ones were hungry and wanting to eat. Hugh asked Ian if he could borrow his trap so he wouldn't have to go back home to get his own. Ian gladly agreed but seemed a little confused over the purpose of this outing, just as Wren had been. Gillian felt certain that Hugh simply wanted to talk privately with her about his feelings for Felicity, as he had many times before. With everything and everyone at home taken care of, Gillian stepped into the trap with the aid of Hugh's strong hand. He sat beside her and took the reins and they were off. In spite of the heat, the day felt pleasant, and Gillian was confident it would be a delightful outing.

Chapter Two
A Convenient Proposal

During the initial stretch of their drive, Hugh and Gillian exchanged typical friendly conversation, then she noticed that he had become especially quiet. She wondered what he was thinking and felt sure that it had to be about Felicity. While she was thinking of Hugh's probable loneliness without the woman he loved, she was surprised to hear him say, "In spite of living in a lively household, you must get lonely."

Gillian was surprised at how the comment pricked something inside of her that she preferred not to feel. She was equally surprised with how it felt as if he had been reading her thoughts all through the morning. She worked very hard at convincing herself that the lack of male companionship in her life was something that didn't bother her. But there were moments of complete honesty when she couldn't deny that it bothered her very much. Generally she only allowed herself the luxury of such honesty late at night when she was completely alone. But Hugh had just brought it up in a way that she couldn't deny or ignore. And she'd never felt any cause or reason to avoid the truth with him before, which made it impossible to do so now. It was as if her spirit knew that she could be completely open with him, and it spurred the truth of her feelings directly from her heart into the open, manifesting themselves with hot tears that stung her eyes and burned her throat. She turned away from him, determined not to lift a hand to wipe her tears, which would alert him to the fact that they were falling in spite of her best efforts to hold them back. But after a minute of silence she had no choice but to sniffle and knew he would be on to her.

"Is there a reason you don't want me to know how you really feel?"

Gillian wiped her sleeve over her face, knowing it was now pointless to try to hide her crying. "I'm not sure there's *anyone* who knows how I *really* feel."

"Except for those months with Felicity, I've been alone as long as you've been alive," he said. "Do you think I wouldn't understand?" She couldn't comment, knowing he was right. She was simply confused as to why he'd brought it up at all.

Gillian couldn't answer, due to her overwhelming emotion, but he reached over and took her hand and squeezed it, silently expressing that he understood and would allow her all the time she needed to gather her composure. A few minutes later he let go of her hand to guide the horse off the road toward a lovely spot of meadow with a large shade tree, perfect for a picnic. He helped Gillian step down, smiling at her as he did so. She was glad that she'd gotten control of her tears and hoped that the evidence of them was not too prevalent on her face. She knew for a fact that when she'd been crying, she often had a red splotch below her left eye that didn't fade for several minutes, or perhaps longer, depending on how long she'd been crying. It was a telltale sign that her parents had picked up on many years earlier, which made it difficult to keep any secrets from those who knew her well—unless she could remain disciplined enough to only cry late at night when no one would see her until the effect had vanished. Hugh didn't comment on whether the evidence of tears was on her face; but then, he wouldn't. He was much too polite for that.

While Hugh settled the horse in a place where it could graze comfortably, Gillian set out the picnic on a heavy quilt that the family used exclusively for the purpose of spreading on the ground for such activities as picnics or resting in the shade out in the yard. It had never been used on a bed.

"Oh, it looks delicious!" Hugh said with enthusiasm as he sat down at the other side of the blanket, keeping his boots on the ground beyond its border.

"Not much variety," Gillian said in reference to the sliced bread and butter, cold pork slices, and some scrubbed vegetables from the garden.

"It's sustaining and flavorful," Hugh said. "What more could we ask for?"

Gillian smiled at him, thinking of the contrast of Brother Skimpole complaining just this morning about the lack of variety in his meals.

"What are you thinking?" he asked with a facetiously suspicious tilt of his head.

"Nothing important," she said. "Let's bless the food."

"Would you like me to do that or would you—"

"Yes, please," she said and listened while he prayed with simple humility and gratitude. Hugh was a man who took every opportunity—even the blessing over a meal—to thank God for things that most people would never give a second thought to. Gillian always enjoyed hearing him pray; it reminded her of the truly valuable things in life and made her feel a little closer to heaven. His voice quivered slightly as he thanked the Father for the atoning sacrifice of Jesus Christ, and for its healing power in their daily lives. The spoken amen was followed by some seconds of pleasant silence as the prayer settled around them, offering a perfectly secure and pleasant atmosphere.

They ate and chatted pleasantly. Gillian was relieved that he didn't bring up her loneliness, as he'd done while they were driving, but she felt confused that he didn't bring up his own. She'd felt certain that the purpose of this excursion was his need to have some private conversation about what she knew was his most difficult daily trial. When they'd finished eating, he helped put the dishes and other things back into the wicker hamper, which was set aside. Gillian leaned back against the tree and stretched out her legs. Hugh lay on his side, leaning his elbow on the blanket and his head in his hand. He still kept his boots off the blanket, even though Gillian had told him it was all right to do otherwise, since that was the blanket's purpose, and she had her own shoes on it. He just smiled; then his expression became serious, and she wondered if he would finally come to the purpose of their getting away together like this.

"You're very good to me, Gillian," he said, looking directly at her.

"Good to you?" she echoed. "It's the other way around, Hugh. Beyond my own parents, no one is more good to me than you are. You always have been. If I am good to you, Hugh, it's only because I follow your example." She smiled at him. "It takes no effort to be good to you."

"Whether or not it does, I want you to know that I'm grateful. I still remember so clearly that day I found you when you were lost in the woods. I never imagined that you would become my best and truest friend. I wonder if you realize that I can talk to you more comfortably than anyone. Even as comfortable as I feel with your father—he's a very dear friend to me—there's just something about the way you and I can talk that is so important to me. I want you to know that. No one knows me better than you do."

"The feeling is mutual," Gillian said, even though she knew that she'd not shared with him her deepest wish, her deepest secret. And yet he seemed to know how she felt without her having said anything. That had been made evident by what he'd said while driving that had induced her tears. She wondered then if she knew *his* deepest secrets. Or maybe that's what this conversation was leading to.

Gillian had barely entertained the idea that there *was* a secret in his heart before he said, "I love you, Gillian."

Her heart quickened with the possibility that he meant something more than the close, familial-type relationship they'd always shared. She immediately convinced herself that was *not* what he'd meant, only to hear him say, "I've been holding back for a long time now, Gillian, not wanting to offend you or make you feel uncomfortable. I didn't want to stand in the way of your finding love with a man closer to your own age. But I sense your loneliness, and I can't help wondering if this is how it was meant to be." His voice quivered as it had during the prayer. "I can't hold back any longer, Gillian. I love you."

Gillian felt an equivalent quivering in her stomach that rippled outward to her every nerve until she realized she was shaking. Her eyes were locked to his, frozen there in some kind of shock. She had not seen this coming, had never imagined it as a possibility, never considered being prepared for such a declaration. And now what?

While she was struggling futilely to move past the shock and say something appropriate, Hugh added with fervor, "It's been fifteen years since I lost Felicity. We've all endured some hard things in those years, and I've watched you grow from a child into a beautiful woman. But you are not only beautiful on the outside; I know for a fact that you have a beautiful heart, a beautiful spirit. Those are the things I love about you."

Gillian quickly assessed that she could say exactly the same about him. She loved him too. But he was talking about a romantic kind of love that she'd never even imagined evolving between the two of them. The very idea was so foreign to her that she couldn't even gather her wits enough to know how to respond.

"I know this must come as a shock to you," he said, once again proving that he could practically read her mind. Or perhaps her expression left nothing to the imagination. "So . . . just listen to what I have to say, and then . . . you can think about it . . . let it settle in . . . and we can talk when you feel ready to talk about it. Is that all right with you?"

Gillian attempted to nod, but it was only a very slight motion of her chin moving downward. He took it as her approval and went on. "You and I are in the same place. I don't mean geographically. Well, we *are* in the same place geographically, but . . ."

Gillian realized then that he was nervous. She'd rarely if ever seen him ruffled by anything. But his stammering and the expression on his face made it evident that his stomach was probably in knots, and his heart was likely pounding as hard as her own.

"We are in the same place," he repeated. "We're both trying our best to do everything right, but we're doing it on our own while everything around us is about families and marriage and *not* being alone. We're both lonely and hurting for it. We understand each other, we care for each other. I will provide your every need, Gillian. You will never go without anything, most especially the care and tenderness you deserve. We can have our own family . . . together. We can stop wasting years and make something meaningful out of what we share."

Hugh moved to his knees, and Gillian became aware of her own breathing. He took her hand and held it firmly, which heightened her awareness of her own trembling. But it also made her realize that he was trembling too.

"Gillian," he said and took a deep breath. She took note of how he let it out with somewhat of a quiver just before he added, "I'm asking you to be my wife."

She took a sharp breath to try to take that in, but she couldn't draw enough air into her lungs, so she had to try again, and again, until she could hear herself almost gasping audibly, and she knew that he could hear it too. She was surprised to hear her own voice, and even more surprised by the words that she spoke when they hadn't seemed to even pass through her mind before they'd escaped. "Your proposal is very convenient, Hugh."

"I love you, Gillian." His eyes turned downward. "But I know I could never expect you to feel the same toward me. I can't force your heart, but I can give you a good life." He looked back up at her. "If you define that as convenient, so be it."

Gillian tried to accept what had just happened while he continued to hold her gaze. Realizing she *couldn't* accept it—at least not without some serious pondering—she jumped to her feet and walked away, needing time to herself. She hoped that he wouldn't feel offended by her abrupt departure, but she figured if he knew her half as well as he claimed, he would understand and give her some space to think.

Hugh watched Gillian walk away and wondered if he'd done the right thing. He lay back on the blanket and put an arm over his eyes, sighing with the emotional weight of this entire situation. He'd hoped that by now he might feel a little lighter, that declaring himself to her might lift some of the burden he'd been carrying around for years now. But he didn't feel lighter at all. He only felt as if the burden had been shifted to Gillian's shoulders, and he couldn't help but feel that weight on her behalf. It seemed he'd been feeling what she felt for as long as he'd known her. In spite of all his best efforts to resist taking on her emotions and struggles, he couldn't get through an hour without thinking of her and feeling as if her burdens were his own. He'd been praying for weeks, perhaps months, to know whether he should take this step. Once he'd felt confident that it was the right course, he'd prayed equally hard for the courage to do so, and for Gillian's heart to be softened. Now his life was hanging in the balance. If she refused his proposal, nothing would ever be the same between them. The friendship they'd always shared would be permanently altered by an awkwardness that he'd just initiated. He'd stepped through a door and he could never go back. The problem was that he'd pulled Gillian through that door as well.

On the other hand, if Gillian accepted his proposal, his potential happiness was impossible to comprehend. He could visualize a life with her that lured him to believe all of his years of emptiness and wanting might be compensated for in ways beyond his imagination. Just thinking about it made him feel that, like Alma in the Book of Mormon, he might know joy that exceeded his pain. But he didn't want to tell Gillian that. He didn't want her to feel responsible for his happiness. And he certainly didn't want her marrying him out of some kind of pity or charity. While he never expected her to be able to love him the way he loved her—and he was all right with that—he still wanted her to accept his proposal because she believed he could make her happy, that they could share happiness together. It wasn't the first time he'd wished that he wasn't so much older than she was. But then, if he'd not been a grown man with many of life's experiences behind him, he would not have been living in Nauvoo on that day little Gillian had been lost in the woods. He could not wish away certain aspects of his life without eliminating other key elements that contributed to the man he had become. He only hoped that he was man enough to make a woman like Gillian Brierley happy, and that she would be willing to accept that possibility into her life.

* * * * *

Gillian walked as quickly as she could manage toward another tree in the distance, the only possible refuge from the sun that she could see. Once she knew she was far enough away from Hugh to have some privacy, her tears came in torrents as she walked. She cried as if someone she loved had died, even knowing that the evidence of that red splotch would be on her face to let Hugh know just how emotional she'd become. She couldn't believe it! Wondering how long Hugh had been secretly feeling this way made her head spin. Wondering how she would ever respond to such a proposal made it spin even more until she had to stop walking and hang her head in order to keep from feeling faint. She dropped to her knees and lowered her head farther when her sobbing overtook her. The heat of the afternoon sun spurred her back to her feet in order to seek the refuge of the shade tree that beckoned to her from not too far ahead. She was grateful to arrive beneath its cooling branches, and she sat on the ground there, wondering why Hugh's declaration of love felt so heavy to her. A wonderful man had just expressed pure, unselfish love for her. He had offered her everything he had to give. Why could she not feel joy in that? Perhaps it was simply her need to adjust to something that presently felt so unfamiliar. She'd simply *never* considered this possibility, and she felt as if she'd been immediately transported to a foreign land where she couldn't speak the language or find her way in the streets.

Gillian's tears finally settled into thoughtful silence. She hugged her legs to her chest and laid the side of her face on her knees while she considered all of Hugh's fine qualities, and how she respected and admired him. She asked herself if it was the age difference that bothered her, and the answer was an immediate no. She'd always felt like an equal to him. Even when she'd been a child and he'd taken a role in helping look after her, she'd always felt like he treated her with the respect of a peer. If it wasn't the age difference, then what was the problem? What made her feel like this *was* a problem, rather than something to be happy about? It only took a few minutes for her to firmly find the answer to that question. Hugh had defined it very clearly. How well he knew her! *I know I could never expect you to feel the same toward me. I can't force your heart.* He was right. She *didn't* feel the same kind of love for him that he felt for her, and neither of them could force such feelings. But maybe it didn't matter, she concluded. She knew that she loved Hugh. It just wasn't the kind of magical, heart-stopping love that she'd always imagined feeling. As much as she wanted that kind of love, perhaps she needed to be mature enough to recognize that turning down a marriage proposal from such a man would be ludicrous. He loved her in every possible way, and she loved him and admired him enough to know that they could be happy together. Then what held her back? Of course, it had only been a short while since she'd been made unequivocally aware of his feelings. He wouldn't expect her to make a decision quickly or without sincere prayer and pondering. She needed to allow herself adequate time to come to terms with this possibility and make a decision with a confidence that could only come through the guidance of the Holy Spirit. She knew well how to hear the voice of the Lord, and He would surely guide her in this matter above anything else that had ever occurred previously in her life.

Gillian heard footsteps and looked up to see Hugh approaching timidly, his hat in his hands. "Forgive me for disturbing you," he said and stopped walking, staying at a reasonable distance. "If you need more time, I'm happy to give it to you, but . . . it's been more than an hour, and I'm thinking I should take you back so your parents don't worry."

"Of course," Gillian said and came to her feet. "Forgive me. I lost track of the time."

"I understand," he said. He was afraid she might just move past him and try to pretend that nothing had changed. But she stood to face him, looking into his eyes as if she might find the answers there. He knew she'd been crying long and hard by that telling red splotch below her eye, but he didn't comment. "Are you all right?" he asked, wanting to touch that little red splotch that he'd first seen there when she'd been a child living in Nauvoo.

"It's a lot to take in," she said and forced a smile, "but I'm certain I'll be fine. I just need some time."

"Promise me that you won't stop talking to me. Take all the time you need, but don't stop talking to me."

Gillian put a tender hand on his arm; her touch quickened his heart. "I don't want anything to change between us, Hugh. I want us to always be friends, no matter what happens."

"I want the same," he said. "But you must know that being friends from now on will be more difficult. It will never be the same."

He saw her look deeply at him long enough to take in his meaning. Then she nodded at the same moment that enlightenment filled her eyes and sadness took over her countenance.

"I'm sorry for that," he said, and she looked surprised.

"For what? Why would you apologize?"

"I'm sorry for changing what we share. If you decide that you don't want to marry me, we'll never be able to pretend that it wasn't considered. And now you know how I really feel. A part of me believes it would have been better left unsaid, but I had to take the risk, Gillian. I couldn't forever wonder if keeping my feelings to myself had denied both of us the opportunity for greater happiness. Do you understand what I'm saying?"

"I do," she said and hung her head, pondering it for a long moment. "I just . . . need time."

"Of course. I understand. In the meantime, I'm hoping that you'll not feel awkward with me around, because I don't think that I could ever keep myself away from your family—no matter what happens."

"And I would never want you to," she said. He felt some relief when she smiled—regardless of how brief and stilted it was. "Whatever happens, Hugh, we will always be friends. I'm certain we should be mature enough to work around a little bit of awkwardness."

"I do hope so," he said, praying that it would never come to that. He wanted her to be his wife, and he knew in his heart that proposing to her was a step that God had wanted him to take. Now he could only put the matter in God's hands and keep praying.

"Come along," he said, guiding her back to the trap. They walked the distance in silence, but it didn't feel as tense or awkward as he might have expected, and he had to be grateful for that. Since he'd already shaken off the blanket and put it and the hamper into the trap, he helped her step up into the little carriage and made certain she was comfortably situated before he stepped in himself and guided the horse back to the road. The drive passed in complete silence, but Hugh tried not to let it get to him. He knew she needed time to think, and he'd never expected this to be easy for either of them. He could only pray that the outcome might be the one he hoped for.

Back at the house, Hugh helped Gillian step down from the trap. She took the hamper and blanket and politely thanked him for a lovely outing, then their eyes met and it became evident that no attempt at normalcy would ever eliminate the profuse evidence that their relationship would never be the same.

"Take care of yourself," he said gently, "and please . . . if you need to talk . . . talk to me."

"Of course," she said and took him off guard when she kissed his cheek. She took a few steps, then turned back. "Are you coming in?"

"No . . . thank you. I should be getting home . . . get some work done. I'll take care of the trap and . . . Thank your father for me. I'll likely see you all tomorrow."

Gillian nodded and walked on toward the house. Hugh watched her go, wondering if she would hurry to her room and cry some more. His spirit still felt sure that this had been the right step to take, but at the moment his heart didn't feel so sure. He wanted to comfort Gillian's concerns and whatever else might be causing her solemn countenance. But he had obviously contributed to the problem, and he had driven her further away from him emotionally than she'd ever been. But they could never become closer without this inevitable stage between friendship and marriage. He just hoped it ended in marriage.

* * * * *

Gillian entered the house to find it unusually quiet. She cleaned out the picnic hamper and put it and the quilt away. A little investigation let her know that Gavin was taking a nap, with Mont listening for him while he read so that he could care for the little one when he woke up. A neighbor had taken the girls to their home to play with girls near the same age, and the older boys had gone with their father to assist on the farm of a friend who was ill and needed help. Gillian peeked into her mother's room to find her looking toward the window, clearly bored. Gillian felt inexpressibly grateful to just be in the same room with her mother, surrounded by a rare peacefulness in the house, so that she could just ponder what had happened this afternoon and how it had changed her life. She had a decision before her that was daunting, to say the least. And whichever direction she chose to take, she would never be the same.

"Hello," was all Gillian said before she laid down on the bed close to her mother.

Wren put her arm around Gillian and urged her daughter's head to her shoulder. "Well, hello. How was your outing with Hugh?"

"The drive and the picnic were pleasant," Gillian answered honestly.

"Did something go wrong?"

"Not exactly . . . wrong," Gillian said. "Just . . . unexpected."

"What are ye saying?" Wren asked, shifting so that she could look at Gillian's face. Their eye contact provoked Gillian to tears. She squeezed her eyes closed and ducked her head against her mother, just as she'd done as a child. Her tears increased, and Wren asked tenderly, "What is it, my darling? Ye must tell me."

"Oh, Mother," Gillian muttered. "I don't know what to do."

"What do ye mean?" Wren asked and was patient with the silence for only a moment before she added, "Ye must tell me what happened."

Gillian looked at Wren without moving her head from its relaxed position. "Oh, Mother. Hugh asked me to marry him."

Wren looked taken aback, but not entirely surprised. Gillian considered the reasons and said, "You knew! You knew he was going to—"

"He's not said a word t' me," Wren said, "but I've seen the way he looks at ye; the way he wants t' be in the same room with ye; the way he's always concerned for ye . . . more than anyone else."

Gillian gasped. "Has he talked to Father about this?"

"Not t' my knowledge," Wren said. "Ye seem upset. Did ye tell him no?"

"I need time to consider such a decision . . . and to pray."

"Of course," Wren said. "It's the most important decision ye'll ever make. But . . . I would think ye'd be pleased by such a proposal."

"I can't say I'm not pleased," Gillian said. "He's a fine man; I couldn't ask for better. I know we could be happy, but . . ."

"But ye don't feel that way about him," Wren stated as a fact. She knew Gillian well enough that she didn't have to ask.

"No, I don't."

"Perhaps it will turn t' such feelings once ye've opened yer heart t' the possibility."

"Perhaps," Gillian said, liking that idea. If she could feel the kind of sparkle and joy toward Hugh that she'd always dreamed of feeling, then everything would be perfect. And perhaps she was being self-centered to think that she *needed* such sparkle in a relationship. Perhaps it was naive and immature to base her decision on such feelings—or rather, the lack of them. Of course, she would base her decision on the guidance of the Spirit, which would always override any of her own preferences or desires. In the end, she could trust the Spirit to guide her well and she could move forward with confidence according to that guidance. But in that moment the decision felt daunting, and she wondered if something was wrong with her that she didn't feel for Hugh the way he felt for her. Lying there in comfortable silence with her mother's arm around her, she considered the undeniable fact that Hugh Montgomery was a very attractive man. He was fine looking with handsome features, he was well built, and he dressed with good taste. He had natural charisma and every attribute of a respectable man. Then why did she feel so weighed down by Hugh's proposal? Even unhappy?

"Do ye want t' talk about it?" Wren asked and pressed a soothing hand down Gillian's arm.

"I'm certain I should," she said. "If anyone can help me make sense of it, I know it would be you. I just don't know what to think." Gillian verbalized all of her thoughts while Wren listened attentively and offered compassion. Gavin woke up, and Mont brought him in to see his mother for a few minutes before he took him downstairs to play. Gillian verbalized it all again, but the conclusion was still the same. She could only give the matter time and prayer, trusting that she would be guided by the Spirit to make the right decision. Wren had little advice to give Gillian that she didn't already know, but it still helped to hear it coming from someone else. Gillian's mother completely understood her desire to feel the deep and passionate love that she knew her parents shared, but there was no denying the fact that Hugh Montgomery was a good man and he would make an excellent husband.

"Ye could do much worse," Wren said. "I wonder how many people are truly happy in their marriages. I suspect that most married people struggle in one way or another. Ye know for yerself that in spite of the love we share, yer father and I have our differences and our family isn't perfect."

"But the two of you love each other so deeply."

"We do, yes," Wren said. "But ye have a different life, Gillian. This problem can only be solved between God and yerself."

"Of course."

"And I think I need t' say that . . . well . . . we all love Hugh very much. He's a part of the family, and we're all comfortable with him. But ye can't let that sway yer decision. If ye know that ye're doing what God wants ye t' do, then ye need t' trust God t' take care of the rest." Gillian looked hard at her mother, not quite certain of her meaning. She clarified firmly, "Ye need t' let God take care of Hugh. As much as he cares for ye, his happiness is not yer responsibility. Marry him if it's right for ye, and if it's not, don't let yerself be feeling guilty or unhappy because of his situation."

Gillian nodded her understanding, grateful that her mother was such a wise woman. Realizing the time, she tore herself away from Wren's comfort and went downstairs to make some supper. They would have to manage with salt pork and fried potatoes—again. It was the only thing she could pull together in a short amount of time with the ingredients available. She was stirring potatoes when the girls were brought home. After they had washed up, Gillian put Rachel to work setting the table, and she sent Sarah out to the garden for some tomatoes that could be sliced to add some variety and extra nutrition to the meal. The food was nearly ready when Ian and the boys arrived, and they hurried to wash up while Gillian took a supper tray up to her mother. She knew that Wren hated missing meals with the family, but it couldn't be helped. She needed to stay down for her health and the welfare of the baby, and the family couldn't all fit in the bedroom at once beyond their kneeling there together for prayer at the end of each day. That was when Wren had the opportunity to see her family all together and enjoy their company.

At the supper table, Gillian felt distracted from the usual banter and interactions until her father said, "I thought Hugh might stay for supper."

Gillian felt startled by the mention of his name. "He . . . said he would probably see us tomorrow."

Ian nodded while he was chewing. He swallowed and asked, "Did you have a nice picnic?"

"Very nice, thank you," Gillian said, then popped a fork full of potatoes into her mouth in order to avoid expounding. She was grateful when her father became distracted by the girls talking about their playtime with friends earlier, and he didn't pursue the topic of her outing with Hugh.

After supper, Gillian stepped out the back door to shake the crumbs off the tablecloth. She was glad she had when she saw her neighbor, Benny Miller, in the corner of the yard, looking at the flowers growing there. And Gillian wasn't surprised at all to hear the voice of Benny's mother calling his name from across the fence. Gillian hung the tablecloth over the porch railing and hurried across the lawn, calling to Sister Miller, "He's here!"

"Thank you!" Sister Miller called back. "I'll be right there."

Gillian just hovered near Benny, keeping an eye on him until his mother could come around the fence. Sister Miller was a good lady, but Gillian had never been able to have a truly comfortable conversation with her. She'd lived a hard life, and Gillian respected her convictions. But the woman had an abrupt way about her, and Gillian never engaged in conversation without coming away feeling a bit awkward. In fact, Gillian simply felt awkward with both sets of neighbors, and the principle of loving thy neighbor had not always been easy for her. The elder and younger Mr. Skimpole were their neighbors to one side, and on the other were the Millers. Gillian was a person who always tried to be charitable to others and to understand that every soul had worth in the sight of God. But she did wonder why—of all the wonderful people in this community—they had ended up with the most odd neighbors.

Sister Miller was an active churchgoer, and the gospel meant a great deal to her. She was a robust woman, somewhat heavy but full of nervous energy in spite of the effort it seemed to take to move her large frame from one place to another. She was always busy caring for her family and compensating for all that her husband did *not* do. Mr. Miller was *not* a churchgoer. He had reluctantly come west with his family when the only other choice for him was to *lose* his family, since his wife and children had eagerly embraced the gospel and were determined to live among the Saints. The Millers' children were all raised and out on their own now except for Benny, who was physically a grown man with the mind of a child. Mentally he'd never evolved past the abilities of a three-year-old. Benny was a gentle soul who loved everyone he met. Everyone who knew him loved him and was patient with his limitations—except for his father.

Gillian had observed the interactions of her neighbors enough to know that Sister Miller put a great deal of effort into keeping Benny out of her husband's way. Mr. Miller came and went from his job at the sawmill, usually went out drinking in the evenings, and was generally unkind to his wife and son. Gillian had observed her parents offering many kindnesses to the Millers, but most of them had been pridefully shrugged off. Mr. Miller refused to accept any kind of charity from *those Mormons,* and Sister Miller was forced to take the same stand in order not to encourage any more grief from her husband.

Gillian put a hand on Benny's arm, speaking to him first, being careful not to startle him. For all of his childish nature, he was large in stature and Gillian had seen him fly into a tantrum that could be somewhat frightening, given his size.

"I did see a butterfly," Benny said in a voice that Gillian could only understand because she'd learned the nature of his intonations.

"Was it a pretty butterfly?" Gillian asked.

"A pretty butterfly," Benny said.

Sister Miller then arrived, took her son by the arm, and gently urged him to go home with her. She thanked Gillian with barely a glance in her direction. Gillian went back into the house, taking the tablecloth with her.

The remainder of the evening was busy, as usual. Gillian supervised the children with cleaning up the kitchen and doing evening chores while her parents spent some time together. Ian kept little Gavin with him so that Wren could be with her youngest child. Ian made certain that each of the children spent time with their mother every day so that she could remain abreast of all that was going on in their lives. The day ended, as it always did, with the family gathering around Wren's bed to read together from the scriptures and to pray. When Wren was not confined to bed, this ritual took place downstairs in the parlor. Gillian had not been able to forget about Hugh's proposal, even though she'd been very busy. But when the quiet of scripture study allowed her mind to more fully take hold of it, she found it challenging to remain composed, and she was glad that her father didn't ask her to offer the prayer. Then she focused on helping get the younger children settled into bed before she went to her own room, sighing as she closed the door behind her, not certain if she was relieved or frightened to be alone with her fragile emotions. Now that she *was* alone, Gillian felt a desire to cry, as if it might ease the pounding of concern and dilemma in her head. But she couldn't summon a single tear. She felt numb and uncertain about what to think. Long after she'd gone to bed, she just stared at the ceiling, wishing just the slightest breeze might magically appear to stir up the air in the room just a bit. Even with both windows wide open and not even a sheet over her, she still felt sticky with sweat. She knew that by morning the room would have cooled to a comfortable temperature, but morning felt so far away, especially when sleep was so boldly eluding her.

Gillian pondered the situation of her life and the possible paths before her in regard to Hugh's proposal. She prayed, then pondered, then prayed some more. The only thought that kept sticking in her head was simply that any woman would be a fool to turn down such a proposal, especially when there were no other obvious options within her social circles. She reminded herself that she had time to make this decision. There was no rush. She didn't need to decide that night, and she knew that Hugh would be kind and patient in allowing her all the time she needed. Still, a part of her believed that she'd already gotten her answer. A woman *would* be a fool to turn down such a proposal. And she didn't consider herself a fool.

Chapter Three
The New Arrival

Gillian was nudged awake, then felt startled as she came out of sleep to hear the urgency in her father's voice.

"I need you, sweetheart," he said. "Your mother's labor has started. I need you to sit with her while I go for the doctor."

"Of course," Gillian said and was quickly upright. She reached for the lightweight robe that she had left over the foot of the bed, glad that the house felt much cooler now and that wearing the robe over her nightgown felt comfortable.

"Thank you," Ian said and pressed a quick kiss to her cheek. "I must hurry. You know what to do."

Gillian nodded and said, "Everything will be all right."

"I pray so," Ian muttered and hurried back to his bedroom with Gillian right behind him.

She entered the room to see two lamps burning low on the bedside tables. Wren was propped up against pillows, as she had been most of the time for weeks now. But the pain in her countenance was immediately evident. Ian put a knee on the bed to bend over and kiss Wren, first on the forehead, and then on the lips.

"I'll hurry," he promised. "Gillian is here, so you won't be alone."

Wren nodded but didn't speak. Ian hesitated a moment, then rushed from the room. Gillian moved to her mother's bedside, working hard to suppress her trepidation. If *she* felt trepidation, she couldn't imagine what her mother must be feeling. The experience of childbirth was horrible to observe; it surely had to be even more horrible to endure. Wren never complained, and she always declared that it was more than worth it to give life to a child. But the actuality of getting from this moment to the point when the child had arrived safely seemed presently unbearable. Gillian had been old enough to help her mother through the last two births and a miscarriage that had happened between Rachel and Gavin. She knew how the process worked, and she'd learned how to assist the doctor and how to encourage her mother through the pains and the bearing down that was necessary to expel the child from the womb. But her knowledge and experience didn't make it any easier to observe the suffering her mother was about to endure.

With Ian gone, Gillian made herself comfortable, sitting on the bed to face her mother. She held her hand, and Wren offered a wan smile. "I'll be right here," Gillian said.

"I could not ask for a more precious daughter," Wren said. She endured a contraction, then added, "I'm grateful that ye're my friend as much as my daughter . . . and for all ye do t' help me . . . and the family."

"I couldn't ask for a better mother," Gillian said as another contraction came on. The contractions were close together, and Gillian knew what that meant. Hopefully it would all move very quickly, and they could have this over and done before lunch, and Wren could be resting peacefully with a new baby at her side. Gillian held to that image and smiled at her mother while her hand was squeezed tightly.

"If it's my time t' go," Wren said, and Gillian forced a calm face to hide the way her stomach knotted, "I know ye'll help care for yer brothers and sisters, and . . ."

She endured another contraction. As it faded, Gillian hurried to say, "There will be no such talk. You know very well that I will always help with the family, but you're going to get through this."

"I don't want ye t' sacrifice yer own happiness for the sake of yer siblings, Gillian. They need ye, but ye must keep balance in yer life. Do ye understand?"

"I understand, Mother. Now just . . ." She paused as another contraction engulfed Wren. "Now just focus on the present and we'll get through this."

Wren forced a smile. "Thank ye for being with me. I know it isn't easy."

"I just consider it an opportunity to be very prepared when I have my own children. Then *you* can hold *my* hand."

"I will!" Wren said with enough conviction to soothe Gillian's fears over wondering if Wren had experienced some kind of premonition that this was her time to go. Convinced that her concerns were just something she needed to get out of the way, she wiped her mother's face with a cool rag that had been left within reach, and continued to hold her hand, determined to get through this with as little drama as possible. With all the experience Wren had at giving birth, this should surely be her easiest delivery yet.

Ian returned with the doctor more quickly than Gillian had anticipated, and she felt grateful to have the doctor's capable hands present. There were very few doctors available, and they were kept very busy. Ian had made the decision weeks ago that a doctor needed to deliver this baby, rather than a midwife, or—as was often the case—other women who had personal experience but little or no medical training. Gillian wondered if Ian's prior decision had some significance; either way, she was glad to have the doctor here now. She also felt grateful to have her father in the room. He was not a man to wait elsewhere while his wife was suffering. While doctors generally preferred that the husband wait elsewhere, Ian had asserted his intention to be present, especially when it came to the children that had been born under horrific circumstances in Far West and while crossing the plains. Now Ian sat on the edge of the bed, holding Wren's other hand, encouraging her with loving words and reassurances that all would be well.

Since the doctor was also a priesthood holder, the first order of business was for Ian and the doctor to give Wren a blessing. She continued to suffer through contractions while the blessing was given, and Gillian continued to hold her hand while the men had their hands on Wren's head. The blessing was beautiful and offered great comfort and a bold reminder that Heavenly Father was mindful of Wren's suffering and that the Atonement of the Savior would compensate for this trial. Wren was promised great joy in eternity for her sacrifices in bringing forth this beautiful family. But the blessing did not say anything directly about whether Wren would survive this ordeal, or whether she would be able to yet enjoy being with her family here in mortality. Gillian tried not to think about what *wasn't* said and to focus instead on the sweet comfort that had been offered.

With the blessing completed, the doctor checked Wren and said that she was moving along quickly and could start pushing soon. They all shared a sigh of relief at the news and a hope that it would be over quickly. Knowing it would only get more intense from here on, Gillian took the opportunity to escape just long enough to put on a respectable skirt and blouse and pull her unbrushed hair back into a ribbon. She returned to resume her vigil.

Wren quickly reached the point when the doctor told her to start pushing, and again Gillian hoped it would be over quickly. Her thoughts were abruptly interrupted by a firm impression in her mind. *Get the children out of the house. They need to be elsewhere.* She gasped as it settled in, then wondered over the possible reasons. Wren's last childbirth had happened at night, and the children had slept through it. The one before that had been during the day, but the older children had cared for the younger ones downstairs, and there had been no trauma or undue alarm for them. Wren had always managed to keep her suffering quiet enough that it couldn't be heard audibly outside of the room unless someone was right outside the door. Gillian concluded that it wasn't for her to try to predict the reasons for the prompting; she simply needed to act on it.

"I'll be right back," Gillian said to her father. He nodded, and she hurried from the room. She found Harry still sleeping and carefully nudged him awake. The room was barely light with the coming dawn.

"What is it?" he asked, looking at her through squinted eyes.

"Mother is in labor, and I just have a feeling that it would be better if you and the other children spent the day elsewhere. I can't explain more than that. I know you understand."

"I understand," Harry said and sat up. She was glad to know that he was a fine young man who lived close to the Spirit so that he *would* understand. "What do you want me to do?"

"I need you to go and get Hugh. Just tell him we need his help. Let me know when he's here so I can speak with him. As soon as you get back, have Alfred help you take care of the animals and do the necessary chores so that you can leave until evening."

Harry nodded. "I'll take care of it."

"Thank you," she said and kissed his cheek. "You're a darling."

Harry forced a tiny smile, then asked, "Is she going to be all right?"

"We can only pray that she will be," Gillian said, and he nodded. With the exception of the two youngest children, they all knew that childbirth brought risks, and they also personally knew families who had lost a wife and mother that way. It was a fear they all shared and couldn't deny. They simply had to trust in the Lord and know that He would not take their mother before her time. They could only pray that it was not her time and that she might be allowed to come through this and continue to be their mother here on the earth for years to come.

Gillian returned to her parents' bedroom, hoping that the baby might be almost here and her prompting would end up coming to nothing. But she found her mother in terrible pain, and the doctor showing some concern. Apparently the baby was positioned incorrectly and not exiting the womb in a normal fashion, which boiled down to the fact that it wasn't exiting the womb at all. Gillian held tightly to her mother while the doctor attempted to alter the baby's position, a process that was so painful for Wren that Gillian wished desperately she could take some degree of the pain from her or do something to help this process along. She felt utterly helpless and terrified, and seeing her own feelings mirrored in her father's expression only deepened her heartache. Throughout the process it was obvious that Wren was finding it more difficult to keep her manifestations of pain silent. She was clearly trying very hard, and Gillian knew that she didn't want to alarm the children. But the prompting to have the children removed began to make sense. Gillian wondered if this meant the pain would get worse. She also wondered how long it might go on. Both questions tightened her already knotted stomach.

Time passed while the agony continued with no apparent progress, but the doctor remained positive, determined to do everything in his power to get this baby delivered safely. The problem was that doing so was bound to be excruciatingly painful for Wren. Until the baby was delivered, she was going to be in agony. There was no way around it.

A quiet knock on the door startled Gillian to the reminder of what she'd assigned Harry to do. "I'll take care of it," she said and graciously exited the room, grateful for a moment of fresh air and the opportunity to take a deep breath.

"Hugh is here," Harry said. "He's downstairs. Alfred is already in the barn. I'll go and help him."

"Thank you, Harry," Gillian said.

"Is Mother going to be all right?" he asked as if she should know the answer to that question. She didn't have the answer, but Harry was very mature and she knew she needed to be honest with him.

"The doctor is doing everything he can, but it appears there is a complication with the position of the baby. Just go about your day and keep praying."

"I will," he said and hurried down the stairs. Gillian followed more slowly, trying not to think about her present situation with Hugh. Such things didn't matter right now. He was a family friend and they needed him. She found him pacing the hall, his hat in his hands.

"What can I do?" he asked eagerly the moment he saw her. His genuine desire to help warmed her and deepened her respect. In her head she heard clearly, *Any woman would be a fool to turn down such a proposal.*

Focusing on the moment at hand, she said, "There may be some complications. I had a strong impression that the children should be out of the house. I won't even venture to guess why. They can help each other with getting dressed and gathering what they need. I'm certain there are friends and neighbors who can take the younger ones. You know who those people are. If the children are playing with friends . . . if they're in homes where they feel comfortable . . . they won't even be thinking about what's going on."

"I understand," Hugh said.

"The boys are seeing to the animals. If you could just . . ."

"You don't need to say anything else," Hugh said. "I know what to do. I'll see that they're taken care of. I promise. Just . . . be with your mother."

"Thank you, Hugh," Gillian said and tried not to give in to the temptation to cry at the evidence of his willingness to be so charitable.

"A pleasure," he said and pressed a quick kiss to her brow. It was brief and brotherly in and of itself, but since it had never happened before, she couldn't deny the implication in regard to how their relationship was changing. She ignored that for now and tried to smile. "We will all pray together before we leave the house, and my prayers will continue through the day. I'll check back, and if you're still up there with the door closed, I'll know it's not over. If you need anything, leave a note on the kitchen table and I'll take care of it."

"Thank you," she said and hurried back up the stairs, knowing they both needed to take action and she had no time to ponder or analyze anything in regard to her relationship with Hugh *or* her mother's frightening condition.

Gillian resumed her position at her mother's side, horrified by the deepening evidence of her agony. She tried to remain calm and supportive, while her father occasionally passed her a discreet glance that expressed his terror. Gillian remained engaged in the situation as the doctor attempted again to reposition the baby. Wren groaned and writhed and clenched her teeth with a tightness that was painful just to observe. With half an ear Gillian listened for familiar sounds in the house and knew that the children were up and about. She could imagine Hugh herding them and making certain all was well. Gillian heard the outside door close with a familiar subtle sound resounding through the house, then everything was very still. She breathed some relief to know the children were taken care of, and there was no household responsibility that couldn't wait. She felt impressed to let her mother know that such was the case. Perhaps if she knew the children wouldn't overhear her, she could relax more through whatever this process might entail. Her theory was proven correct when Wren nodded in response to the information; then at the next sign of pain she cried out as if vocalizing the pain fully might help her to better endure it.

As the struggle continued and Wren's evidence of pain heightened, Gillian more than once noticed her father discreetly wiping away tears. Gillian had no choice but to do the same. But she knew her father had to be exercising the same self-restraint that she was. A few silent tears didn't begin to vent what they were feeling. The doctor's concern was obviously deepening, even though he did well at concealing it.

Gillian's heart pounded when the doctor looked directly at her father and said, "Brother Ian, I need to speak with you."

"If there's something ye need t' say, Doctor," Wren said with surprising firmness, "ye can say it in front of me. Whatever it is, I'll know eventually, now won't I."

The doctor sighed deeply and nodded. Gillian could hardly breathe and recognized from her father's expression that he was suffering from the same symptoms. The doctor then spoke in a straightforward manner. Even though Wren and Gillian could clearly hear what he was saying, he spoke directly to Ian. "If I don't get this baby out of her, she'll die. And she'll die painfully. Whether or not the baby is alive, I cannot begin to know. We must act quickly."

Ian nodded but couldn't speak. Gillian watched as he turned to meet Wren's eyes. They shared some kind of silent communication that mingled fear of what had to be endured and the fear that she wouldn't make it through. Gillian could almost imagine them both pondering that this moment might be their earthly farewell. The aching that tightened her own heart felt unbearable. She couldn't imagine what they might be feeling. In that moment Gillian felt a deep, incomprehensible gratitude to know that Ian and Wren had been sealed to each other, along with their children, following their forced exodus from Nauvoo. As soon as it had been possible, they had been some of the first in line to partake of the blessings of that crowning ordinance in that beloved temple. Gillian felt sure that her parents were considering their own gratitude in that moment, knowing they would be together forever, no matter what might happen now. But even with that knowledge, the thought of losing Wren at this time was unthinkable. Gillian wanted to curl up next to her mother and cry like a baby. But she needed to be strong—for both of her parents. Beyond the doctor, she was the only other adult in the house, and she needed to *act* like an adult.

Ian turned back to the doctor and asked with a croaking voice, "What are you saying, exactly?"

"We need to do a caesarean section; we need to remove the baby surgically, by cutting open the abdomen. And we need to do it now. I have a small amount of ether available that should help her sleep some through the worst of it, but I don't want her to sleep too deeply; that brings on other dangers. And the recovery could be very difficult."

Gillian heard her mother whimper and felt her grip tighten. She watched as Wren and Ian exchanged another difficult gaze that implied silent communication. As if Wren didn't want there to be any question of her feelings, she spoke firmly to the doctor while her gaze didn't leave her husband. "Do it. Do it now. We must get it over and done with."

The doctor hurried to prepare, giving Gillian some orders on what he needed. She was horrified to realize that he needed her to stay near his side and hand him his instruments as well as rags to soak up the blood. Ian was to hold Wren's upper body to the bed to prevent as much movement as possible, given the chance that her body might respond to the pain even if she were asleep, or the sleep might not be deep enough to eliminate all of the pain. Just before the doctor was ready to begin, the ether was administered, and Wren drifted almost immediately into a strange sleep. Gillian hoped it would be sufficient to spare her from the pain, but she wondered if she would ever see her mother awake and alive again. Given the entire spectrum of the situation, Gillian wondered what new heights of agony Wren would endure in contrast to what she'd already suffered in the last few hours.

The experience was more horrible than Gillian could have ever conjured up in her imagination. She kept praying silently while she tried to keep her focus where it needed to be. She envied her father for not having such a close view of the surgery, but neither of them could avoid being keenly aware of what was happening. Even though Wren seemed mostly unconscious, she still writhed and whimpered in response to the pain. Gillian felt inexpressible gratitude to know that the children *were* out of the house. She thanked Heavenly Father for that prompting, and she thanked Him for allowing them to have someone like Hugh in their lives to assist with making that happen quickly and efficiently. *Any woman would be a fool to turn down such a proposal,* Gillian heard in her head, then she forced thoughts of Hugh out of her mind, praying that this would be over quickly and that the results would not be disastrous. She wondered how it might be if, after all of this suffering, the baby didn't survive. She wondered how it might be if her mother didn't survive. She refused to think of either possibility for more than a moment, and concentrated her efforts on feeling needed as the doctor kept giving her orders to hand him this or that or to do one thing or another. She'd never pictured herself being so closely involved with such a medical procedure, but there she was, and she had no choice but to see it through. More than once she felt a little woozy from the sight of all the blood, but she kept praying and managed to keep herself together enough to help her mother through it.

When it seemed like it would never end, the doctor reached into the open hole in the womb and gently pulled the baby out. Gillian gasped at the sight of it, so real and so human. She took a quick glance at the clock and realized it had only been a few minutes since the surgery had begun. The doctor had been quick and efficient, in spite of how the procedure might have seemed to go on and on.

"Look," Gillian said when she realized her father was looking at her mother, oblivious to what had just happened. She heard him gasp, and they both became intently focused on watching the doctor's hands stimulate the baby, which was still attached to its cord. He turned it mostly upside down and gently slapped its little back, explaining briefly that he had to get any fluid out of the way so it could breathe. A moment later they all heard the baby take in a breath, then another. Then a healthy wail broke the silence, and all of the witnesses to the miracle laughed with relief and pleasure.

"It's a girl," the doctor said and handed the baby abruptly to Ian so that he could focus on cutting the cord and completing the surgical procedure. Once the cord was cut, Ian wrapped the baby in a little blanket and set it carefully close by so that he could focus his attention on helping Wren remain still through the remainder of the ordeal. The baby's crying didn't seem at all a distraction or a concern; it was rather a reassurance that she was healthy and strong. This new little girl would just have to wait until her mother was cared for before she could receive any further attention. Ian held tightly to Wren while the placenta was removed, and they all thought it was over except for the process of stitching her back up. Then the doctor declared that something was not right. Wren was bleeding excessively, and he concluded that the only way to stop it was to surgically remove the uterus. Since she was already open, it was the obvious option. Ian told him to go ahead, and he continued to hold to Wren. Gillian continued to try to keep her wits about her while she assisted the doctor. She knew that if an actual doctor had not been here to know what to do, Wren and the baby would have surely died. As it was, they couldn't be certain that Wren would yet survive. But the baby *had* made it and was doing fine. They could be grateful for that. Gillian just prayed—continually—that the rest of the outcome would be favorable.

Gillian was aware of the baby laying nearby at one side of the bed. Her crying quieted, and she began to look around as if to take in the world she'd just entered. Her eyes were bright and full of interest and seemingly wise. *A new little sister,* Gillian thought, and then had to focus fully on helping the doctor deal with the inordinate amount of blood. There seemed to be blood everywhere. But Gillian tried not to think about that. She imagined her mother having this behind her, healing, and returning to health.

It seemed forever before the surgery was finally completed and Wren was all stitched up. Every minute of it had been grueling, but the doctor declared that it had gone well—all things considered. The bleeding had stopped, and he had no reason to believe Wren wouldn't recover completely, as long she didn't get some kind of infection. Infection was always a risk with anything like this, he told them. But they would take good care of her, and they would keep praying and hoping for the very best.

Once the drama had died down, the doctor examined the baby more closely and declared her to be healthy and strong by all accounts. He was gracious enough to help clean up, but Gillian felt overwhelmed by the amount of blood-soaked linens that were left in the laundry tubs to soak. Wren merged slowly back into a groggy consciousness and wept when her daughter was placed in her arms. But she was obviously in a great deal of pain. The doctor gave Wren some laudanum to help her sleep and to hopefully ease the pain somewhat. With Wren resting and the baby bathed and sleeping, Ian held his new daughter and sat close to his wife. Gillian made certain everything was in order in the bedroom before she left them with some peace and quiet, determined to make headway with this laundry while the children were gone so they wouldn't be exposed to any evidence of what had taken place. She was just about to get started when she heard the back door and went into the kitchen to investigate. She wasn't surprised to see Hugh, since he was one of few people who might walk into their house without knocking. He'd said he would check back, and he would leave a note if necessary. He looked startled to see her there, then his eyes moved down and widened in horror.

"Good heavens!" he muttered. "What's happened?"

Gillian looked down to see a great deal of blood on the front of her skirt and blouse. She hadn't noticed and therefore hadn't thought to change her clothes. "Oh, my!" she said and turned her back to him. "I'm glad the children didn't see me this way. I had no idea it was . . . there."

"What happened?" he repeated. "Is she . . ." He couldn't finish.

"She's fine . . . relatively speaking," Gillian said, keeping her back to him. She was actually glad for an excuse not to look at him. "We just need to hope she doesn't get any infection." Silence reminded Gillian that she hadn't answered his initial question. "She . . . uh . . ." Tears came, and Gillian cursed them. She'd managed to hold them in for hours, and now, with Hugh here, they just had to come out. But she had to finish her explanation. "The baby had to be delivered by caesarean . . . surgically," she added in case he didn't know what the word meant. "Then the bleeding was so bad that . . . the uterus had to be removed."

"Good heavens," Hugh said again.

"She won't be able to have any more children," Gillian said, her voice more steady, "but the doctor says that's probably a good thing, given her age and how difficult the last couple of pregnancies have been." Gillian sniffled and wiped her nose on her sleeve. "I'm certain she'll be in a lot of pain for a good long time, and very weak for even longer. I can't . . . even imagine how she . . . endured it."

Gillian struggled again with tears that were determined to be shed, her back still to Hugh. She was surprised when he put his hands on her shoulders and asked gently, "And how are you?"

If not for the blood all over the front of her clothes, she might have felt tempted to just crumble in his arms and weep. As it was, she simply said, "It was horrible. It was so horrible." She sobbed, then attempted to choke back her tears, then sobbed again.

Hugh tightened his grip on her shoulders. "What can I do?"

"The children are all—"

"In good hands, for as long as you need them to be. I'll bring the boys back this evening to care for the animals, or I'll do it myself. What needs to be done here . . . now?" Gillian couldn't think and didn't answer. He asked, "Have you had anything to eat? What about your father? Your mother? Is she up to eating, or—"

"Mother is sleeping . . . mostly. I don't know if she's up to eating, but . . . I should prepare something for her just in case. And Father needs to eat, of course."

"And you," he said. "You need your strength. I can help with that."

"I can manage, Hugh," she insisted. "There's no need for you to—"

"Please let me help you," he said. "After all these years on my own, I'm not so bad in the kitchen."

Gillian simply nodded and wiped her face on her sleeve. She looked down at herself and said, "I need to change my clothes and get the laundry hung before the children come back."

She hurried up the stairs, and once alone in her room, the tears came forth unleashed, and she cried the way she'd wanted to ever since her mother's condition had become precarious. Once she'd vented enough emotion to be able to manage, she changed her clothes and brushed her hair so that she could pull it back in a ribbon and not have it look so unruly. She then took a deep breath and opened the door of her room to once again face what was necessary. She wasn't sure if having Hugh in the house was helpful or distracting. She had to focus on the drama at hand and appreciated his help. Avoiding any thought of his proposal seemed best for the time being. She peered quietly into her mother's bedroom to see that Wren appeared to be resting peacefully, and her father appeared to be dozing on the bed beside her, the baby sleeping close to his chest. He'd helped raise many babies and was comfortable with handling them.

Gillian left them all to rest and went straight to the bathing room downstairs, where the tubs that were used both for laundry and taking baths were kept. The blood appeared to be coming out of the linens into the cold water where they'd been soaking. She scrubbed the stains out with some good, strong soap, then rinsed them thoroughly while she was vaguely aware of productive noises coming from the kitchen. Gillian tried not to think about Hugh. And she tried not to think about what she had witnessed since she'd been awakened early this morning. The only other option was to allow her mind to wander into nothingness, and she kept it there while she took the clean linens outside and hung them on the clotheslines to dry.

* * * * *

For a week beyond the birth of Gillian's new sister, Wren barely ate and mostly slept, aided by the medicine the doctor had left with her. He'd checked back a few times and declared that she was doing as well as could be expected. The fact that a week had passed with no indications of infection was a very good sign, and they were all extremely grateful. The baby was doing very well, and it was considered a miracle that she had survived the ordeal of her birth and that she was thriving so well on her mother's milk, in spite of her mother's weakened state. The name they chose for the baby was Deborah, and it quickly seemed to suit her. Everyone in the family enjoyed holding her and contributing a little bit each day to her care. In spite of Wren's obvious pain and weakness, the joy on her face was obvious as she observed her new daughter among the rest of the children. She declared that she felt a completeness about her family that she'd not felt before, and she felt peace over knowing she was finished bringing children into the world.

Ward and Patricia, who were very close friends of the family, came by the day after Deborah was born to visit and to assist in any way possible. Although Ward had been blind from childhood, he had a certain charm in keeping children entertained, and he was fairly handy in the kitchen if the right things were put within his reach. Patricia and Wren had been so close for so many years that Patricia could help with almost anything in the household and know exactly what to do. Gillian appreciated their help and their company, given that the entire family had been somewhat traumatized by the event. Having Ward and Patricia stopping by regularly and spending time with the family had a soothing effect on all of them.

Gillian kept busy running the household so that her father could mostly care for her mother and the baby. Hugh came and went, interacting with the children in his typical way and helping here and there, wherever he was needed. He didn't even hint at wondering if Gillian had come to any decisions, or even if she'd given his proposal any thought at all. He was simply there, stalwart and firm as always. He was dependable and kind and caring, and Gillian knew she would be a fool to turn down his proposal. When Deborah was ten days old, Gillian knew in her heart that this was her answer. She discussed it with her mother, who was now spending more time awake with less need for the medicine. They concluded that sometimes the answer to prayers was simply so obvious that there didn't need to be a strong confirmation of the Spirit; sometimes a simple, quiet peace over the matter was all that a person could expect. Gillian couldn't deny that there was a peaceful calm inside at the thought of marrying Hugh. It didn't excite or thrill her, but she believed she could be happy with him. And practically speaking, there were no other options. He was a fine and decent man, and he loved her. What more could she want? She just had to find the right time to tell him.

The very evening after Gillian had discussed her decision with her mother, Hugh came with candy for the children and he accepted Gillian's invitation to stay for supper. He offered to help her in the kitchen, and suddenly it became evident that they were alone in the room, standing side by side in front of the stove, and the words just came out of her mouth. "I want to accept your proposal, Hugh."

He stopped stirring abruptly and set aside the large, wooden spoon. Without moving any farther, he said, "Did I hear you correctly?"

"I want to marry you," she said, turning to face him. "You're a good man. I could not ask for a better husband. I would be a fool to turn down such an offer, and I thank you for it."

He smiled, then he laughed. "Oh, Gillian," he said, his voice a bit husky, "this makes me so happy."

"I'm glad," she said, returning his smile.

"And what about you?" he asked. "Are you happy?"

Gillian measured her words carefully. "I can't pretend that I feel for you the way you've claimed to feel for me, but I do feel peace over this. There is a great deal of happiness that can be found from such peace."

"I understand," Hugh said, sounding only mildly disappointed. Of course he'd known from the start how she felt, and this was what he'd expected. She only hoped that she could be a good wife to him and that he could be as happy as he hoped he would be.

"Have you spoken to anyone about this?" he asked.

"Only my mother."

"Has she said anything to your father?"

"I don't believe she would have without asking me if it was all right, but I can't say for certain."

"I should talk with him . . . officially."

"Of course."

"Until I do . . . we'll keep it between us."

"Yes, that would seem wise," she said, wondering how long it might be until their engagement would be made public. She wondered how that might change their lives. She couldn't even imagine.

Gillian was hoping they might be able to discuss their plans a little more thoroughly, but the girls ran through the back door, and a flourish of loud giggles came with them. The remainder of the evening was busy and noisy as usual, and then Hugh had to leave, having promised some neighbors that he would care for their animals since the husband was ill. Gillian walked him out to where his horse was tethered. He took hold of her shoulders, smiled, and pressed a kiss to her brow. She smiled in return, but couldn't help feeling some awkwardness in the moment.

"I'll see you tomorrow, then," he said and untethered the horse. "Probably in the evening. I have some work to catch up on." As he was mounting, he added, "And I'll speak with your father as soon as I can make the opportunity."

Gillian nodded. "Good night, then."

He nodded and smiled in return, then rode away. Gillian stood there in the fading light of a summer evening, hoping that she had done the right thing and wondering why she should even doubt it.

* * * * *

When James MacBrier finally set foot into the valley of the Great Salt Lake, he could *not* believe how many weeks it had taken him to get there, and how utterly miserable he'd been practically every hour of his travels. Arriving with a wagon company and quickly realizing that such an event drew a great deal of attention, he just attempted to remain invisible and take it all in with watchful eyes. What he saw around him didn't necessarily convince him that the journey had been worth it. There was evidence of a thriving community, with many prospering businesses and beautiful homes. But the streets were dusty, and the air was hot and dry. There was still a rugged feel to the city that was different from anything he'd ever seen or felt before. He hoped for the thousandth time that his decision to come here had not been a mistake. After all he'd gone through to get here, he would hate to have to turn around and head east again. But then, as he considered his *real* reasons for coming here, perhaps the distance from any viable civilization was a good thing. Possibly the miles he would have to travel to get to anywhere of consequence could work in his favor. All in all, he figured that Salt Lake City was a good place to hide. And all he was truly interested in doing was just that: hiding.

James rode the horse he'd purchased back east when he'd realized that the only way to get to Salt Lake City was to travel with a wagon company headed in that direction. It hadn't taken him much effort to connect with a company of Mormon immigrants. They'd all been comparatively friendly, and were pleased to learn that he was going to stay with his relatives in the West. Those who could speak English had wanted to know if he too was a Mormon, and he quickly became skilled at declaring his firm disinterest in their religion while maintaining respect for their beliefs. For the most part, people were kind and made an effort to help him feel included, but he preferred to keep to himself.

He had spent weeks traveling at a slow and steady pace, annoyed by the dust and the bugs and the heat. Or if it wasn't hot it was raining, and the mud became a demon. He'd carried his personal items on his horse with him, and he'd spent his nights underneath the stars when the weather was fair, and underneath various wagons when it was rainy. He'd made an arrangement with a family at the beginning of this endeavor that had served him well in regard to having something to eat along the way. He had made a generous contribution to their food supply, and they in turn had included him in their meals so that he didn't have to personally transport food or put very little more than minimal effort into its preparation. The Nielsen family was kind to him, and he didn't feel uncomfortable with them while they shared their meals prepared around campfires. But they many times declared him to be quiet and shy. He didn't consider himself to be either; he simply had absolutely nothing in common with these people and no desire to talk. So, he just allowed himself to be labeled as shy and endured each day, looking forward to arriving in the famed Salt Lake Valley where he could hopefully find a place of refuge among this branch of his family.

James had known for as long as he could remember that not long after he'd been born, his uncle had gone to America to start a new life in regard to a particular religious group that was gathered there. James had vague memories of his Uncle Ian visiting once when James was just a child. Other than that, all he knew was what he'd heard from his aunt, his uncle, and his grandmother. They all loved and missed Ian and his family and spoke of them often. They sometimes read letters aloud that they'd received on a regular basis. James therefore had some inkling about what their life was like in the American west, and he knew a little bit about their religious beliefs. He had no interest in religion; God had done nothing for *him* that inspired any desire for devotion or loyalty. But he had a very big desire to find a life where people didn't know the truth about him; a place where he could hide from the past and never have to look at it again.

The only problem now was finding his relatives who lived in this city, as they were his reason for choosing this place instead of any other. When he finally found the right house, he was relieved to see that it was a large, beautiful home, surrounded by a lovely fenced-in yard. It was nothing like what he'd grown up with, but then it seemed that there was little in the world that was comparable to his native Brierley. And this appeared to be actually much nicer than he'd expected—in spite of knowing that his uncle had been raised as the son of an earl under much more opulent circumstances.

James tethered his horse to the fence and opened the gate. He walked slowly to the porch and took a deep breath as he knocked at the front door, hoping this would go well. He wondered for a moment what he'd do if he wasn't at the right house. Or given the number of weeks it had been since he'd left Scotland with a copy of a letter from his uncle in hand, he feared—not for the first time—that the family might have moved elsewhere in the meantime, and he would have to continue traveling in order to find them. He'd considered more than once sending a telegram from one of the cities in which he'd stopped along the way, but he'd resisted, perhaps fearing that if Ian Brierley knew he was coming, he might move his family simply to avoid being found. James felt certain that his *other* uncle, the current Earl of Brierley, might have written to his brother about their problem nephew. If that was the case, he might well get the door slammed in his face, and he'd still be confronted with the dilemma of having to turn around and go back. Or at least find another place to hide.

Chapter Four
The Contender

From the other side of the door, James heard the running footsteps of what he guessed to be at least two children, maybe more. Multiple voices called out competitively, "I'll get it! I'll get it!" Apparently answering the door was a big event, or at least some kind of privilege. He knew his uncle had several children, but he honestly didn't know *how* many, and he'd never bothered to keep track of their names and ages through the information received in letters that were addressed to other people in the family.

The door was flung open, and James looked down to see a lanky boy who was taller than the two girls in front of him. When none of them spoke, James said, "Hello."

"Hello," the littlest girl said eagerly, and he smiled at her. The others didn't speak and looked more cautious.

"I'm looking for Ian Brierley. Is he your father?"

"You talk like him," the little girl commented, and James chuckled. Since he'd been raised in the same home in the same country as Ian, they certainly would have the same accent.

James smiled at her again, then looked at the boy, hoping to get a straight answer.

"Yes, he's our father," the boy said and stepped back. "Come in and I'll get him."

"Thank you," James said and stepped inside. He knew he looked like he had a thousand miles of dust on him. He probably did. The girls didn't seem to notice, however. They just stood there and stared at him, the younger one smiling and the older one looking skeptical. She closed the door and kept staring while James hoped that his uncle would appear soon. He tried to think of something to say, but he couldn't come up with one single point of possible conversation.

James heard the approach of footsteps and looked up, but instead of his uncle, a blonde-haired woman near his own age appeared at the other end of the hall, saying as she did so, "Did I hear the . . . door?" Just before the last word came out of her mouth, she stopped abruptly and looked at him as if she'd seen a ghost. He wasn't certain what had caused such a reaction in her, or why she continued to stare at him. But he had no doubt about why he couldn't keep himself from staring at *her*. Never in his life had just *seeing* a woman initiated such a response in him. His heart quickened, his palms became sweaty, he felt hot from the inside out but consumed with a sudden chill. A quick logical assessment made it clear there *was* no logic to such an experience. By all appearances, she was not the kind of woman he would have ever felt drawn to. She was no doubt beautiful, but in a simple way that generally would not have held his attention. Her attire implied a practical life, and her countenance betrayed something that felt entirely foreign to him. But he couldn't stop staring. His ears started to ring, and for a moment he almost feared becoming light-headed. He wondered how this encounter would evolve if he had to suddenly take a step in order to get close enough to a wall to find support so he wouldn't teeter like a drunken man. He'd never believed in destiny, never believed in such fanciful things as love at first sight— until now. He'd never felt so completely attracted to a woman; but it was more than that. Attraction was not a sufficient explanation. He felt drawn to her, as if something that had been missing in his life was now standing before him. The journey felt worth it. And everything that had preceded it didn't seem as bad as it had felt a minute ago.

"That's my sister," the littlest girl said, startling James from his trance. But he noticed that it startled the reason for his trance as well. She glanced away and chuckled uncomfortably, putting a hand unconsciously to her heart. James didn't even have to wonder if he'd had the same effect on her that she'd had on him.

"Your sister is very beautiful," James said, and the unnamed sister looked at him again, as if she couldn't force herself not to. He saw an unmasked intrigue in her eyes, and he had no trouble knowing that she could see the same in his.

Gillian startled herself to the realization that she was staring at this man, which brought her to an awareness of the pounding of her heart. With the hope that reverting to practicality might ease the undeniable tension, she asked, "May I help you?"

"He wants to see Papa," Rachel answered for him while he continued to stare at her.

"Mont went to get him," Sarah reported.

Gillian nodded and forced herself to look elsewhere, but it only lasted a moment. Her eyes moved back to his as if she had no control over them whatsoever. He was a little taller than average with a lean build and dark, wavy hair that hung to the bottom of his neck; his brown eyes were tormenting her, and she didn't even know his name. She did think that he looked vaguely familiar, but she couldn't quite put her finger on just why that was the case.

"Would you like to sit down?" she asked, again hoping to ease the tension.

"Oh, thank you, but . . ." he looked down at himself, "no. I've just come into the city with . . ."

He seemed unable to finish due to being flustered, and she guessed, "A wagon company?"

"That's right," he said, looking at her again.

Fearing that she might actually go weak in the knees if she continued to stand there, looking like an utter fool, she hurried to say, "I'll go and see where my father might be." She rushed around the corner, out of his view, and leaned her back against the wall, pressing a hand over her pounding heart. Was this what she'd been waiting all her life to feel? Was this that magical feeling she'd given up hoping for? Or was it just some ridiculous notion she'd be wise to ignore? If it *was* some indication of deep attraction, she had to wonder what kind of cruel twist of fate would bring this man through her door the day *after* she had committed herself to marriage. And now she'd just stood there in the hall like some kind of ogling schoolgirl, likely giving this man the impression that she was available. Well, she wasn't. That's all there was to it. And if they had any more interaction whatsoever, she would have to make it immediately clear that she was committed elsewhere.

Gillian tried to gather herself together enough to go and find her father, then she heard him coming down the stairs with Mont on his heels. She quietly eased out of their view, hoping to remain close enough to overhear something about who this man was and what he wanted.

"Hello," she heard her father say with pleasant curiosity. "I was told you were looking for me."

"I am indeed," James said, forcing his thoughts away from his sudden obsession with the blonde sister—who would then, of course, be this man's daughter; his cousin. Focused on his uncle, he felt his heart pound for an entirely different reason. He'd been anticipating this meeting for many months, and the journey to get here had been ridiculous, to say the least. "You're Ian Brierley?" he asked, just to be certain.

"I am," Ian said and extended a hand. James shook it firmly as Ian added, "And you are?"

James took a deep breath, knowing that all he had to do was speak his name to either be welcomed or kicked out—depending on this man's interpretation of what he'd been told through letters. "I'm James MacBrier," he said and added quickly, "your brother's son."

He saw enlightenment in Ian's eyes, then a smile. "I know who you are," Ian said with a chuckle as he threw his arms around James to give him a firm, fatherly embrace—oblivious to the dirt on James's clothes. He drew back and took James's shoulders into his hands. He was a little taller than James, and bore a definite resemblance to other members of the family that James had grown up knowing. Ian's hair was a little darker and a little more curly than his own, but he recognized some similarity in their features.

"How in the world did you get here?" Ian asked.

James glanced self-consciously at his clothes. "I should think it's obvious."

"Of course. There's only one way, really," Ian said. "But . . . why? Why would you come all this way?"

"That's a long story," he said, "but I guess I could sum it up by saying that I just needed a fresh start."

"If you'd sent a telegram, we could have met you when you arrived; we could have been more prepared and—"

"I don't want to impose," James said. "I have money and I can get a room if you'll let me know where there's something available, and I can—"

"I wouldn't dream of having you stay elsewhere!" Ian said eagerly.

"We have a tolerable guest room, and you're welcome to stay here as long as you need."

James wondered then if his uncle *didn't* know the truth about him. He couldn't imagine this good man inviting him to live under his roof if he had actually been warned about his reputation. He felt certain it would be fair to warn him, but he wasn't sure how to get the conversation to that point.

"Come and sit down," Ian said, motioning toward a lovely parlor.

"Oh, thank you, but . . ." James glanced down at himself again. "I really should clean up before I—"

"Nonsense. This house can handle some dust. It's a common factor where we live." Ian urged James into the parlor while at the same time addressing the three children who were still hovering close by. "This is your cousin, James . . . all the way from Scotland. I haven't seen him since he was a very little boy." He touched the littlest girl on the nose. "He was about your size." He then said to James, "This is Rachel." The littlest girl looked up at him and smiled. "And this is Sarah," he said, referring to the other girl. "And this fine young man is Mont, which is short for Montgomery."

"Hello," Mont said politely.

"Hello," James replied.

Ian sat down. James brushed off the back of his breeches the best that he could before he sat across from him, but remained at the edge of his seat. "So, tell me, James," Ian said, "why you—"

"Please call me Jamie. My friends all did. The family always called me James, but it never settled very well with me to be truthful. I'm sure bearing the name suited my father well enough, although I never knew him so I can't say for sure. Perhaps you would know the answer to that."

"Yes, I believe the name suited him," Ian said.

"Glad to hear it," Jamie said. "As for me, it always felt a little too formal, so I've become rather attached to Jamie." He chuckled. "Sorry for the lengthy explanation. I think I'm a little nervous."

"No need for that," Ian said. "We're glad to have you here, Jamie. Are you hungry?" Before Jamie could answer, Ian said to Sarah, "Go and tell Gillian to set an extra place at the table for supper." To Rachel he said, "You go and help your sisters get supper ready." To Mont he added, "Go and tell your mother that your cousin James has come from Scotland, and I'll bring him up to meet her a little later. See if your mother needs anything, and watch out for Gavin."

The children all left to follow his orders, and Jamie had to admit he felt a little more relaxed without the extra three sets of eyes sizing him up.

Gillian made a quiet dash for the kitchen once she'd heard that her sisters had been sent to find her there. She managed to be nonchalantly standing at the stove when they entered with instructions that she pretended not to have already overheard. She put the girls to work, certain her father would prefer they remain busy while he had a chance to visit with the new arrival.

"Is your wife not well?" Jamie asked his uncle.

"She had a baby less than two weeks ago," Ian said, his eyes hinting at some kind of trauma even before he finished his explanation. "It was a terrible ordeal and required an emergency surgery to save her life. She's doing well, all in all, but she's very weak and still experiencing a great deal of pain."

"I'm sorry to hear it," Jamie said. "Perhaps the timing of my arrival is not good, or—"

"Nonsense," Ian said. "She'll be thrilled to meet you, and . . . well," he chuckled, "she met you when you were a baby, but—"

"But you left for America not many months after I was born."

"That's right," Ian said. "And the one time I went back, I went without her."

"I'll look forward to meeting her . . . again," Jamie said, his mind preoccupied with the blonde woman he'd seen. Then it clicked in his mind. Gillian. Ian had told the little girl to tell Gillian to set an extra place. He knew that name. Gillian had been named after his aunt, Ian's sister. She was actually the daughter of Wren's sister, who had died at sea. Gillian had been left an orphan, and Ian and Wren had raised her as their own. She wasn't actually a blood relative of his, but still family. Either way, feeling the way he felt could be complicated. He wondered if Gillian was the woman he'd seen. He hoped so.

Jamie felt certain his uncle was full of questions, but he felt awkward with his dirtiness and said, "If I'm staying for supper, perhaps I should get cleaned up first, and—"

"Oh, of course," Ian said and came to his feet. Jamie did the same. "Wait right here for just a minute."

Once alone, Jamie turned to survey the room more closely. The furnishings and decor had a simple, almost rugged quality to them, but that was understandable, as secluded as they were. He suspected that almost everything in the room had been handmade by people here in the valley. He wondered once again what would motivate people to live this disconnected from any real society. He knew the answer to that question was religion, but that didn't seem like nearly enough of an answer to him. Perhaps with time he would come to understand, although his desire to understand didn't mean he would ever want anything to do with it. He'd found a place to start a new life. That was all he cared about.

Ian came back into the room, saying, "Come along." They crossed the hall and walked through a room that looked like a very simple version of a library or study, with a desk and some sparsely filled bookshelves and little else beyond a couple of chairs. Ian opened a door on the other side of the room and motioned Jamie through it. Once inside, Ian drew back the curtains, then opened the window with a groan. It hadn't been opened for a while.

"It won't be as hot in here as it is upstairs," he said. "It's not much, but it's adequate."

"It's more than fine, thank you," Jamie said. At one time he might have thought otherwise, but he'd been sleeping on the ground for many weeks now. The room looked very comfortable. It was small and furnished only with a narrow bed, a bureau with three drawers, a little table by the bed, and a single chair.

Ian opened another door to show him a tiny closet. "I've told my older boys to care for your horse and bring your things in." He walked back out of the room, motioning for Jamie to follow him. "In the meantime, you can get cleaned up in here. I've left some of my own clothes in here. I'm betting you have nothing clean at the moment."

"That would be correct."

"Until we get some laundry done for you, I think you can manage with something of mine."

"That's very thoughtful," Jamie said. "Thank you." They passed through a kitchen area where he hoped to get a glimpse of the woman he'd become smitten with, but he only saw the two little girls setting dishes on a large table.

Ian led him into a room with two large tubs and a stove where three pots of water were steaming. Barrels with more water sat nearby, as well as towels, soap, shampoo, and the clothes that Ian had spoken of. "We always have water heating for evening washing up. You go ahead and use what you need to bathe. We can heat more when you're finished."

"Thank you," Jamie said, desperately craving a good bath but hoping he wasn't putting anyone out too much. "You're very kind."

Ian just smiled. "It's good to have you here. Just leave the dirty clothes . . ." he pointed to a large basket in the corner, "there, and they can be washed tomorrow."

"I don't want anyone to have to—"

"It's not a problem," Ian insisted. "As soon as you're done here, supper should be on."

"Thank you," Jamie said again, and Ian left, closing the door behind him. Jamie noticed a lock on the door and latched it before he put the water and soap to good use. The last real bath he'd enjoyed had been somewhere on the other side of the Mississippi River in a hotel. If he'd known then how long he'd be going without a decent bed or the opportunity to bathe in hot water, he wondered if he would have made the journey. It was good he hadn't known.

Jamie enjoyed his bath but still tried to be quick about it, not wanting supper to be delayed for him. He found that Ian's clothes fit him rather well, except for the need to roll up the shirtsleeves, and the breeches bunched up a bit over the top of his boots, since they were a little too long. But it was better than putting his own clothes back on, when they all needed laundering very badly. He felt more inclined to find out where he could purchase some new clothes first thing tomorrow. There was no comb available in the room, so he did his best to smooth his hair back off his face with his hands. He was also accustomed to shaving in the evenings and had done so last night before bed, but the dark hair on his face grew quickly. Looking into the tiny mirror, he knew he looked decidedly scruffy, but it would have to do for now. He didn't want to go searching for his shaving items, and since he was already clean and dressed, he couldn't shave without creating a new mess.

Wanting to leave the room in order as much as possible, he took note of the small, low door that opened to the outside, making it possible to dump the dirty water and have it run into the dirt outside the house. He emptied the tub and did his best to leave it clean, then he moved water from the barrels into the pots on the stove so that it could be heating for others to use.

Unlocking the door, Jamie knew he should have been wondering what it might be like to share supper with his uncle's family. He'd been wondering things like that for weeks. But all he could think about was the blonde woman he presumed to be Gillian. His heart quickened to think of even being in the same room with her. To sit at the same table and share a meal made him fear that he might turn into a bumbling fool. It occurred to him that he could really use a drink, but he knew better than to ask or to expect that there would even be liquor in the house. He'd spent many weeks traveling with a band of Mormons. He knew well enough their views on liquor, and he didn't want to offend his budding relationships with these people by bringing their attention to his penchant for drinking. If his uncle didn't know about that through letters he'd exchanged with their common relatives—or if he was too polite to allow it to impede their reunion—Jamie wasn't about to remind him of it. He'd gone many weeks without drinking. Surely he could manage now. And maybe this was the fresh start he needed in order to put such a habit behind him for good.

Gillian heard the door to the bathing room open, and her intense preoccupation with Jamie MacBrier provoked a fresh quickening of her heart. She felt utterly terrified to even be in the same room with him, but at the same time she felt so drawn to him that she could likely just stare at him for the entire evening and somehow be more fulfilled as a woman than she had ever been. How was it possible to feel that way about a person when they'd barely laid eyes on each other? And what purpose could such feelings have when she was already committed? The very idea of having this newcomer living under their roof was as thrilling as it was tormenting. She was so confused that she both wanted to break down in tears and burst forth with laughter. The contradictions in her feelings tempted her to believe that Jamie MacBrier had triggered some kind of deeply rooted insanity inside of her.

Gillian heard footsteps come slowly into the kitchen and she looked up, trying very hard to appear nonchalant. But the sight of him provoked a reaction inside of her even more intense than what she'd experienced earlier. The absence of trail dust combined with the white shirt and dark breeches had a startling effect. His dark hair looked more wavy now that it was wet. She found herself wanting to touch that hair, and she wondered what it might be like to kiss him. Certain that such a thought must surely be wicked, she abruptly looked back at the pot of boiling potatoes in front of her. She lifted one out with a spoon and pricked it with a fork to test its doneness.

"You must feel better now," she said, focused on the need for the potatoes to cook a few more minutes.

"I do, yes," he said, his voice stirring her. "Thank you." He cleared his throat with an indication that he felt some nervousness. "Is there something I can do to help you?"

"No . . . thank you. Just . . . have a seat, if you'd like, or . . . you can wait in the parlor, or—"

"I'll wait right here, if that's all right," he said and slid a chair away from the table that was set for dinner.

Gillian couldn't protest, but as he sat down where he could look directly at her, she wondered if she could bear it.

"Are you Gillian?" he asked, and she glanced at him in surprise. "I heard your father use the name. I just wondered if that's you, or if—"

"Yes, I'm Gillian," she said, stirring the pot of peas.

"Then I know well who you are." The statement was spoken with such confidence that Gillian felt unnerved. She couldn't keep herself from looking at him as he said, "You were born to Wren MacBrier's sister on the crossing to America, and your mother died soon afterward. Your father had died before you were born. Since I was born not long before Ian and Wren left for America, you and I are very near in age."

Gillian thought about that for a long moment while she stirred the peas again. Stories she'd heard of her family's relatives in Scotland came together in her head. "Then I suppose I know well who *you* are."

Jamie held his breath. How much *did* she know? And how might she feel about him based on the information she might have been told? He wasn't out to keep any secrets from her or anyone else. He knew well enough how painful the disclosure of a secret could be, and he was convinced that no secret could be kept forever. He could only hope that Gillian wasn't the kind of person to judge him harshly for events of the past.

Gillian went on to say, "You were raised by the Earl of Brierley and his wife because your parents are both dead as well."

"That's right," Jamie said. "My mother right after I was born, my father months earlier. Ironic that we would have that in common."

"It *is* ironic," Gillian said, stunned by the depth of that irony in light of what she was feeling.

Jamie felt determined to take this opportunity to clear away the most important issue, if only so he wouldn't have to dread it coming up. "The biggest difference would be that your parents were actually married."

She looked startled by the comment, and he knew from her expression alone that she hadn't known that about him. He wondered for a moment if he shouldn't have told her, but his convictions about secrets answered that question for him. He was not going to pretend to be anything different than what he was. He had no problem being known as a scoundrel if he'd earned that title, but he could not tolerate hypocrisy—in himself or anyone else.

"But that has nothing to do with *you,* or who you are."

Her insistence warmed him and felt strangely healing in ways he could never tell her, but he had a long way to go in healing completely over the fact being discussed. There was only one thing he could think of to say, and he hoped it would close the conversation. "That's what they tell me."

"They?" she asked, and he wondered where all the people were who had a place set at this table. He became momentarily distracted by the number of plates set out and wondered how big this family was. He wished he'd paid more attention to what he'd been told about his uncle's family.

When an interruption didn't save him from acknowledging her question, he said, "The people who actually care about me who don't want my illegitimacy to damage me—as opposed to everyone else who knew me my entire life and looked down on me while I had no idea *why* they were looking down on me."

By some force beyond her control, Gillian set the spoon down and pulled out a chair so that she could sit to face him. She felt so deeply overcome with warmth and compassion that it felt impossible to hold it all inside. She wondered where such feelings originated. She'd always considered herself a warm and compassionate person, but this was different. It was as if she could truly feel what he felt, and her desire to soothe and comfort him was overpowering. "You didn't know?" she asked, finding it impossible to believe she'd only met this man less than an hour ago.

He shook his head and looked down, but only for a moment. Their eyes connected the same way they had when they'd first looked at each other earlier in the hall. She felt like an entirely different person when he looked at her like that, and she wondered what kind of strangeness could account for such a feeling. He sighed, and she sensed that there was no easy way for him to answer her question. Without thinking about it first, she reached out and took his hand, squeezing it gently. She didn't realize what she'd done until he gasped and looked down at their hands. She'd done it the same way she would have taken Hugh's hand, or one of her parents or siblings. It was a common gesture among the family and close friends and she'd meant no implication beyond compassion, but given the unmasked effect they had on each other, she wondered how he might perceive what she'd done. Now that she was holding his hand, she couldn't very well withdraw it. She just kept looking at him, waiting for him to answer the question.

Jamie had difficulty remembering what course the conversation had been on when he realized Gillian had clasped his fingers with hers. Her touch made his hand tingle with a magical effect, as if he'd been touched by an angel. He looked into her eyes and saw a compassion and gentleness there that he'd never felt from anyone. As much as he'd felt loved and accepted by his grandmother and his aunt, he'd never had a woman exude such perfect concern. He felt in that moment as if he could bask in her genuine comfort and mercy and become a completely different man from the one who had entered this house.

"You didn't know?" Gillian repeated, hoping to prod them out of this intense silence.

Again Jamie shook his head, then he told her what he'd never wanted to talk about with anyone. "Not until my grandmother's death a few years ago. I believe she'd always had good intentions to tell me when the time was right, but when is it the right time to tell someone such a thing?" He chuckled with no sign of humor and looked down, hoping that if he didn't look at her eyes he might be able to concentrate more on the conversation. "I was very close to my grandmother. My aunt and uncle always made me feel included, and I cannot fault the way they treated me. But it was my grandmother who made me feel truly loved and accepted . . . in spite of my circumstances. When she died, the full truth of my circumstances came to light. I realize now that her being alive had somehow inspired people in the community to keep their mouths shut; as if her presence in the world had some kind of threatening effect on them. Once she was gone, people started to talk; they said things they'd always been thinking but hadn't dared say to my face. Once I realized the whole truth, I could never hope to stay there and have any kind of normal life. I'm not sure I can, anyway—not when I know what I do about myself."

"But this has nothing to do with you, Jamie," she said, and he had no choice but to meet her eyes again. Her familiar use of his name—as if she'd known him for years—provoked a fresh quickening of his heart. Her sincere kindness lured him to come out of himself in ways he never had before. He took in her words like a dry sponge soaking up fresh water. "Surely the choices made by your parents could not be altered by you; a child has no control over such things. You can only take what you've experienced and do your best to make it into something valuable for *you.*"

While Jamie had never heard such wisdom applied to his own circumstances, he had to admit, "I suppose that's what I'm doing here. I needed a fresh start . . . away from people who know the truth."

Gillian smiled and tightened her grip on his hand, which increased the tingling sensation. "Then I hope you find what you're looking for."

"Maybe I already have," he said. Gillian didn't realize the implication was personal until he lifted his free hand to touch her face. She wanted to protest and retract from his touch. But the part of her conscience that was trying to be convinced of her commitment to Hugh was completely overpowered by an inexplicable, instinctive connection to this man. She became even more lost in his gaze, something that had become startlingly comfortable and familiar. Her heart quickened further, and her stomach fluttered. She instinctively lifted her hand and put it over his where it rested against her cheek. He leaned slightly closer, and she wondered if he might try to kiss her. Even Hugh had never kissed her lips. In fact, she'd never been kissed by *any* man.

Every nerve in Gillian's body reacted to the possibility of having Jamie MacBrier kiss her, then a knock at the back door startled her so badly that she gasped and bolted out of her chair and away from Jamie's touch as if she'd been struck by lightning. She was vaguely aware of Jamie chuckling, but it was an awkward kind of chuckle, as if he too had been so startled that he wasn't sure how to respond. She hurried to the stove, suddenly concerned that the peas and potatoes would be overcooked and that the first meal she would serve to Jamie would be pathetic.

"Come in," she called while hurrying to move the peas off of the heat of the stove.

She wasn't surprised to have Hugh enter the room. She *was* surprised by the stark feelings of guilt that smothered the magic she'd been feeling with Jamie.

"It's just me," Hugh said, and by the time he had closed the door, Gillian had moved the potatoes off the heat as well.

"Hello," she said, glancing over her shoulder at him, which brought her to an awareness that he had noticed a stranger in the room. Jamie was on his feet, and the two men nodded at each other.

"This is James MacBrier," she said. "He's just arrived from Scotland."

"With the company that came in today?" Hugh asked with genuine interest.

"That's right," Jamie said.

"A relative," Hugh said with an eager smile. "It's remarkable how much you resemble Ian . . . and how you speak like him."

"That explains why I thought you looked familiar," Gillian said.

Jamie felt pleased by the comment but didn't have a chance to respond before Hugh said, "There's definitely a family resemblance."

He held out a hand and Jamie shook it firmly. "It's a pleasure to meet you, Mr. MacBrier."

"Oh, Jamie, please. I loathe formality."

"We're all very casual here," Gillian said, wondering if Hugh would be so pleased to meet Jamie if he had any idea what was going on in her head—and in her heart. While she was talking she tested both the peas and potatoes for doneness and found them to be perfect. A blessing.

As she went to drain the water from the potatoes, Hugh stepped forward, saying, "Here, let me help you." He took the colander from her and held it while she dumped the potatoes into it over the sink.

"Thank you," she said, then they did the same with the peas. She put lids over both pans to keep the food warm until the pork loin came out of the oven.

With the task done, her attention returned to the unfinished introductions. With a glance toward Jamie, she said, "This is Hugh Montgomery. Hugh has been a friend of the family since . . . well, since I was a little girl."

"They're the only family I've got, really," Hugh said, "so I make a nuisance of myself as often as I can get away with it."

He chuckled, and Gillian said, "Never a nuisance."

"Perhaps I could take some lessons," Jamie said lightly to Hugh, and both men laughed. Gillian was glad to see them getting along well, but then neither of them yet knew that Jamie's appearance had created a huge dilemma in her heart—in little more than an hour. What was she thinking? It was preposterous to think that she could back down on her commitment to Hugh based on her first impressions of a man she knew nothing about.

Jamie said, "Would that be the same Montgomery that Mont is named after?"

"You have a good memory," Gillian said. "Yes, the very same."

"A distinct honor," Hugh said to Jamie. Then turning back to Gillian he said, "I believe some of the children are in the yard. Should I have them come in and wash up?"

"Yes, please," Gillian said. "I'm going to take a tray up to Mother, and then we can eat."

Hugh nodded again at Jamie, who nodded in return. Gillian focused on removing the pork loin from the oven and slicing off a portion for her mother.

"Can I help you?" Jamie asked after the door had closed behind Hugh.

"No, thank you," she said without looking at him. Jamie actually felt a little jealous of the way that she had allowed Hugh to help her, but then he'd seemed to know what to do. He was obviously very comfortable in this house. Hopefully, with time, Jamie could be the same. He wanted to be by her side and help her with every little task for the rest of his life. He chided himself for such ridiculous thoughts, but at the same time he couldn't discredit the feelings that had spurred them.

Sensing some kind of tension in the air that he didn't understand but refused to ignore, Jamie said, "Is something wrong? Did I do something to make you uncomfortable?"

Gillian looked at him, surprised by his straightforward manner and taken off guard by the question when she had no idea how to answer it. He hadn't done anything wrong, and the reasons for her discomfort were something that he could not possibly understand. She considered it a very tiny lie when she said, "No, of course not."

She focused on preparing a plate for her mother, adding some butter to the potatoes and peas once they were on the plate. The butter melted over the hot vegetables as Gillian put the plate and some eating utensils on a tray, along with a large glass of water.

"I'll be right back," Gillian said and tossed Jamie a smile before she hurried toward the stairs. "Make yourself at home."

Jamie watched Gillian walk away, confronted once again by a quickened heartbeat. Then a mass of children exploded through the back door. Along with the three he'd met earlier, there were two older boys who both looked well on their way to being men in their physique but who still had the faces of little boys. He knew he'd looked much the same not so many years ago, but the irony of that deepened when he recognized similarities in their features and coloring to his own. Two of the younger children he'd already met had lighter hair, but these boys were both dark. The younger of the two looked curiously at Jamie but didn't comment; the older one showed a great deal of maturity when he stepped toward Jamie with an outstretched hand, saying, "You must be our cousin. The kids were talking about you. James, isn't it?"

"Call me Jamie," he said, shaking the boy's hand.

"I'm Harry, and that's Alfred."

"Hello," Alfred said and offered a passive wave.

"Hello," Jamie said. "It's a pleasure to meet you both."

Harry then nudged his brother with an elbow. "We'll just hurry and get washed up." They went into the bathing room where the younger three children had gone, and the noise level coming from the room was impossible to ignore.

Hugh then came in the back door carrying a very young boy in his arms. Jamie wondered how many children there were. Including Gillian, he could tally seven at the moment. But he'd been told there was a new baby, and he wondered if there were more. Eight children? His aunt and uncle in Scotland had four, and that had seemed like a large family. He'd known of people in the community with large families, but he'd never associated with them closely enough to be part of such a situation. It was overwhelming to think of seeing to the physical and emotional needs of so large a family!

"This is Gavin," Hugh said to Jamie, obviously noticing that Jamie's attention was on the child.

"After my grandfather," Jamie said. He didn't remember the man, but he knew his name well.

"That's right," Hugh said and took the little one into the bathing room to wash him up. Jamie listened to the commotion and heard the older boys making some effort to get the younger ones to hurry along. Hugh's voice joined them in trying to help establish order, and he also teased the children in a comfortable way that provoked some giggling. The laughter elevated the noise level, but it made Jamie smile.

Gillian took the tray into her mother's room to find her father sitting on the edge of the bed with the baby in his arms. Ian saw her and stood to lay the sleeping Deborah in her bassinet.

"I was telling your mother about Jamie," Ian said. "He seems like a fine young man."

"He seems that way," Gillian said for lack of anything better to say. She didn't know if she was thrilled or upset by the way her heart and stomach responded to the mention of his name, but she fought to keep her expression disinterested. It occurred to her that her father might not have any idea of the changed status between her and Hugh. But her mother knew, or at least she knew Hugh had proposed. She'd not yet had an opportunity to tell Wren that she'd actually accepted Hugh's proposal and they were just waiting to take care of the formalities.

"Here's your supper," Gillian said, setting the tray over her mother's lap.

"Oh, it looks delicious!" Wren said, her weakness and pallor still so readily evident that it was difficult not to feel concerned. "What luck that ye would have a pork loin in the oven when our visitor showed up."

"Luck indeed," Gillian said, thinking of some of the meals that she threw together for the family that would not have been nearly so nice as this. Simple as it was, it exceeded many things she might serve to unexpected company. "But then," she pointed out, "if he's going to be living with us, he'll soon realize how simple a cook I am."

"You're an excellent cook," Ian said. "If he's going to live with us, he'll have to take what he gets and accept who we are. We're not trying to impress him."

Gillian wanted to protest. She desperately wanted to impress him, but knew that trying to be anything more or less than herself would be ludicrous. Given her relationship with Hugh, she wondered why she would even entertain such a thought.

"Is something wrong?" Wren asked, startling Gillian.

"No, I'm fine," she said with a convincing smile.

Ian bent over the bed to kiss Wren on the brow. "After we're done with supper you can meet Jamie," he said.

"I'll look forward t' that," Wren said.

"Do you need anything else right now?" he asked with his typical kindness and concern.

"I'm fine for now," Wren said with a smile toward her husband. Gillian watched them for a moment, just as she'd been watching them for years. She wanted what they shared, and she wondered if she'd made a mistake in believing that she could find it with Hugh. She could hardly believe the circumstances she'd gotten herself into, and she didn't know what to do about it. But for now, there was a hungry family downstairs to feed and Jamie MacBrier to impress.

Chapter Five
Unwanted

Supper erupted into typical chaos as soon as the blessing had been spoken. Of course, the children all had good table manners and were polite and appropriate. But they all had a great deal to talk about, and their bantering and teasing were always noisy. Gillian wondered how it all might appear to Jamie. He seemed to be taking it all in with good humor, but occasionally his expression betrayed that he'd never seen anything like this before. He asked Ian lightly if he had any other children hidden away besides the new baby.

Ian chuckled and said, "Only the two who are already married."

Gillian could see that Jamie had not expected an answer that would add to the number. "That is . . . amazing," Jamie said.

"Ten all together," Ian said with pride. He glanced around the table, as if to make eye contact with every child. "A beautiful family."

"Indeed," Hugh said with enthusiasm, but his eyes were focused on Gillian. She noticed and smiled circumspectly at him before turning away. She couldn't help being aware that both Hugh and Jamie were discreetly preoccupied with her. She tried not to look at either of them, fearing the implications of what her eyes might betray either way. She needed to tell Jamie the truth, but she wondered how to do it and when she might find the opportunity. The very thought put her stomach into knots, and she wondered why. She had to believe that Jamie would actually care, or she wouldn't feel such a reaction.

Ian finally got the children to quiet down so that he could have Jamie tell him all the news from Scotland. Jamie could only report how it had been many months earlier when he had left there, but they quickly started talking about people they both knew—both in the family and in the community—and they seemed to be thoroughly enjoying the conversation. When Jamie was asked about his reasons for traveling all this way, he simply said, "I just felt the need for a new start."

Once supper was over, Ian put Sarah in charge of Gavin and told the rest of the children they needed to help him clean up the kitchen.

"Gillian," her father said with what appeared to be a quick wink, "why don't you take Jamie upstairs to meet your mother. Take your time and let us take care of this."

"Very well," Gillian said, concealing her mixed emotions. She wondered if her father would have made such a request if he had any idea about Hugh's proposal of marriage. Then it occurred to her that Ian might actually be enlisted in some form of matchmaking. Did he sense the attraction between her and Jamie? And if he had noticed, then she had to wonder if Hugh had noticed it as well? They were both sharp men. Was she a fool to think she could conceal Jamie's effect on her? She wondered if Hugh would be taking the opportunity to speak with her father while she was upstairs entertaining Jamie and her mother. The irony was horrible, but what could she do?

With the children clearing the table, Gillian could do nothing but come to her feet and motion for Jamie to follow her. She caught a smile from Hugh and smiled in return, hoping he was oblivious to any change in her. On her way up the stairs it occurred to her more fully that she knew nothing about Jamie MacBrier. She did know that he did not share her religious beliefs, and she could never marry a man who didn't. Along with that, she couldn't imagine ever telling Hugh that she'd changed her mind about agreeing to marry him. It would break his heart, and she just couldn't do it! She'd been prayerful about her decision to marry Hugh. She hadn't known that Jamie would be arriving, but God had known. Surely she needed to have the integrity to stand by her decision. Still, she couldn't deny the cloud of confusion surrounding her over the entire matter.

Gillian was keenly aware of Jamie coming up the stairs right behind her. He didn't have to say a word or make a sound beyond the step of his boots on the stairs. She could feel his presence as if it radiated some kind of tangible warmth. The feeling added to her confusion. In her mind she knew what she needed to do. She'd already made her decision and she needed to stand by it. Didn't she?

Distracting herself with practical reasons for having Jamie in her company, she turned to him once they'd reached the top of the stairs, and said to him quietly, "My mother has hardly come out of this room for months now. She was down in bed before the birth, and then the birth itself—as my father told you—was extremely difficult for her."

He was walking slowly beside her in the hallway, and said with compassion, "It was very difficult for *you.*" Gillian looked up at him and wondered if her eyes were so easy for him to read. He verified it when he added, "You were there?"

"Yes, I was there," she said and felt a little choked up. "It was horrible, to be truthful."

"You're a very brave woman."

Gillian stopped walking and chuckled to force back her temptation to sob as the effect of the memories caught her by surprise. "How do you know I wasn't just a blubbering fool, making matters worse with my own screaming and crying?"

"That doesn't seem at all like you," he said. "I would think you were more likely to be calm and reliable, even though you *wanted* to scream and cry."

Gillian became lost in his eyes again. How could he know her so well? How could he so perfectly understand one of the most horrible experiences of her life? His knowledge and compassion for her seemed to come so easily, as if it cost him no effort whatsoever; as if he just *knew* her, when in truth he could know next to nothing about her.

"I *did* want to scream and cry," she admitted, then forced herself to look away and move on toward her mother's room. "Thankfully, Mother is recovering well, and I must admit my gratitude in knowing that she won't be able to have any more children. She's the kind of woman that would give her life to bring a child into the world, but her family needs her. She's recovering slowly, and I'm certain she'll be thrilled to meet you. Having a new face to look at and some company is always a delight for her." She smiled and knocked at the partially open door. "I'm certain the two of you will have much to talk about."

"I'm certain we will," Jamie said, returning her smile. She realized then how truly remarkable his smile was. She could get lost in simply looking at it, if she weren't already in danger of becoming lost in his eyes.

"Come in," Wren called softly, and Gillian pushed the door open. The baby was sleeping on the bed next to Wren.

"Mother," Gillian said, motioning to Jamie as he entered the room, "this is Jamie MacBrier; Jamie, my mother, Wren Brierley." As she stated the names, Gillian thought of the story she'd been told many times of how Ian and Wren had made the decision to change their surname when they'd become Americans. Rather than holding to the very Scottish *MacBrier,* they had chosen *Brierley,* which was the name of the magnificent castlelike house in the Highlands where Ian had been raised. It was a lovely surname, and Gillian was proud to use it, in spite of knowing that legally her surname was something else. But she was a part of this family for the span of her mortal life, and she loved sharing their name. She wondered if Jamie might also choose to change his name if he intended to remain here in America, but that was a question to be saved for another conversation.

"What a fine pleasure this is," Wren said, reaching out her hand toward Jamie. "Come sit beside me and tell me about yerself."

Jamie felt something warm and comforting already, just being in the same room with Wren Brierley. Her accent reminded him of home. It was different from his own, and from Ian's. She'd obviously been raised among the common people, and without formal education. But it brought to mind many friends and people in the community where he'd grown up, and it touched him.

There were chairs in the room, but when Jamie put his hand into hers, Wren urged him to sit on the edge of the bed so that she could see him more clearly. She squeezed his hand tightly and held on to it for several seconds. He liked the feel of her hand; it reminded him of his deceased grandmother, who was the only person he could say had truly understood him. He immediately became aware of the close relationship that Gillian shared with her mother. He couldn't help watching her as she helped her mother sit up a little more comfortably against the pillows behind her. Then she sat on the other side of the bed as Wren began asking Jamie questions about her homeland and Brierley and the people they both knew. Wren tired quickly, but it was evident she enjoyed the conversation at least as much as he did, and she made him promise to come and talk to her every day. She expressed hope that he would be staying with them for a good, long time, and that he would decide to stay here in the valley permanently.

"We're family," she said, again taking his hand to squeeze it. "And family should be t'gether."

"You're very kind," Jamie said, resisting the urge to add that in the hours since he'd arrived, he'd fallen hopelessly in love with this woman's daughter, and with any luck he would be able to make himself even more a part of the family very soon.

As Jamie stood to leave the room, Gillian leaned over her mother and put a tender kiss to her brow. "I'll check back in a bit," she said. "Is there anything you need right now?"

"I'm fine, but thank ye, dear," Wren said. She smiled at Jamie. "Just make certain this precious young man has what *he* needs to be comfortable here."

"I'm being well cared for," Jamie said. "Don't you worry about me."

"Oh, I'm not worried," Wren said with a smile and a subtle glance that passed from him to Gillian and back again. He felt certain she'd noticed the way he and Gillian couldn't seem to keep from looking at each other. It was likely difficult *not* to notice, he concluded. He felt as if it had to be literally glowing from his face. He'd never experienced anything like this, and he knew such feelings had to be life altering.

Gillian led the way out of the room while Jamie thanked Wren once again for the pleasant visit and expressed how very good it had been to meet her. She returned the compliment, and Jamie followed Gillian into the hall. She closed the door, then walked toward the stairs, but Jamie couldn't overlook this opportunity to be alone with her.

Gillian was surprised to feel Jamie take hold of her arm to stop her. She turned to face him, then wished she hadn't. Her resolve had a way of disintegrating in the face of his gaze.

"Now, where were we?" he asked in a whisper. With her mother's bedroom door closed, and everyone else downstairs or out of the house, there wasn't any risk of being overheard. His whisper seemed more an attempt to express something in regard to what he was feeling. "In the kitchen," he clarified, "before we were interrupted." She gasped as he took hold of one of her hands, then pressed his other hand to her face. "I think it was something like this," he said, and the next thing she knew, his lips were pressed to her brow. Hugh had kissed her there, but it had never been like this. Jamie's kiss was sweet and tender, but filled with silent emotions and implications that Gillian had never imagined possible from a simple gesture of affection. She sensed that he didn't want to offend her but he'd not been able to hold back. She felt so thoroughly taken aback by the effect of his kiss that she could hardly breathe. It lasted longer than she'd expected, and she slowly opened her eyes to see him doing the same, as if he were awaking from a pleasant dream. She knew exactly how he felt.

"Forgive me," he said as if to directly verify her thoughts. She looked into his eyes and found his face so close to hers that she could feel his breath. "I simply couldn't resist another minute. It's been so long since I've kissed a woman, I was afraid I might have forgotten how."

Gillian wondered by the way he was looking at her if he intended to kiss her lips, and she didn't know if she could survive such an experience in her present frame of mind. She felt unnerved at the very idea of him having kissed other women. Given the fact that he didn't share her religious beliefs, she wondered what else he might have shared with other women. But she told herself that such possibilities didn't really matter when what she had to tell him would put a stop to this here and now.

"There's something I need to say," she said quietly. With as close as he was standing to her, no volume was necessary.

He didn't comment, but she saw him steel himself, as if to be prepared for a harsh blow. She took a deep breath and forced the words out of her mouth, but she closed her eyes when she said them, unable to look at him. "You should know . . . Jamie . . . that Hugh and I are practically engaged."

Jamie felt as if someone had just slugged him in the chest. He felt as if the hourglass of his life had just flipped over and he was being shoved through the tiny neck in the middle. While he felt certain that her marrying *anyone* but him had to be a mistake, he couldn't deny that he was a stranger to these people. He'd just stepped into their world with no idea who they were or what was going on in their lives. His sudden and unexpected feelings for Gillian did not change where she might be in her life. Still, he couldn't just stand back and do nothing, given the way he felt. As ludicrous as it seemed, he could not deny the way he felt.

"Practically?" he countered quietly without stepping back. "Does that mean *not quite* engaged? Or does it mean engaged for purely *practical* reasons? He's *practically* old enough to be your father. He seems like a nice enough man, but . . . are you sure he's the right man for you?"

"Of course he's the right man for me!" Gillian insisted, wishing it hadn't sounded so defensive, especially when Jamie's left eyebrow went up in response to her tone. But how could she not feel defensive when he'd seemed to read her mind? She *had* agreed to marry Hugh for purely practical reasons, and he *was* old enough to be her father. It wasn't the age difference that bothered her, but the other certainly did. But she'd agreed to marry Hugh, and she wasn't going to back down on that agreement simply because a handsome and charismatic man had caught her attention. In a voice that was more calm and self-assured, she added, "We haven't announced our engagement yet because he hasn't officially spoken to my father. That's just a technicality. I've agreed to marry him, and that's that. I just thought you should know."

"Well, thank you for informing me, Miss Brierley." He finally took a step away from her, and Gillian hated the distance. She also hated the evidence that he was actually angry. "Does anyone else know?"

"Only my mother." She didn't clarify that her mother knew Hugh had proposed but didn't know that Gillian had accepted. But she planned to tell her right away. She needed her mother's support and wisdom more than she ever had.

"So, it's a secret," Jamie said.

"For now."

"I can't help wondering why you would let *me* in on the secret when I'm *practically* a stranger."

Gillian felt alarmed by the question but remained unruffled. "I just thought you should know," she said.

"Given the fact that I just kissed you, it would certainly be valuable information." His anger came out in the form of biting sarcasm, but

Gillian couldn't blame him. She didn't know him well enough to have predicted how he would respond to the news, but she did know he had strong feelings for her. She'd seen it as clearly as she'd felt it herself. She wasn't surprised by his anger. In a strange way it was somewhat validating; it meant she hadn't imagined what she'd seen in his eyes and felt in his kiss. It felt good to mean that much to someone, but at the same time she'd never imagined when she'd gotten out of bed this morning and mentally planned out her day that she would be breaking a man's heart.

Gillian was hoping to escape this conversation, certain that by tomorrow Jamie would have settled with the fact that she was not the woman for him. But she was completely taken aback to see tears glistening in his eyes, while his chin quivered subtly at the same time. She could see him visibly fighting back his emotion, and knew he felt embarrassed by it. But she also saw a determination in him to say something more. She wanted to escape before her own emotion came to the surface, but she owed him the decency of finishing the conversation.

"You don't love him!" he said with the confidence of stating a cold, hard fact.

Gillian turned away, unable to deny it. "I'm committed to him. He and I are the same."

"*We,*" he said hotly, motioning back and forth between them with his hand, "are the same."

"Not in the ways that matter," she insisted. "You know nothing about me, about what matters to me. And I know nothing about you."

"Precisely! Which means you can't just . . . flick me away like an unwanted fly before you even consider giving me a chance."

His plea struck Gillian deeply, but while she was considering how to respond to it, he said with barely controlled anger, "If that's it . . . then it would seem I know where I stand."

He turned to leave and she put a hand on his arm to stop him, saying his name as if she had loved him for a lifetime. "Jamie."

He turned to look at her, his eyes mingling hope with cynicism. "What?" he asked, the cynicism dominant in his voice.

"It's . . . complicated. It's not my intention to hurt you. How could either of us have anticipated what's happened today?"

"Well, it happened. I would think it's obvious that you have a choice to make, and yet it's evident your mind is already made up, so I'll just . . . bow out. But don't expect me to do it graciously."

Gillian saw a vague hint of his chin quivering again, which strongly contradicted the anger percolating in his eyes. He hurried away before she could say anything else, but she suspected he didn't want her to see any further evidence of his emotion. She stood there, stunned, wondering how so much turmoil and heartbreak could have occurred in her life in a matter of hours. She'd betrayed Hugh and hurt Jamie deeply. And no matter how she looked at it, she was caught in the middle of something that felt impossible to solve without hurting one or both of these men even further.

Since her father had said he'd have the family take care of everything in the kitchen, Gillian turned around and went straight back to her mother's room.

"Are ye all right?" Wren asked when she saw Gillian's expression.

Gillian closed the door and leaned against it. "No, I'm not all right. I don't know if I've ever been less all right."

Gillian just shook her head, not knowing where to begin. As if to give her a moment to gather her thoughts, Wren said, "Jamie seems t' be a fine young man." She laughed softly. "And the way the two of ye were looking at each other made the room more bright; I swear t' ye that it did."

Gillian squeezed her eyes closed and grimaced.

"What is it?" Wren asked. "Talk t' yer mother."

Gillian just said it, still relying on the door behind her for support. "Last night I told Hugh I would marry him."

She heard Wren gasp but still didn't open her eyes. Then her mother said with slow deliberation, "Oh, I see. And then a stranger walked int' yer life and everything went from gray to colored."

Gillian opened her eyes. "You make it sound as if that's a *good* thing!"

"Isn't it?" Wren asked, surprised.

"Mother," Gillian said, moving toward the bed where she sat on its edge and leaned forward, "he knows nothing of our religious beliefs, and we know nothing about *him.*"

"Except that he has awakened something in ye that ye've never felt before."

Gillian couldn't deny the statement; she couldn't even acknowledge it. But she knew her mother was right. Wren apparently knew it too, when she added with gentle confidence, "He *has* awakened something in ye, has he not?"

"He has," Gillian said, "but I don't know what to do with it. Hugh is a good man; he's everything a woman like me could ever ask for in a husband. There is no reason why I shouldn't be thrilled with the opportunity to marry such a man and share my life with him."

"Except that in all the years ye've known Hugh, he's never made ye feel the way ye've felt for Jamie just this evening."

Gillian groaned at hearing the truth and the dilemma it had created. She attempted once more to put forth her defense. "There's nothing practical at all in what I'm feeling; I'm certain of it. Hugh is kind and decent and good. How can I possibly even consider—"

"Oh, my darling," Wren said, "ye're thinking too much. Ye've got to drop down out of yer head and trust yer heart. Of course we're taught t' study a problem out in our minds, and we have t' use common sense, but when we are striving t' live close t' the Spirit and do the will of our Father in Heaven, we have t' trust our feelings. It's through our feelings that the Spirit speaks t' us, my darling. Ye cannot move forward with such a decision until yer mind and yer heart are in agreement. As I see it, yer head is telling ye that ye should marry Hugh, but yer heart is drawn to Jamie. Ye cannot go forward until they are both in agreement."

Gillian felt both calmed and alarmed by her mother's wisdom. It made perfect sense, and she knew that Wren was right. But it only made the situation all the more complicated, especially since she had just utterly alienated Jamie with her attempt to declare her situation. She felt a sudden need to find him and offer some clarification, to tell him that she simply needed some time. And she would have to tell Hugh the same. The very idea of having such a conversation felt so difficult to face that she had no comprehension of how she could do it. But she had to. She couldn't deny what she was feeling, and she needed to try to behave with some maturity and wisdom—no matter how difficult the situation might be.

Gillian thanked her mother and shared a careful embrace with her before she hurried down the stairs, determined to find Jamie and ask to have a private word with him. She thought of what she would tell him, that she'd spoken impulsively, that she needed to speak with Hugh, and she needed some time to get to know him better before she made any decisions. She imagined him smiling, and her heart quickened at the thought. It quickened further and sparked a fluttering in her stomach as she recalled him kissing her brow. His tenderness and simple affection had warmed her deeply! Her feelings of betrayal toward Hugh were smothered by the thrill, and she consoled herself with the fact that she could not make the most important decision in her life based on guilt or a desire not to hurt Hugh's feelings. She knew it would be hard for him, but she had to do what was right for herself—not in selfishness, but according to the guidance of the Holy Spirit. That was the only way for her to know the path that her Heavenly Father would have her take. And she needed to watch and listen closely and wait for that path to be illuminated.

Gillian found most of the family gathered in the parlor. Hugh was there visiting with her father, but since there were children in the room, she had to assume he'd not yet spoken to her father about their engagement. She hoped not.

"Where is Jamie?" Gillian asked. She saw Hugh's brows go up slightly and wondered if the enthusiasm in the question had alerted him to the change in her. Or perhaps he had observed more over the supper table than she had chosen to believe. She pushed thoughts of hurting Hugh away for the moment, unable to face them.

Ian said as if it were nothing, "Oh, he said he needed some fresh air, wanted to explore the town a little. He rode out a while ago; said not to wait up for him. I told him I'd leave the back door unlocked."

Gillian felt certain she didn't conceal her disappointment any better than she'd concealed her enthusiasm a moment ago. She attempted to smooth it over by nonchalantly saying, "It's not important. I just . . . wanted to make certain . . . he has what he needs, and . . ."

"He said that he did when I asked him," Ian said. "The boys went out to see to the animals. As soon as they come in, we'll gather for study and prayer."

Gillian nodded. "I'll just . . . be in the kitchen."

She hurried there, fearing what her expression might betray. She was glad to find the kitchen in perfect order, but wished there was some task she could focus on in order to distract her thoughts. She wondered how long it might be until she could speak with Jamie. She panicked to recall that he had left feeling angry. He'd said not to wait up for him, and she wondered where he might actually go in this city where he could be out that late. There were very few possibilities, but they all made her a little queasy. It occurred to her that if Jamie was the kind of man to spend the evening drinking and fraternizing with the undesirables of the community, then she was perhaps completely disillusioned in believing he might be a potentially suitable husband.

Gillian wondered if Hugh might stay to have study and prayer with the family, as he did on occasion. She also wondered if he might seek out an opportunity, after the children had gone to bed, to speak with her father. She wondered if she should ask Hugh to wait, then wondered if it would be best to just go forward—all dependent on whatever Jamie might be doing at this moment.

She was startled to hear Hugh say from behind her, "Are you all right?"

"I'm fine," she lied and gave him a convincing smile. "It's just been a big day. How are you?"

"I'm fine," he said, also offering a persuasive smile. But Gillian sensed that perhaps he too was lying. She wondered if he'd sensed what she was feeling, but she didn't know how to ask and preferred to avoid it altogether. "I need to go." She expected him to kiss her brow, as he had done the last time they had parted. But he didn't, and she wondered if that was significant.

"Have you spoken to my father?" she asked, both fearing and hoping that he had.

"Not yet," he said. She expected him to say that he simply hadn't found the right opportunity, or offer some other explanation. But he didn't. He smiled again, but it seemed mildly forced. "I'll see you soon."

"Take care," she said, and he went out the back door.

Gillian stood there in the kitchen for minutes after the door had closed. She thought of the possibilities of what Hugh might be feeling, and she wanted to sink to her knees and cry like a baby. Why couldn't she just feel for him the way she felt for Jamie? Why couldn't this be an easy equation? And why did it seem inevitable that whatever the outcome of this situation might be, one of these men would come away with a broken heart? Who was she to break a man's heart? What had she done to end up in this situation? It was ludicrous!

All through study and prayer, Gillian couldn't keep her mind away from her dilemma. She felt equally worried for Jamie and Hugh, wondering what each of them was doing right now, what they were thinking, how they were feeling. The depth of concern she felt for both of them implied that she felt some kind of love. She *did* love Hugh. She always had. But not the way a woman should love a man. What she felt had no hint of romantic love or passionate love. And yet that was exactly what she felt for Jamie. But she didn't know him well enough to know if she loved him. It was accurate to say that she'd fallen in love with him, which simply was not the same thing. It was possible for one to lead to the other, but never possible for one to be enough in and of itself.

After family prayer and study, Gillian exchanged the usual good-nights with her family members and left her mother in her father's care. She went to her room where she normally would have dressed for bed, brushed out her hair, and cleaned her teeth. She did the brushing and cleaning, but remained in her clothes, hoping at any moment to hear Jamie come through the back door so she could speak to him. She opened her personal copy of the Book of Mormon to read, as she always did at bedtime, but she couldn't focus and closed it again. She knelt beside her bed and said her usual nighttime prayers, offering extra pleading in regard to this situation. She asked God to help her know what to do, and to bless both Hugh and Jamie, to comfort them, guide them, and protect them. When her prayer was done, she paced the floor, then she went quietly downstairs when it occurred to her that perhaps Jamie had already come in and he'd done it so noiselessly that she'd missed it. She found his room empty and the back door still unlocked. She then started pacing the kitchen, keeping an eye on the clock. She'd purposely set a lamp close to it so that she could tell at a glance what time it was. Eleven o'clock came and went. Midnight passed. One. Where on earth could he be? And what could he be doing? She began to feel worried, then *deeply* worried. She prayed and stewed over what to do, recalling a story about her parents that had practically become a legend in their family. They had been living in New York City when she was just a baby. They had been desperately trying to find the location of the Mormons and had finally discovered that they were in Nauvoo, Illinois. Her parents had written a letter to the Prophet Joseph Smith, hoping for some kind of response that would make it possible for them to join the Saints. Ian took the letter out to mail it and was struck by a passing carriage while crossing the street in the fog. After hours of worrying, Wren had finally gone to the police station and they had guided her to the hospital. Of course, Ian had come through just fine, but Wren couldn't tell the story without expressing how she'd feared that her husband had been badly hurt or, even worse, that he might be dead.

Gillian began to wonder the same now. If Jamie *had* been hurt, no one in town would know who he was or who to inform. At ten minutes after one, Gillian finally went upstairs to wake her father. She didn't want to disturb him, but she didn't know what to do, and it was out of the question for her to go looking for her missing cousin. If Jamie *was* loitering in some unfavorable establishment, a young woman certainly couldn't go in such a place without subjecting herself to other potential problems.

"What is it?" Ian asked in a panicked voice after she'd gently nudged him awake.

"I'm sorry to bother you," Gillian whispered, grateful to see that she'd not disturbed her mother, who was sleeping deeply, likely aided by the pain medication that she still took at night. Only the baby's crying seemed to reach past her lethargic state when she was in such deep sleep. "Jamie's not back yet. It's past one. I'm worried . . . and I don't know what to do."

Ian sat up and shook his head as if that might bring him closer to coherency. "*Why* are you even awake?" he asked, taking note that she was still dressed.

"I needed to talk to him," she said, and Ian's eyes showed some suspicion but he said nothing more. Knowing he needed to get dressed, she added, "I'll be downstairs."

Only a couple of minutes later, Ian joined her in the kitchen. "Are you sure he's not in the house somewhere?"

"I'm positive. I just checked his room again. Do you have any idea where he could be?" she asked, not wanting to suggest what she was thinking.

"There are a few possibilities," Ian said with chagrin, heading toward the door.

"Be careful," Gillian said, stepping onto the back porch with him. At the same moment, they both saw two horses and two men at the end of the long drive. One man was helping the other down from his horse. They both stumbled and laughed in a way that made the evidence of their condition sink into Gillian's heart like a dagger. Her stomach smoldered as she watched Mr. Miller from next door help Jamie walk toward the back porch. Mr. Miller wasn't terribly steady on his feet, but he was a lot more so than Jamie, who barely seemed to know where he was.

Mr. Miller looked up to see Ian and said, "Before he got too drunk he told me he belongs to you."

"In a manner of speaking," Ian said, his voice expressing more disappointment than disgust. Gillian was prone to feel more the other way around. Or perhaps it was more that she would *rather* feel disgust than disappointment. If she fully acknowledged the depth of her disappointment, she would crumble into a heap of childish tears.

Ian stepped off the porch to ease an arm around Jamie to support him. "Thank you, Mr. Miller," Ian said, "for getting him home safely. You're very kind."

"Maybe he'll do the same for me next time," Mr. Miller said with an obnoxious laugh.

"Can you get home safely?" Ian asked him.

"Oh, yeah. I'm used to it," he said as if being accustomed to drunken behavior might be something to take pride in.

Ian turned to Gillian and said, "Help me get him to his room, then I'll take care of his horse."

Gillian put her arm around Jamie, wishing that being close to him now could have had the effect on her that it had earlier. Now she just felt heartbroken and sick to her stomach. He reeked of cigarette smoke and liquor. Worst of all, she knew that her rejection of him earlier had surely contributed to this. Of course, she knew it had been his choice to go out and get drunk. But she still felt some responsibility, and it tore

at her conscience. If she had been more open to the idea of giving him
a fair chance in light of what they were feeling, perhaps it might have
inspired him to be his best self, rather than descending into his *worst*
self. On the other hand, if this was an indication of the kind of man
that Jamie MacBrier was, then perhaps it was best that she knew now.
In truth, she could never even consider marrying a man who would
engage in this kind of behavior. By the time they had Jamie to the bed
in his room, Gillian knew that it was best she'd not yet said anything
to Hugh. It was best to press forward with her original plan. She just
needed to pretend that what had transpired between her and Jamie had
not transpired. He was clearly not the man for her. It was not even a
matter to be considered.

Gillian watched as her father pulled off Jamie's boots and tossed
them. Jamie hovered somewhere between delirium and a drunken
hysteria exhibited by brief bouts of laughter. Unable to watch this
scene any longer, she said to her father, "I'll take care of his horse. It's
probably best if *you* deal with this."

"Probably," Ian said with a weighted sigh.

By the time Gillian was out the back door, hot tears were stinging
her eyes. Alone as she was, she made no effort to hold them back.
Taking hold of the horse's reins, she started to sob and didn't stop.
She managed to light a lantern in the barn, remove the saddle and
bridle, and secure the horse in a stall while she sobbed as if her
heart might burst right out of her chest. And she wondered why.
She'd not even known this man today at lunch. How could he have
stepped into her life and wreaked such havoc in so short a time?
She felt certain his appearance was nothing more than some form of
opposition meant to test her. And she could only remain true to her
convictions, and do what she knew had to be done.

Knowing all was well in the barn, Gillian composed herself and
wiped her tears before she headed back to the house. She found
her father sitting in the kitchen, his arms folded over his chest. He
didn't look at all happy. But she couldn't blame him. He'd taken his
nephew into his home without hesitation, and now he was probably
wondering what he'd done. She was glad for the very dim lamplight
that would not reveal that telltale red splotch on her face. She
locked the back door and expected her father to stand up, or to say

something. When he did neither she sat down as well. He looked at her as if he were trying to figure something out. Knowing her father well, she could imagine his mind churning with his disappointment over Jamie's behavior, and his wondering what he was going to do about it. She was completely unprepared to hear him say, "He's in love with you."

"What?" Gillian countered, astonished. To actually hear the word *love* spoken in regard to this situation unnerved her already frazzled nerves. "What on earth would make you think such a thing? We barely know him!"

"He just told me," Ian said.

Gillian chuckled uncomfortably and looked away. "He's drunk. Men say and do all kinds of foolish things when they're drunk."

"That's a true statement," Ian said and sighed loudly, his voice suddenly distant. "And I once expressed that same idea to your mother. Do you know what she told me?" Gillian said nothing. She'd never heard *this* story before, and she wondered what point her father could possibly be getting to. "In essence, she told me that sometimes liquor removes inhibitions and makes a man say what he might not say otherwise." She was startled when he added, "Gillian, look at me." She did so, quivering inside. "Is it true?"

"Should I know the answer to that question?" she asked, knowing the defensiveness in her tone implied her guilt.

"You're a sharp and insightful woman. I saw the way he looked at you today, and you at him. The two of you had a chance to talk. I think you know how he feels about you. And I think it has something to do with his reasons for drinking tonight."

"I cannot be held responsible for his drinking."

"No, you cannot, but I can't help him if I don't understand what's going on. Is it true?"

Gillian looked away and couldn't speak. She was choking on the sudden heat in her throat, and she couldn't hold back the tears that came with force and slid down her cheeks.

"You mustn't judge him too harshly," Ian said in a gentle voice.

Gillian looked at her father. "What do you mean?" she asked, feeling as if there was something more to this conversation than she'd been able to perceive.

"Gillian," he said, "when your mother said that to me . . . about liquor making a man say what he might not say otherwise . . . she was talking about me, and the first time I'd admitted to her that I love her." Gillian gasped but still couldn't speak. "She was angry with me for being drunk, and she had a right to be. I was frequently drunk, Gillian. It's a time in my life I'm not proud of, but the facts of my past cannot be changed. I had a serious drinking problem for years. If your mother had not been patient and forgiving, where would any of us be?" He leaned more toward her. "I would never want you to put yourself in a position where you might be hurt—for any reason. Do you understand me?"

"Yes."

"I'm simply saying . . . don't judge him too harshly."

"Father," she said, knowing it had to be said, "I'm going to marry Hugh."

Ian leaned back as if he'd been hit with a hot wind. He'd obviously had no idea that this was brewing. "Are you?" he asked as if he questioned her judgment. Or perhaps he meant to imply that she should question her own judgment.

"I've already told him that I would. He didn't want anyone to know until he'd spoken to you officially, but . . . Jamie showing up like this does not change the fact that I've already told Hugh I would marry him."

Ian was thoughtful a long moment. "Hugh might disagree with that if he knew what I know. It's late and we're both tired and overwhelmed. I'm going back to bed." He stood up and put a hand on her shoulder. "You're a wise and spiritual woman, Gillian. You'll know what to do as long as you let the guidance of the Spirit overcome your own fears and desires." He sighed loudly. "I'll sit with Jamie in the morning until he comes around. In spite of this, we don't want him to feel unwanted."

Gillian felt guilt in recalling her last conversation with him. "Perhaps he already does."

"Then we'll have to work on that." He kissed the top of her head. "Get some sleep. It's too late at night to be stewing over such things."

When Gillian hesitated to stand, Ian took hold of her arm and urged her to her feet. He picked up the lamp from the table and they walked together up the stairs, but nothing more was said until he told her good night at the door to her room. Gillian had to force herself to change into a nightgown and actually get into bed. She was so overcome with so many thoughts and feelings that she felt certain she would never be able to sleep, but her next awareness was daylight in the room and the sound of noisy children in the hall. It was rare for her to not be up and dressed before the children were awake. She hoped her father was managing all right, because she didn't feel at all like getting up. Of course, the older children were well versed in caring for the younger ones, but she wondered if she should be in the kitchen cooking breakfast. She wondered for a moment what the family would do once she married Hugh and lived elsewhere, then she checked her thoughts, wondering whether that was the right course. In spite of what her father had said about not judging Jamie too harshly, she didn't believe he could even be a fair candidate for marriage. The chasm between their lives was simply too wide and too deep.

Chapter Six
The Problem

Jamie came reluctantly awake to a familiar sensation. He'd been drinking, and far too much. He became aware of being in a bed, but couldn't remember getting there. He forced his eyes open just enough to get a glimpse of his surroundings and didn't find them familiar at all. He rolled over and groaned from the pain it prompted in his head. He took another glimpse and found some vague familiarity that eventually led his thoughts to recalling that this room was in his uncle's house; the room he'd been given to stay in. He felt some relief to know that he'd made it to a safe place last night after his drunken escapade, but he felt utterly ashamed to realize that the family was likely now aware of his bad habit, and that his uncle would probably throw him out on the street before lunch. He'd surely missed breakfast. Through the fogginess of his aching head, he reasoned that leaving was probably best, after all. Gillian's declaration had shattered his motivations for staying here. He'd fallen for her hard and fast, but she'd made it clear where she stood. And Jamie knew he couldn't remain here and watch her live her life with another man—especially a man she didn't love. The irony would simply be too horrible to endure.

"Are you awake enough to have a conversation?" Jamie heard his uncle say, and he grimaced from the shame more than from the pain in his head.

"Marginally," Jamie said and forced his eyes open. He couldn't see his uncle and assumed he was on the *other* side of the bed.

When he attempted to lift his head to see, he heard Ian say, "There's no need to sit up. I'm certain your head would rather stay where it is. But I do think we need to talk."

Jamie *did* sit up, and managed to get a pillow behind his head so he could lean against the wall at the head of the bed. "I'd like to attempt a tiny bit of dignity," he said.

"Fair enough," Ian said.

A minute passed without him saying anything else, and Jamie decided to just get to the inevitable point. Perhaps he had more hope of maintaining some degree of dignity if he spared his uncle from having to deliver the bad news. "I don't blame you at all for not wanting me here. I can stay at a hotel until I can make arrangements to head back east, and—"

"And then what?" Ian asked, sounding surprised.

His tone encouraged Jamie to open his eyes and try to focus on his uncle's face. He saw disappointment in his eyes, but surprisingly, there was no evidence of anger. "I'm not certain what I'll do exactly," Jamie said, "but I don't think my being here is a good idea. Given your Mormon principles, my bad habits are not very compatible."

"I can't argue with that," Ian said, "but I don't know what makes you think that would mean I want you to leave. I do *not* want you to leave. In fact, I very much want you to stay. I think we need each other."

Jamie turned to look at him more directly. "How is *that?*"

"You need family. You need a stable environment. To go wandering around some foreign country with no idea where you're going or what you're doing is not going to solve this problem."

"This *problem?*"

"Convince me," Ian said, his voice now betraying a hint of anger, "that this is *not* a problem."

Jamie sighed and closed his eyes. "You've got me there. But I am not your responsibility. And my *problems* are certainly not your responsibility."

"You're an adult, Jamie. You and your problems are no one's responsibility but your own. However, we're family. And families help each other get through their problems. I have a suspicion that since my mother died you didn't feel like you were getting the support you needed from the *other* branch of the family."

"Why would you suspect that?" Jamie asked, suspicious of his suspicions.

"Because I know my brother at least as well as you do," Ian said. "He's a good man and he's been a good brother to me, but I know that the two of you haven't necessarily shared a warm relationship. I suspect his wife was always very kind to you."

"They were both very kind to me," Jamie said.

"But they never really felt like your parents, did they," Ian said as if he already knew. "You always felt like an orphan."

"Are you psychic?"

"Not at all." Ian chuckled mildly, then he sighed. "Let's just say that I've been able to read a great deal between the lines of the letters I've received from Scotland over the years." He chuckled again. "Actually, it would be more accurate to say that my mother admitted more than once that she felt concerned for that very thing. She tried to be a mother figure in your life, but she knew it just wasn't the same when you were being raised along with your cousins, yet knowing you didn't have the same parents."

"I never wanted for anything," Jamie insisted.

"Except acceptance," Ian said, and Jamie had to fight not to let the statement provoke him to tears. Did that mean it was true? Apparently. Ian sighed again. "Well, that's one thing you'll get here. I strongly disagree with trying to drown your problems with liquor. It only causes more problems. Trust me on that. I can't make you not drink. I am asking that you not expose my family to it in any way."

"How can you be certain I won't do that?"

"I can't."

"But you're still going to let me stay here?"

"I don't believe you traveled all this way—under the circumstances that have to be endured to make the journey—just to expand your horizons. Like I said, we need each other."

"I can be humble and gracious enough to admit that I could really use a family," Jamie said, "but I don't see where *you* could need *me* at all. Have you got some degrading, menial labor that needs to be performed?"

"Maybe," Ian said with a chuckle. "But that's not what I mean."

"What *do* you mean?"

"That's something we'll discuss at another time," Ian said. "For now, I'd just like you to try and fit in with the family as much as possible. There are things you can do to help if you just take notice and help where it's needed."

"Of course," he said. "I have no intention of being a leech, or expecting something for nothing."

"I know that," Ian said.

"How do you know that?"

Ian leaned his forearms on his thighs and looked closely at Jamie. "Believe it or not, Jamie, you and I are a lot more alike than you might think."

"MacBrier blood and all that," Jamie said, sounding mildly sarcastic.

Ian remained unaffected by the comment or the tone. "It's much more than that, but sharing MacBrier blood is no small thing, and I will never take it lightly. I hope you don't, either."

"I have a deep respect for my heritage," Jamie said, "but that's not what you're talking about."

"No, it's not."

"Then what?" Jamie asked. "Or will you keep me in suspense over that as well?"

"I was once where you are," Ian said straightly.

"Where I am?" Jamie asked. "I don't understand."

Ian sighed again. He looked away, then looked at Jamie firmly. "I don't talk about this much anymore. It's long in the past, and I prefer to leave it there. But I can't count how many times I woke up with a hangover and had no idea how I'd gotten where I was."

Jamie looked at his uncle hard, trying to imagine such a thing being true. He simply *couldn't* imagine. "You're not just saying that to patronize me, are you?"

Ian let out an ironic chuckle. "First of all, I'm not the patronizing type. Secondly, why would I want you to believe something about me that I'm utterly ashamed of? I'm trying to tell you that I have empathy for what you're going through. The only real difference I see is that you probably have a better excuse to drink than I did. Facing what you've learned about your life is no small thing. But drinking isn't going to make it go away; it will only make it worse. The craving for liquor can be difficult to contend with when there are thoughts in your head that you don't want to be thinking."

"You *do* know what it's like," Jamie admitted. "How do you recommend that a man might overcome such cravings?"

"For me, it was when my fear of what might happen while I was drunk became more powerful than my fear of facing the reality of my life. I wouldn't recommend getting to that point. I would recommend that you stop now and find other things with which to occupy yourself."

"Such as?"

"We can work on that," Ian said. "But we should make one thing very clear between us." Jamie waited for some kind of reprimand or warning in regard to his household rules, but he said with the same firmness, "You should not be drinking in order to avoid facing the way you feel about Gillian."

Jamie was so stunned he almost choked. He managed to keep it to a mild cough, then said, "The way I . . . feel?"

His attempt to sound innocent was apparently futile when Ian said, "You told me last night when I was helping you to bed that you're in love with her . . . but she doesn't want you." He allowed a moment of silence to let that sink in before he added, "Is it true?"

Jamie coughed again. "It seems entirely illogical to be able to know such things when I've been here less than twenty-four hours."

"There are many things in life that are entirely illogical, Jamie. But I think that *you* need to figure out whether or not it's true. And you will make more progress with that if you remain sober."

Jamie wanted to mention that Gillian was going to marry Hugh, but she'd said that her father didn't know yet. Regardless of whether he did, it wasn't Jamie's place to bring it up. Instead he pointed out something that should have been obvious. "She would never have a man like me," he said as if it were a final conclusion. That's how he felt.

"I don't think that you even know what kind of man you are, Jamie. You've never had a chance to really figure that out when it hasn't been so long since you learned the truth about your parentage. If you don't know what kind of man you are, then how could she possibly know?"

Jamie was intrigued by the principle, but he felt more stuck on the other point of Ian's comment. "You know the truth about my parentage."

"Of course I know," Ian said. "Your father's death is still one of my most difficult memories. It was a horrible day in my life. And you were brought to us after you were born. Wren and I were not living at Brierley at the time. Your mother's maid brought you to us. We were the first ones in the family to lay eyes on you, and even then you looked like your father. In spite of the circumstances, your existence was a sweet gift to us."

"Perhaps I should have come with you to America in the beginning."

"I can't say it didn't cross my mind, but my parents needed you. You were a great boon to their lives. You gave them so much joy. Now that they're both gone, perhaps it's right for you to be with us. I am glad to have you here."

"Well, I'm glad to be here," Jamie said. "And I'm especially glad you're not kicking me out. I truly *don't* know what I'd do."

Ian stood and said, "I want you to feel welcome here, Jamie, and I want you to know that you can talk to me—anytime, about anything. I mean it."

"Thank you," Jamie said. "And I'm certain you'll let me know if I get out of line."

"Oh, I'll let you know," Ian said, moving toward the door. "Get cleaned up and come to the kitchen. I'll heat up your breakfast."

"I can heat it up," Jamie said. Ian's hand was on the doorknob when Jamie added, "Why *did* you drink?"

Ian thought about it. "I would have to say that the answer to that question is complicated, but there were two prominent reasons. One is that a dear friend of mine was killed, and I blamed myself for his death."

"And the other?"

"I was in love with Wren and didn't know how to tell her, because she was in love with someone else. There's hot water in the bathing room. I'm going to town in a little while. Why don't you come with me and we'll get you some new clothes."

Jamie nodded, and Ian left the room. He sat there for a few minutes just trying to take in the conversation and all of its implications. Ian Brierley was as sharp as he was kind. Jamie just hoped that he could have the self-discipline to not disappoint his uncle any further. Beyond that, he couldn't think of anything to hope for. Gillian was determined to marry Hugh. And while Jamie wanted to be here with Ian and his family, he did *not* want to see Gillian with another man. Perhaps he would eventually end up leaving anyway. For now, he had nowhere else to go, and Ian had been right. He needed a family. For all that his heart felt broken over Gillian, he could at least be grateful that he had a family, and that they were willing to accept him in spite of his bad habits.

* * * * *

Once Jamie was adequately cleaned up, he entered the kitchen to see Ian setting a plate on the table—and Gillian with her back to him, consumed with some task that was keeping her hands busy.

"Feeling better?" Ian asked Jamie.

"Somewhat," Jamie said. Gillian didn't turn or acknowledge him.

"The food has been blessed," Ian said, motioning toward a chair.

"Thank you," Jamie said and sat down, unable to see Gillian from this particular chair. "You're very kind."

Jamie heard Gillian slam something on the counter. The noise made his head wince, but he wondered if the slamming had been necessary to her task, or some indicator of the mood she was in. As if Ian were attempting to clear the air, he said, "Gillian waited up for you last night."

Jamie felt mortified at the thought. Did that mean she had seen him blind drunk? Probably. That explained the slamming. Hoping to ease the situation, he said, "That was very thoughtful of you. Thank you."

Gillian made no comment. Ian sat down nearby and said, "I think she wanted to talk to you."

"I'm certain that could be arranged," Jamie said, wishing he could see her.

"I'm certain it could," Ian said when Gillian still didn't comment.

"I've got a very busy day," she said and hurried out of the room.

Jamie said to Ian, "Perhaps you should take a vote on whether to let me stay."

"She would be the only one opposed to it, and she would lose," Ian said. "But deep inside, I believe she wants you here. She's just angry because . . . well, I think it's because she's disappointed in your behavior last night. But she understands the principle of forgiveness. Just give her some time."

"I'm not sure time will make much difference," Jamie said. "I don't want to break any confidences here, but she made it very clear where I stand."

"And that's why you went out and got drunk?" Ian asked.

Jamie leaned back. "I suppose that had something to do with it."

Ian turned more toward Jamie. "I would never pretend to fully understand my daughter, but I do know one thing for certain. She's confused right now. Don't let her confusion rub off on you."

Ian stood up and left Jamie alone with his breakfast. "Too late for that," Jamie said to the empty room, then he pressed a hand to his forehead, groaning from the hovering pain in his head, and the confusion he felt on several accounts that only amplified it. "You're such a fool," he muttered to himself and tried to gather enough fortitude to face the day—and to face Gillian. If she would even talk to him. His relief at being allowed to stay—and being fairly reprimanded by his uncle—was overshadowed by the prospect of living under the same roof with Gillian. Given the way he felt about her, it wasn't going to be easy. He wondered if he could balance out the blessing of having a family with the torment of loving a woman who wanted nothing to do with him.

Jamie was glad to get out of the house with Ian. He liked his uncle and felt surprisingly comfortable with him. Some of the children asked to come along. Jamie would have been fine with that if it weren't for the noise they made and his persistent headache. Ian told them they could come next time. He gave them all assignments regarding chores in the house and yard and helping care for their mother and each other.

The two men set out together, sitting side by side on the seat of a wagon with a long bed. Ian explained that they needed to pick up some grain for the animals and some food supplies for the family. "And I know an excellent place where you can get some ready-made clothes," Ian said. "We have some talented seamstresses in town. I'm certain you can order some custom-made things as well. The available fabrics are somewhat limited, but we manage well enough."

"So I've seen," Jamie said. "Don't worry about me. I'm grateful to have whatever is available."

"I've noticed that," Ian said.

"Noticed what?"

"That you're grateful for whatever you have. Forgive me if this makes you uncomfortable, but I just have to say that growing up as you did—as *we* did—it would be easy to expect the best of everything. But you don't. I think that says something about your character."

"Does it?" Jamie asked. "My grandmother raised me on humility and gratitude."

"Since your grandmother is my mother," Ian said, "we were raised by the same woman. But you could have rebelled against her teachings.

You chose to take them into your life and live them. If you had come here with certain high expectations, I might not have been so eager to keep you under my roof. Or rather," Ian chuckled, "I'd be eager to give you some lessons in humility and gratitude."

Jamie managed a one-syllable chuckle, but his head hurt too badly to exert himself any more than that. "I can only imagine what *that* might entail. Although, I'm happy to do anything you would like me to do—in order to earn my keep."

"Don't worry about that. I'll keep you busy."

"I'm not worried about that," Jamie said. They were silent a couple of minutes before Jamie said, "Isn't your wife a seamstress?"

"Yes, and she does excellent work. She was the tailor's daughter. That's how I met her. She still enjoys sewing, but the children have kept her very busy, and now she . . . well, she's just too weak to do it now. But she's on the mend, and we're grateful for that."

Jamie didn't miss the unspoken implications that came through clearly in Ian's tone of voice. "You almost lost her, didn't you?"

Ian glanced at him, seeming surprised by the question, then he looked straight ahead and his expression became very somber. "Yes, it was rather horrid. I really thought she was going to leave us. I'm grateful every minute of the day that she didn't."

"Apparently your mother's teachings have sunk in well," Jamie said.

Ian chuckled. "There was a time when she likely wouldn't have thought so."

"But you turned out tolerably decent," Jamie said with light sarcasm.

Ian chuckled again. "Eventually. And so will you."

Jamie felt surprised. He seemed to mean it. "How do you know?"

"I just have a good feeling about you, Jamie MacBrier."

Jamie felt mostly guilt and shame, certain he would eventually let his uncle down and he would have to admit that he'd been far too optimistic. He felt he had to say, "Maybe you should check yourself on that."

"And maybe you should raise your expectations of yourself a little."

Jamie wasn't sure how to do that under the circumstances. A part of him believed that having a woman like Gillian in his life could certainly raise his expectations of himself, but he couldn't count on another person to make him become a better man. He had to do that for himself, and he wasn't sure he wanted to. He chose to change the subject.

"Would it be more appropriate for me to use the name Brierley . . . instead of MacBrier? As you've done?"

"That's entirely up to you," Ian said. "We felt good about changing the name, but they're both fine names."

"I suppose I'll have to think about that," Jamie said.

Ian went with Jamie to buy some new clothes and to order some others to be made. He also ordered some new boots and some shoes that would be proper for Sunday use. Since Ian had insisted that Jamie purchase a suit of clothing appropriate for church attendance, he needed shoes as well. Jamie only had to hint at preferring to avoid church attendance for Ian to make it clear that if he was going to live under their roof, he would be attending church with the family.

"You don't have to embrace our beliefs," Ian said, "and you don't even have to like it. You're welcome to hold to your own opinions on the matter, as long as you either keep them to yourself or express them appropriately and with respect. But if you're a part of the family, then you need to participate in our daily prayer and study and attend church with us on Sundays."

"Very well," Jamie said, trying not to sound as skeptical as he felt.

Ian gave him a conspiratorial smile. "You *did* say that you would be happy to do anything I would like you to do—to earn your keep." His smile widened, and he winked. "You did say that, didn't you?"

"I did say that," Jamie said with mild chagrin. Ian just chuckled.

At the general store where Ian purchased a number of supplies, Jamie got himself a few things that he needed, most specifically a new comb and razor and some shaving soap. With his purchases made, he browsed in order to kill time while Ian's purchases were put in order. He was looking at some lengths of ribbon when he heard Ian say, "You should buy Gillian one of those."

"Should I?" Jamie asked, certain she'd just throw *any* gift in his face.

"She always likes a new ribbon for her hair."

"Does she?" Jamie asked, wondering why Ian would be encouraging him to do such things when he surely believed that Hugh Montgomery was a far better man to care for his daughter.

"Trust me," Ian said and moved on.

Jamie decided to trust Ian, not thinking of any reason why he shouldn't. He bought a cream-colored ribbon and watched as it was carefully folded and put into a little bag.

On the way back to the house, Jamie asked Ian if he enjoyed living here in Salt Lake Valley. His answer surprised Jamie. "We enjoy living in peace among people who share our beliefs."

Jamie thought about it for a minute in light of some things he'd heard discussed among the Mormons he'd traveled with to get here. A part of him wanted to know more, but a bigger part of him preferred to avoid anything to do with religion. The whole God issue just made him uncomfortable, but he knew that God was the biggest reason his family members had ended up in this out-in-the-middle-of-nowhere desert. He didn't understand, and he wasn't sure he wanted to.

Back at the house, Jamie helped Ian unload the wagon. Harry and Alfred also helped. They all just had time to get washed up before lunch. It was a simple meal of bread and cheese and vegetables from the garden, but it all tasted heavenly to Jamie after being on the trail for so many weeks. He tried not to think about Gillian, and tried even harder to avoid looking at her when it became evident she was avoiding looking at him. He focused his attention instead on her younger siblings, trying to memorize their names and learn more about them. He couldn't deny that his uncle had a beautiful family, though the size was a bit overwhelming.

When the meal was over, Jamie offered to help in the cleanup efforts, but Gillian curtly said, "No, thank you," and went about her business. He caught a discreet glance from Ian that seemed to plead for his patience. He could certainly be patient, but to what end? Would it simply be to keep peace in the household so that he could stand by and watch her marry a man she didn't love? The very idea made his stomach churn. He forced thoughts of such a possibility out of his mind and chose instead to invest in the hope that Gillian might come around. Even though he hadn't come right out and said as much, Ian seemed to be on his side. Encouraging him to buy a hair ribbon for her was a big clue. He just wasn't certain how to go about actually giving it to her when she was putting a great deal of effort into avoiding him.

Later in the afternoon, Jamie noticed that Gillian was alone in the yard, hanging wet laundry on the clotheslines. He approached her quietly and watched her for a minute while she was unaware, freshly stunned at how deeply she affected him. Without saying a word, he pulled a clean, wet shirt out of the basket at her feet, grabbed some clothespins, and hung it up.

"What *are* you doing?" she asked.

"I should think it's obvious," he said and hung up a small dress.

Jamie glanced toward her and found the intensity of her glare actually humorous. He was unable to hold back a hearty chuckle, but she wasn't at all amused. "I'm just trying to be helpful," he said.

"I would prefer that you be helpful somewhere else," she said and got back to work. He continued helping until she moved the basket out of his reach and glared at him again.

If she wasn't going to let him help, he would just have to . . . how had Hugh put it? He would have to make a nuisance of himself. He chuckled again to think of the irony.

"Yesterday," Jamie said, "you let me kiss your beautiful face, and today you won't even talk to me."

"*Yesterday,*" Gillian said in a spiteful voice, without even looking at him, "I didn't know what kind of man you are."

"What kind of man I am?" Jamie asked, trying not to take her judgmental attitude too personally. But it wasn't easy. "You have no idea what kind of man I am."

"I know how drunk you were last night," she said tersely.

"And my drinking offends you?"

"Yes, it offends me," she said firmly.

"And yet you've made it indisputably clear that you are going to marry Hugh, no matter *what* kind of man I am. Therefore, whether or not I go out and drink myself into oblivion should be of absolutely no consequence to you."

She shot him a defensive glance. But that's what he wanted. He wanted to bring to light the ridiculousness of her attitude, and most of all he wanted her to come around to his way of thinking and send Hugh packing for good. He had nothing against the man. He simply didn't want Gillian to end up with *any* other man.

"I'm simply concerned," she said, focusing on her task, "about the influence you might have on my younger siblings."

Jamie let out a one-syllable laugh. "They weren't even awake when I came in. *You* were awake, however; waiting for me. Why is that, exactly?"

Gillian stopped what she was doing and sighed, but she didn't look at him. She seemed forced to honesty, and he was glad for it, especially when she admitted, "I was worried about you."

"That's very kind of you," he said with sincerity, and she went back to her work. "I would like to point out that you were worried about me because you knew that what you'd said to me was completely ridiculous."

Her eyes shot him a harsh glare as surely as if they'd fired a poisoned arrow, aimed right between his eyes. "Don't make something more out of this than it is," she growled. "You chose to go out and get drunk. I'm not responsible for that."

"No, you're not. But *you* are choosing to believe that my getting drunk is the complete and total representation of my character. Where I come from, people drink—and it's not a sin or a crime. Do you think that a man can just fall out of the sky and land here in your world and instantly be as perfectly noble as you are?"

Jamie saw something soften in her expression, although it was subtle enough that he wouldn't have caught it if he'd not been watching closely. And he knew her rancor was still very close to the surface. He took advantage of the moment and pulled the little bag out of his pocket and handed it to her.

"What is this?" she asked. The element of surprise had clearly thrown her anger toward him off balance.

"A ribbon for your hair," he said, and she looked up at him with a glimmer of the way she'd looked at him yesterday. "Your father suggested you might like it."

"My father?" she asked, completely disarmed.

"Yes," Jamie said, and couldn't resist making a point—even at the risk of stirring up her anger again. "Against all odds and logic, he actually seems to like me." He forced a smile. "Have a lovely day. I suppose you'll be seeing me at supper."

He walked away without giving her a chance to retort—not certain if she would retort with kindness or fury. But he hoped he'd said enough to make her think about what she was doing, and how she was behaving. For a short while he felt pleased over the conversation, then he thought of the full gamut of his feelings since he'd laid eyes on her yesterday and he became downright depressed. He wondered why he was even trying. He felt certain there was nothing he could ever do or say to compete with a man like Hugh Montgomery, and he was fooling himself to believe that he could ever truly be a contender for Gillian Brierley's heart.

* * * * *

Gillian stood there by the clothesline, holding the little bag in her hands, watching Jamie walk away. She felt so deeply confused that she wanted to sink into the ground and disappear. She looked at the bag, wondering what to make of such a gift. She *did* love having a new ribbon for her hair. Of course her father knew that. But why would he have suggested it to Jamie? Did her father actually *want* Jamie to give her gifts? For what purpose? Did he simply want there to be peace in the house? Was it a peace offering? Or was it intended to be more? Surely her father couldn't be proposing Jamie as a candidate for her heart! He'd heard Jamie admit to his feelings—albeit in a drunken state—but surely Ian Brierley would not want his daughter to marry such a man!

Gillian determined that she could not stand there and assess her father's motives—or Jamie's. She simply opened the bag and let the creamy-colored ribbon fall into her hand. "Oh, it's lovely," she whispered and let it slide between her fingers, imagining the difficult journey it had made to get here to the valley, probably from back east somewhere.

The thought suddenly occurred to her that Jamie was probably spying on her from a distance. She put the ribbon back in the little bag and shoved it into her apron pocket before she hurried on with her chore. She felt angry with herself for being so preoccupied with Jamie, when she wanted with all her heart to feel such feelings for Hugh. How might it be to have such powerful feelings for a man who was fine and upstanding? Instead she was being tormented by a situation that had no chance of a favorable outcome. But she knew what she had to do. The path of her life had been very clear until Jamie MacBrier had walked through the door. She needed to remember that path and keep pressing forward with the faith that all *would* be well. As long as she prayerfully strived to do what she knew was best, surely all would be well. And she believed in her deepest self that marrying Hugh would be best—for everyone. She just had to do it.

Gillian finished with the laundry, then enlisted the help of her younger sisters in cooking supper. She tried not to react when Jamie arrived in the kitchen a few minutes early. He was wearing new clothes and looked fairly respectable—except for the thick, dark stubble on his face that made him appear somewhat scruffy. It suited him, she thought. But the overall effect of Jamie MacBrier standing in the kitchen made her heart and stomach flutter in competition with each other.

"Hello," he said.

"Hello," she replied and forced herself to look away. "Thank you for the ribbon," she added, not wanting to be ungrateful. "It's lovely."

"You're welcome," he said, sounding pleased. "Is there something I can do to help?"

"No, thank you," Gillian said.

"You can help me set the table," little Rachel said eagerly.

"Oh, I'd love to," Jamie said and listened attentively to Rachel's instructions about arranging the forks and knives just so. Gillian became briefly distracted with observing his tender interaction with her little sister. When she realized he was staring back at her, she looked abruptly away but heard him chuckle. The girls appeared to be oblivious to the silent interactions of the adults in the room; she hoped it would stay that way. She could only imagine how they might tease her or ask awkward questions if they began to sense the tension—and the reasons for it.

While Gillian finished putting supper together, she concluded that knowing what she had to do didn't change her feelings for Jamie. And feelings were just feelings. She had no control over what she felt. She could only control how she acted on what she felt. She'd been taught that principle from a very young age. She also knew that her feelings for Jamie didn't change knowing what she had to do. As if to add an exclamation point to that thought, Hugh knocked lightly at the back door then came in even before Sarah could get to the door. Sarah was thrilled to see him and jumped into his arms with a giggling hug. Rachel left her post at the table long enough to do the same. Hugh laughed as he tickled the girls a little, then sent them back to work. He then focused on Gillian, and she saw the warmth and the hope in his eyes. She smiled at him, wishing she could feel the same in return.

"Hello, Gillian," Hugh said.

"Hello," she replied, and they shared a momentary gaze before she turned back to her work at the stove. "We'll be eating soon. I'm glad you're here." More for Jamie's benefit she added, "Rachel and Sarah always set a place for you. The family doesn't feel complete without you here for supper."

"I'm glad to hear it," Hugh said. "Eating supper at home alone holds very little appeal."

"I can appreciate that," Jamie said with sincerity, and Gillian almost felt angry with him for being *kind* to Hugh.

"Hello, Jamie," Hugh said, forced away from his attention to Gillian.

"Hello, Hugh," Jamie said, wishing he could find something wrong with this man. But even as little as he knew him, he appeared to be absolutely flawless. Jamie resented it, but he couldn't help but respect him. Attempting to keep the mood light and hoping to create some camaraderie between them, Jamie added, "I've been trying to follow your good example and make a nuisance of myself."

Hugh chuckled. "Perhaps you're better at it than I am."

He obviously meant it with light sarcasm, as if the word *nuisance* was truly meant to actually mean exactly the opposite. But Gillian said, "No doubt about that."

"He's not a nuisance!" Rachel said with firm authority. "He's helping me set the table."

Jamie put another fork neatly into place and said lightly, "And I'm very good at it, if I do say so myself."

This made the girls giggle, which drew Gillian's attention for just a moment. Then the boys all came in, passing through the kitchen on their way to the bathing room to get cleaned up, the older ones all working together to keep track of and assist little Gavin.

They all heard Ian call from upstairs for Sarah to come up. She ran out of the room, calling over her shoulder for Rachel and Jamie to finish the table and make certain it was done right. She came back not a minute later and said with glee, "Papa wants us to set another place at the table. He's bringing Mama downstairs for supper."

The announcement spurred great excitement among the girls, and Jamie said, "Quite an event, apparently."

"Indeed," Gillian said. "I can't count how many weeks it's been since we all sat together for a meal. She was down in bed for many weeks before the baby came."

Jamie wondered if her congenial conversation was an indication that the things he'd said earlier—or the gift he'd given her—had produced some positive effect. He figured it was more likely that she would not speak to him unkindly with Hugh present. Whatever the reason, he decided to just enjoy being in the same room with her. Even so, he felt torn as to whether he should allow himself to believe she might change her mind in regard to her marriage plans, or if he should start getting used to just thinking of her in a cousinly sort of way.

When the table was set for the correct number of people, Jamie marveled that so many people could gather around a table under the circumstances. The table was certainly adequate, but barely. He recalled the enormous dining tables in enormous dining rooms back at Brierley. But those tables had never been filled. The family occasionally had guests over for dinner, but they had never held large social events. The mood and atmosphere here in the home of Ian Brierley was entirely different, but in a good way. Jamie had never *dis*liked sharing meals with the Scottish branch of his family, but he felt glad to be here with the American one. In spite of his hovering turmoil over his feelings for Gillian, he was sincerely glad to be here. Ian's gracious attitude had helped a great deal, and he felt sincerely grateful for his uncle's compassion and acceptance.

Jamie was thinking about Ian when Ian came into the room, carrying the sleeping infant. He carefully laid little Deborah in a cradle, which Jamie now realized had been there at the edge of the room all along. Obviously, it was likely a common thing for the baby to sleep where the family was gathered.

"Keep an eye on her," Ian said to his daughters collectively. Then he noticed the men in the room. "Oh, hello, Hugh. How are you this evening?"

"Well, and you?"

"Excellent, thank you," Ian said, then he smiled at Jamie. "And how are you?"

"Very well, thank you," Jamie said.

Ian looked back and forth between the two men for a moment, as if he intended to say something else to both of them. But he just smiled and went back up the stairs.

Chapter Seven
The Revoking

Just as the children were helping Gillian put the meal on the table, Ian entered the room, carrying his wife in his arms. He set her carefully on a chair, and she grimaced a bit as she tried to get comfortable. Ian's attentiveness and concern was answered by a warm smile as their eyes met, and the love they shared was glowingly evident. Jamie observed their tenderness with an aching kind of hope. He wanted to feel that way about someone and to have that person feel that way about him. Specifically, Gillian. He wanted to share that kind of life with Gillian. But his hope for such a possibility continually battled with his acute awareness that he could not compete with a man like Hugh Montgomery. Given the fact that Hugh was a fine, upstanding Mormon—and Jamie hardly even knew what that meant—he figured that he didn't stand a chance.

Once Wren was settled in her chair, she looked up to take in her family, all watching her with a tenderness they had clearly learned from their father. The children all applauded, and Hugh as well. Jamie had to join in, even though he hadn't been here long enough to fully appreciate what this meant to the rest of them. He did note the tears in Wren's eyes, however, and even a glimmer of them in Ian's. He turned to steal a glance at Gillian and saw her discreetly wiping tears with her hand. She caught him looking at her and turned away abruptly.

Supper was delicious, and Jamie found the antics of the children very entertaining. In one day he had come to know their names and personalities enough to appreciate the dramatic differences between them, yet he knew they all shared a firm and unmistakable bond as a family.

For all his efforts, Jamie couldn't keep himself from looking at Gillian frequently, and he made no conscious effort to try to disguise what he was feeling. He felt sure that Hugh noticed, and he wondered if Hugh might at some point take the opportunity to make it clear to him that Gillian was taken and he had no right to look at her that way. Until that happened, Jamie figured he could look at Gillian all he wanted. And he found some gratification in noting how frequently Gillian returned his gaze—even though it seemed against her will, and as soon as she realized what she was doing, she looked elsewhere.

The baby woke up in the middle of supper, and she was passed around, with everyone but little Gavin taking a turn holding her for a few minutes. Even Hugh held her and seemed completely comfortable doing so, as if he'd had a great deal of practice holding babies. Ian asked Jamie if he would like to hold the baby, but he politely declined and simply enjoyed seeing how each one of Deborah's siblings took joy in their little sister. He especially enjoyed watching Gillian hold the baby. He wondered exactly what that meant, when he'd never paid *any* attention to *any* woman holding *any* baby *ever* before. But he couldn't help staring, and he wasn't entirely surprised to have her glance up at him. Only a second later she looked at Hugh instead, as if she had in that second convinced herself it was what she should do. The entire situation made Jamie angry, but he felt entirely helpless to do anything about it.

Wren declared at the end of the meal that she'd thoroughly enjoyed being with the family, but she was worn out and hurting and needed to get back to her bed. The baby was fussing by then and needed to be fed. Ian carried Wren up the stairs, while Gillian followed him with the baby. The children all pitched in to help clean up the meal. Jamie felt a little out of place with everyone except him seeming to know what to do. Even Hugh knew what to do. He'd rolled up his sleeves and was cleaning a pot. Jamie rolled up *his* sleeves and stood right next to Hugh, saying eagerly, "Let me help."

"I'll wash, you rinse," he said, nodding toward the small tub of clean water.

"I can do that," Jamie said, and Hugh handed him the clean pot before he picked up a dirty one. Jamie rinsed it quickly, then felt useless again, so he picked up a clean towel and started to dry it. He saw Gillian come back into the room, and smiled over his shoulder at her when she looked surprised—or maybe disconcerted—to see Hugh and Jamie side by side, cleaning the dishes together, no less. The irony made Jamie chuckle.

"Is something funny?" Hugh asked him.

Jamie tried to think of something to say that would not alert his competitor to the true nature of his thoughts. A plausible statement came to him, and he said, "If my friends could see me now."

Hugh chuckled. "I've had that thought a number of times since coming to America. The people I associated with in London—and the things that I did with them—are dramatically different from anything I've experienced in my new life."

Jamie realized then that Hugh spoke with a British accent. Gillian and the other children spoke distinctly as Americans, since they'd all been raised in this land. Ian and Wren still maintained their distinct Scottish accents, and Hugh was clearly from England—London to be precise, as he'd just admitted. Jamie also noted what was obvious. Hugh's accent implied that he was not of the lower classes of England. Jamie had traveled there enough in his life to know the difference. Hugh Montgomery came from a refined and educated background. Perhaps they might have *something* in common—something besides being in love with the same woman. But Jamie wasn't about to admit to *that*.

When the kitchen was all cleaned up, the family was herded upstairs to gather in Ian and Wren's bedroom for what they called study time. Jamie felt a little reluctant to join them, but Ian insisted. Since Hugh was joining them, and he obviously did so somewhat frequently, Jamie figured it would be all right. Technically, Jamie was more a part of the family than Hugh—except that Hugh had the advantage of actually having lived and worked among them for many years.

In the bedroom there were a few chairs, but some of the family members gathered on the bed with Wren, and others sat on the floor. Jamie opted for that, leaning his back against the wall. Having a perfect view of Gillian where she sat on a chair near the bed, he liked the location and felt completely comfortable. The temperature upstairs was hotter than down on the main floor, but an unusual breeze was blowing pleasantly through the windows, taking the edge off of the heat somewhat.

Jamie quickly learned that *study time* meant reading from the scriptures. He'd traveled with Mormons and knew well enough that they believed in a book of scripture that was separate from the Bible but apparently was meant to be a companion to it. He'd many times refused offers and pleas from his fellow travelers to read the book or to join them in their study. Now he was here living under the same roof as a Mormon family, and Ian had made it clear that he expected Jamie to participate in such things. He told himself it was a small price to pay for a room and meals. He could have easily afforded to meet his own physical needs elsewhere, but the warmth and acceptance he'd received here in this home far outweighed the need for a place to live. If he'd only been seeking a place to live, he certainly wouldn't have come this far. And he had no trouble admitting that. He'd been seeking a place where he would feel wanted and where he would belong. And with the exception of Gillian's overt snubbing of him, he'd certainly felt that. In *spite* of her snubbing, he felt wanted here. Enduring study time was a small price to pay.

Everyone who was old enough to read took a turn reading for a few minutes. Even Jamie was expected to take his turn. When they had finished with the studying, every member of the family had the opportunity to share anything they would like to about their day. Jamie felt a little nervous when Hugh was asked how his day had gone; he knew he would be called on next and wondered what he might say. Hugh reported that he'd accomplished some important work, and Jamie learned then that Hugh did the accounting ledgers for some small businesses. He mostly worked from his home, which to Jamie sounded like a very lonely and tedious life. He could certainly understand why Hugh would want to marry Gillian and therefore make his life less lonely and lackluster, but he strongly disagreed with Gillian agreeing to the marriage simply for the sake of practicality—or because she felt sorry for Hugh.

When Jamie was asked about his day, he simply reported that he'd enjoyed going into town with Ian, and that he was grateful for the warm welcome he'd received among the family. Everyone applauded, much as they had when Wren had appeared at the dinner table. Jamie felt a little overcome, wondering if they were all really that happy to have him here. He noticed that Hugh even joined in, but there was some kind of vague reluctance in his countenance. Gillian did *not* join in, and it bothered him far more deeply than he wanted to admit.

Once that was over, the family all knelt to pray. This too was something that Jamie had observed with the wagon company, but he'd never participated. Everyone knelt down except for Wren, who remained where she was. Ian called on Mont to give the prayer, and Jamie was impressed that a boy his age could express himself to God with such ease and sincerity. He prayed on behalf of the family, and he prayed for many others outside of the family as well. He expressed gratitude to have Jamie there with the family. Jamie felt a tiny jolt in his heart at this. Perhaps it was because he too felt grateful. Or perhaps it was something more.

The family then dispersed for bedtime. Hugh made a gracious exit and left for the night, and Jamie went to his room. He felt restless and bored and went into the next room to survey the books on the shelves. He recognized many titles, and had already read a number of them. He wondered what it had taken to get these books here. Since there was little else in the house that wasn't of a practical nature, he had to assume that Ian and Wren put a high priority on books.

Rather than choosing something unfamiliar, Jamie picked up a novel he'd read before, but since it had been many years, he hoped to be able to immerse himself in something comfortable but still not be able to recall exactly what was going to happen. He tried reading for a long while, aware of noises overhead that indicated children still walking—or usually running—upstairs. The house finally became very quiet, and Jamie lay back on his bed, wishing he felt even a little bit sleepy. In truth, what he felt was a strong craving for a shot of whiskey—for starters. He resisted the thought many times, but when the only other avenue his thoughts would take led to Gillian, he finally gave in and left the house as quietly as he could manage.

Once he'd arrived at his destination, it didn't take much effort to find Mr. Miller, the next-door neighbor who had gotten him home safely the previous evening. He didn't necessarily enjoy the man's company, but since he was the *only* man here that Jamie knew *at all,* it was either drink with him or drink alone. Jamie restricted the amount of liquor he drank in order to keep control of his senses somewhat. He preferred to get home of his own accord, and to not cause a stir in the household when he *did* arrive there. Everything was going fine until Mr. Miller picked a fight with another man. Or maybe it was the other way around. Jamie couldn't be certain. Either way, Mr. Miller was in the middle of it, and since Jamie had been drinking with him, the other man assumed that Jamie was somehow involved in whatever it was they were arguing about. Jamie was genuinely an innocent bystander, but he still got kicked out the front door, sporting a black eye and a bloody lip. He felt certain *that* would not sit well with his new family—especially with Gillian.

Since Mr. Miller had more injuries, Jamie returned the favor of the previous evening and helped get him home safely. Mrs. Miller met them at the door, and she curtly thanked Jamie while she glared at him as if he were entirely responsible for the problem. He made certain Mr. Miller's horse was properly cared for, then walked his own horse around the fence and down the long drive to see to its needs. He only staggered a little as he went from the barn into the house, and he was proud of himself for how quietly he went inside and locked the door behind him. Then he turned around and saw Gillian standing on the other side of the kitchen, holding a lamp. He almost cursed but restrained himself, certain that would not aid his cause.

"Do you never sleep, Miss Brierley?" he asked.

"Not since you got here," she said, as if he were entirely to blame and she resented it. He felt some perverse pleasure in thinking that her thoughts of him might have kept her from sleeping. It only seemed fair, since his thoughts of her had driven him to drinking. "I came down to the kitchen for a glass of water and realized the door wasn't locked, then I realized you weren't here. Against my better judgment, I find it difficult to keep myself from worrying about you when you're out and about at all hours."

"I would like to point out that, in contrast to last night, I have managed to get myself safely home without any assistance from anyone." He took hold of the back of a chair to keep himself from teetering and knew that she couldn't help but notice.

"How very impressive," Gillian said with sarcasm. "I would like to point out that you are *still* drunk."

"Only marginally," Jamie said, then grimaced when she took a step closer and held the lamp higher. He told himself it didn't matter; she would obviously see the evidence eventually. But he'd been hoping to delay this conversation until tomorrow, or perhaps it would have been better to have the conversation with her father present. On the other hand, perhaps this would change Ian's mind and he'd have the good sense to send Jamie packing.

"What on earth have you been doing?" she asked, looking closely at his face while he became utterly distracted by looking at hers. "What happened?" she asked when he didn't answer the first question.

"I'm afraid that Mr. Miller got into a fight, for reasons that I do *not* understand. And somehow I ended up in the middle of it. But I did get Mr. Miller safely home." He said the last as if it were a great accomplishment, but she didn't seem impressed.

Gillian felt so overwhelmed with confusion and frustration that she wanted to either scream at him or break down and cry. She forced her commitment to being a charitable person to subdue her emotions. King Benjamin had taught that people should be charitable, even if someone had brought his troubles on himself. She found no reason beyond King Benjamin's teachings to give any aid or assistance to Jamie, but she forced herself to ask, "Do you need anything? May I help you?"

"No, thank you," he said. "I'm fine."

"You don't look fine," she said and set the lamp down to dampen a rag with cool water. She dabbed at the dried blood on his lip, trying not to let her eyes meet his even while she was brutally aware of him staring at her. For all that she felt drawn to him, she could smell the liquor on his breath, and it was a stark reminder of why she could never take a man like this into her life or into her heart. Hearing him catch his breath made her catch her own, and she wondered if it was too late on that last account. She felt angry with him for indulging in such atrocious behavior and making it impossible to even consider sharing her life with him.

Suddenly overcome with the urge to cry, she put the rag into his hand and rushed from the room, saying over her shoulder, "I'm certain you'll manage." She left the lamp on the table and felt her way up the stairs in the dark and into the safety of her own room. With the door closed, she curled up on the bed and wept. She wished that she and Hugh were already married, or at the very least that they could get married quickly so that this problem would be removed from her life. She had expected him to speak with her father this evening after the children had gone to bed, but he hadn't stayed and she wondered why. She made up her mind to talk to him about it tomorrow, certain he would stop by sometime during the day. If she told him she wanted to get married as soon as possible, surely he would be eager to please her. It felt like the easiest and most practical solution to the problem, and she prayed that it would all work together in her favor.

When morning came, Gillian was up early and had bathed and washed her hair before the children were even awake. Since she'd slept very little, it seemed a good idea to just get up and get started on her day. She wasn't surprised when Jamie didn't show up for breakfast. She'd already reported quietly to her father that he had come in late again—and drunk again. She saw disappointment in her father's eyes, but she saw no sign of anger. Personally, she felt both.

When Gillian was clearing the table after breakfast, she was surprised to hear her father say, "Would you take some breakfast to Jamie, please."

"Take?" she countered and knew by her father's expression that it had come out sounding more sassy than her father had ever tolerated from his children—no matter how old or young they might be.

"That's what I said," he stated firmly.

"But surely he's capable of getting up and coming to the kitchen himself to—"

"I'm certain he is," Ian said. "And if my motivation was simply about him getting something to eat, that would be a practical solution."

"What *is* your motivation?" she asked, trying to sound *less* sassy.

Ian sighed. "I realize you're an adult, Gillian, but I'm still your father. Could you simply do what I've asked of you and not make such a fuss? Perhaps if you pay attention to what's going on around you, you'll figure it out."

Ian walked away, seeming more ill-tempered than she had seen him since before the doctor had declared that Wren was going to be all right following the birth of little Deborah. She wondered if his mood was a result of Jamie's drinking, or of her arguing with him. She preferred to believe it was the former, but had a nagging suspicion it was the latter.

Gillian found tasks to keep her busy as long as she could manage while Jamie's breakfast got colder. But she figured cold griddle cakes and ham could be tolerable. She finally took a tray to his room and threw open the door, glad for the way it banged against the wall, and she heard Jamie gasp, then groan. She set the tray on the bedside table, then pulled back the curtains, letting the full light of day into the room.

"What . . . in the *world* . . . are you doing?" he demanded.

"Against my better judgment," she said, "I have brought you some breakfast."

"Why?" he asked, squinting toward the sound of her voice.

"Only because my father asked me to," she said. "Although I can't imagine why. If you choose to go out drinking and miss breakfast due to a hangover, you ought to have to get your own breakfast. It's not my problem that you choose to wallow in the gutter."

"Your opinion is duly noted," Jamie said, sitting up in bed, glad he'd remained in his clothes. "And in this case, I must say I agree with you. In the future, I'll be happy to come to the kitchen and get my own breakfast."

"Good. I'm glad we agree on something."

"I don't suppose I could get a good, strong cup of coffee."

"Not in this house," she said as if she fully preferred for him to be in any other house, anywhere in the world.

"I knew you'd say that," he muttered and put a hand over his eyes, "but I still had to ask."

Gillian hovered close by, as if doing so might help her figure out what her father had been implying. She honestly could not think of a single thing that might be accomplished by her bringing breakfast to Jamie, as if she were some kind of household servant.

"You don't have to stand there and watch me eat it," he said, then smiled up at her. "Although it was very kind of you to bring it. I think your father likes me a lot more than you do."

Gillian refused to comment, but she felt a little unnerved when he stood up to face her. She was on her way to the door when he added, "In fact, I think *Hugh* likes me more than you do. Although he seems a bit dull for a woman like you."

Gillian knew very well that he was trying to goad her. She told herself not to fall for it, but she heard words flying out of her mouth before she even bothered to let them linger for a single moment in her brain. "Hugh Montgomery is the kindest, dearest man in the world, and you could never hold a candle to him!"

"I would never try to dispute *that*!" Jamie countered. "But it's too bad for you that you know in your heart there are ways he could never hold a candle to *me*."

"Don't be ridiculous!" she snapped.

"And don't make a fool of yourself, Gillian," he said, his facetiousness completely absent. "He may be the kindest, dearest man in the world, but you don't look at him the way you look at me."

Gillian looked abruptly away, as if that might keep Jamie from proving that what he'd said was true. Only a moment later did she realize that averting her gaze had made her look more guilty. He chuckled as if to let her know that he'd picked up on the implication of her reaction. But the sound had no indication of satisfaction, and no hint of mocking. It was more a sad kind of chuckle, which was verified when he said, "I actually feel sorry for you at least as much as I feel sorry for myself. I know I could never hope to win the heart of a woman like you, but it doesn't seem right that a woman like you would have to live with the pain of loving a man like me."

"*Loving* you?" she echoed and met his eyes again, anger neatly replacing the vulnerability she'd been feeling. "That's an awfully arrogant assumption."

"Arrogant, perhaps," he said. "But it's no assumption. I *know* what I see in your eyes when you look at me."

"And how exactly do you *think* you know what *I* am feeling?"

"Because I feel it too," he said with such humble sincerity that Gillian gasped. She couldn't keep herself from meeting his eyes even while she knew it would likely condemn her to feeling like more of a hypocrite. *He was telling the truth!* And what was she supposed to do about it? Under the circumstances, such feelings had nowhere to go, and she could never embrace them or make them a part of her life.

"Don't worry," he said, as if he'd read her mind—something he apparently had in common with Hugh Montgomery. "I'm not expecting anything from you. I know better than to think that a man like me could ever end up with a woman like you. I'll just keep *wallowing in the gutter,* as you have so quaintly put it, and mind my own business. And you will marry Mr. Montgomery and have a perfectly wonderful life. He's a good man. He deserves you." Jamie turned to walk away while Gillian convinced herself that she would be relieved to have him gone, but something inside of her wanted to beg him to stay and just be in the same room with her. He abruptly turned back, and she prepared herself to be landed another blow. She never could have been prepared enough, however, to hear him say, "You should bear in mind, Miss Brierley, that I don't think I'm the only man who has noticed the way you look at me. You might want to let your fiancé know that your heart belongs fully to him. With any luck, you'll be able to convince him."

He left the room and left Gillian standing there, her heart pounding and her mouth dry. Then she realized that she was standing in *his* room along with his cold breakfast, and she still had no idea why her father had insisted on having her bring it to him. She felt literally sick to her stomach to think of the possibility that Hugh had noticed what she'd been feeling. But Jamie was probably right. Hugh was a sharp man, and what she felt for Jamie had been too overwhelming for her to believe that she'd been able to disguise it as well as she might have wanted to believe. She hurried out of the room before Jamie had a chance to come back. She rushed out the back door and ran to the other side of the barn where she could be completely alone and try to take in everything Jamie had just said. Two phrases especially kept pounding in her head, one and then the other, as if a pendulum were swinging back and forth between them with great force and undeniable reality. *I don't think I'm the only man who has noticed the way you look at me* battled violently in her mind with Jamie admitting, *I feel it too.*

Gillian sat down on the ground and cried as if there had been a death in the family. She leaned back against the wall of the barn and looked heavenward, praying for strength and understanding, wishing this would all just go away and she could go back to living her simple life, content to live without the prospect of marriage for a while longer.

She was startled to hear Sarah say, "Why are you crying?"

"It's not important," she said and smiled, reaching out a hand for her sister. "When you get a little older you'll understand that sometimes a woman just needs a good cry."

"Are you sure you're all right?" Sarah asked, taking Gillian's hand.

"I'm fine, sweetheart. What are you doing out here?"

"I was looking for you. Hugh is here and he wants to talk to you. He's waiting in the parlor."

Gillian wanted to tell Sarah to give him the message that she wasn't feeling well and now wasn't a good time. She wished she'd gone to her room to have her cry instead of out here. Then she could have been more convincing about the need to lie down and avoid company. As it was, she likely couldn't avoid seeing Hugh without having the whole family knowing about it—including Jamie. Knowing that she needed to act like an adult and get on with her day anyway, she took a deep breath, forced another convincing smile, and said, "Tell him I'll be right in, and . . . please don't tell anyone I was crying. Let that be our secret."

Sarah nodded. "I can keep a secret."

"Good."

"You never told anyone that I keep the candy I saved in the can under my bed."

"No, I never told anyone," Gillian said, and Sarah ran off.

Gillian took a couple of minutes to compose herself and dry her eyes, then it occurred to her that she probably had that pathetic red patch on her face that always showed up when she'd been crying. She figured if Hugh noticed, she could skirt the issue the same way she had with Sarah. She took a deep breath and walked back into the house, wondering if Hugh had spoken to her father while she'd been outside. Glancing at the clock in the kitchen made her realize she'd been outside much longer than she'd realized. The tray she'd taken to Jamie's room was on the table, and the food had been eaten. She wondered where Jamie was now. She wouldn't be surprised to find him in the parlor with Hugh, making light conversation as if they weren't both tugging at her heart, threatening to break it in two.

Gillian entered the parlor to see Hugh there alone, lost in deep thought. He turned when he heard her enter the room, then he stood to greet her. She closed the door for the sake of privacy, mostly not wanting Jamie to pass by and overhear *anything* they might be saying to each other. She expected him to greet her with a squeeze of the hand or a kiss on the brow, but he did neither, and she felt increasingly haunted by Jamie's words. She smiled at Hugh, attempting to appear as normal as possible. She knew instantly, however, that Hugh could see past any efforts she might make to conceal her true feelings.

"Is something wrong?" he asked.

"I'm fine," she insisted and forced a smile, knowing even as she did that she wasn't telling the truth, even as much as she *wanted* it to be the truth.

She attempted to busy herself with straightening the newspapers on the table, but Hugh put a gentle hand on her arm. "Why don't you sit down and talk to me and tell me what's really going on."

Gillian met his eyes and resisted the temptation to lie again and dig herself deeper into a hole that was only making her look like a fool. She took a deep breath and sat on the sofa, remaining at the edge of her seat. Hugh scooted a chair closer to her and sat on it so that he was directly facing her. He leaned his forearms on his thighs and looked directly at her. Knowing this conversation was about to turn very serious, Gillian shuddered inside to once again recall Jamie saying, *I don't think I'm the only man who has noticed the way you look at me.* If Jamie was right, and she and Hugh were committed to complete honesty, then the outcome of this entire situation could be doomed. Making one last attempt to divert the problem, she said lightly, "I'm not sure what you mean, Hugh."

"I mean," he said, taking her hand, "that your countenance and your words are contradicting each other. If you're trying to spare me from hearing something that might hurt me, then your efforts are noble, but under the circumstances, not necessarily productive. We need to be completely honest with each other, Gillian. *Completely!*" To add emphasis to his words, he gave her one of his penetrating gazes that he was famous for. But his kindness and perfect love came through brilliantly, and she knew she *could* be completely honest with him—however difficult it might be. The problem was, he was right. She *was* trying to spare him from being hurt. But perhaps he already knew the truth, and it was more her unwillingness to talk about it that was hurting him.

Gillian took a deep breath and mentally reviewed her life history with Hugh, most specifically the place they had come to. She also considered that she could be honest without going into territory that was too sensitive or uncomfortable. She settled on a firm statement. "I simply had a difficult encounter with Jamie. That's all. I was trying to set it aside and not let it ruin my day." She concluded with another smile that she hoped would soothe him.

Hugh's expression didn't change. "It seems every encounter you have with Jamie is difficult for one reason or another."

Gillian looked down, unable to make eye contact. She wondered how he knew anything about any of her encounters with Jamie. Had he been talking to her parents? Her siblings? Or was she just more transparent to him than she'd believed? She cleared her throat and attempted to smooth this over. "It seems that way . . . although I can't imagine why I let him get to me. His bad habits and less-than-gentlemanly behavior are certainly of no consequence to me."

Gillian heard Hugh sigh. It wasn't a subtle sigh, but rather a weighted breath that came from deep in his chest. She lifted her eyes to check his expression, then wished she hadn't. Her heart began to pound as Jamie's words came back to her again. Hugh *had* noticed, and he was not going to ignore it. Could she have really expected him to? But she felt something crack in her heart even before he said, "You can't lie to yourself, Gillian, or to me—even if your reasons for doing so come from noble intentions." She squeezed her eyes closed, waiting for the inevitable blow. "His behavior *is* of consequence to you because you're attracted to him."

Heat gathered behind Gillian's closed eyelids, then quickly overflowed in hot tears that leaked between her lashes and down her face. It took her a full minute to speak. "I'm not trying to be, Hugh."

"I *know* that," he said, taking her hand. "But that doesn't change the fact that we can't force what we feel. I told you from the beginning that I couldn't force your heart. You can't force it either."

Now that the door had been opened, Gillian found it easy to think of telling him the *rest* of the truth. She pondered her words for only a moment before she opened her eyes to face him, saying with perfect confidence, "And what good is the heart if it draws me to a man like that? He is *nothing* I've ever wanted in a husband. I could never tolerate his behavior. What kind of husband and father would he be? God would never expect me to be fool enough to pursue *any* kind of relationship with a man like that! I admit to feeling some kind of bizarre attraction to him, but that doesn't change where I stand in my convictions. It doesn't change the way I feel about you, Hugh."

He smiled, but it was forced and brief. "Your strength of character is very honorable, Gillian, and I respect you for it. But it would be wrong for you to move forward with *any* decision about your life if your heart and your head are not in complete agreement. Your head wants what I have to offer you. It's comfortable and practical. But your heart wants to be with him. I think you need some time to be certain of what you want."

"What I want?" she echoed and sprang to her feet, shocked by the implication of what he was saying. He remained seated but looked up at her, utterly calm and collected while his eyes betrayed that his heart was breaking. Gillian attempted to repair it, uttering with conviction, "What I want is a man I can rely on, depend on to be there for me. I want a man who will take care of me and be a good father to our children. Not a man who is out drinking; not a man who has no interest in the convictions and beliefs that are most important to me. I want *you,* Hugh. What I feel for Jamie has no bearing on this situation."

Hugh's response came after some silent deliberation and another of those heavy sighs. "Again I have to say that your efforts are noble, Gillian, but you must admit I have some life experience that you don't have. You're going to have to trust me when I tell you that we can't move forward like this. I'm not saying that it won't work out for you and me. I pray that it will. But until you have sorted all of this through, prayed about it, and know exactly where you stand, we cannot pursue marriage. I won't have you wondering for the rest of your life if you did the right thing. How can either of us be happy both knowing that you love another man while you're sharing your life with me?"

"Love?" she retorted in a high pitch that implied a defensiveness she would have preferred to keep to herself. "What I feel for Jamie could by no stretch be *love.*"

"You're a sensible woman, Gillian. I admire the way that you don't let impulsive feelings guide your actions. But quite frankly, I think you're too young and naive to know *what* you feel for Jamie. And until you *do* know, you need to reconsider the path of your life. If you believe that God's hand is in our lives—and I know that you do—then your feelings for Jamie must have some purpose or meaning. If that purpose is for you to learn something valuable about life and love before you and I settle down together, so be it. But you can't close your mind to the possibility that his purpose in your life might be much more than that."

"What are you implying?" Gillian demanded, hating this more by the minute.

Hugh sighed again and looked down. "Perhaps you can make a difference in his life, Gillian. Maybe this isn't just about you and me and what *we* want. Sometimes God's purposes don't take us along the easiest route, but they get us to the correct ending of the story."

"So . . . what?" Gillian asked, wishing she didn't feel so agitated, so frightened. "You're calling off our engagement so that I can freely make Jamie some kind of . . . charity project?"

"Our engagement was never made official, and perhaps this is why. Perhaps—"

"It was official between you and me, even if we had never declared it publicly. Does that mean nothing?"

"It means a great deal," Hugh said. "At least to me it does. Your willingness to marry me is a gift that I will always hold close to my heart, Gillian. But I cannot ignore this turn of events, and neither can you. We must trust in God and move forward, and right now I know that this is the right step . . . for both of us. I can't predict the outcome, and neither can you. I don't think you need to see Jamie as some kind of charity project, but I *do* think you need to look past the defensiveness he arouses in you and be more charitable toward him. The pure love of Christ, administered correctly through the guidance of the Spirit, can go a long way to healing a troubled soul. If he feels drawn to you, then you may be the only one who can get through to him. You need to rely on the guidance of the Spirit, Gillian. You always have; I believe you always will. You can't let him hurt you, and you can never compromise who you are. *That* is the best possible avenue to opening doors for him that he doesn't even imagine exist. How can we judge him for his behavior when he doesn't know what we know? When he's never felt what we feel? He's a damaged soul, and we can't understand *why* or how it's affected him.

But we do know that every soul is great in the sight of God. Whatever our purpose might be in his life, you and I need to step back and acknowledge the truth of what's happening before we move forward."

Gillian wiped tears from her face. "I'm confused, Hugh. Is this supposed to be about acknowledging that I have feelings for Jamie? Or is it about trying to help him spiritually?"

"Both. Perhaps one is meant to draw our attention to the other. Perhaps in spite of all your best efforts, he will continue in his difficult ways and you'll know there's nothing more you can do. But I cannot in good conscience allow you to commit yourself to me when I know that your heart is elsewhere. That's where I have to stand, and I make my stand after much prayerful consideration."

Gillian knew that meant he'd probably realized the truth right away, and she wondered how deeply he'd been struggling with this. The very idea broke her heart on his behalf.

Hugh sighed again and added, "Now that you know where *I* stand, you must prayerfully consider where *you* stand. I will be here for you, Gillian . . . as your friend, the way I always have been. But it can't be more than that until . . ." His voice quivered slightly and Gillian felt as if she'd burst from the unbearable irony and heartbreak permeating the very air around them. "Until we both know for certain that it's the best choice for both of us. Until you can come into this marriage with your head *and* your heart invested in the relationship, I can't condone it. I don't mean that I expect you to love me the way I love you. I *do* mean that your heart has to know that being with me is right—beyond any inkling of a doubt. Do you understand?"

Gillian wiped more tears and sniffled a couple of times. "I understand, but I hate it. If Jamie hadn't come here, then—"

"You can't see it that way, Gillian. He *did* come here."

"The timing is just so . . . horrible; so ridiculous."

"I've seen too much evidence of God's hand in my lifetime to ever believe that any event—or its timing—is mere coincidence or without purpose. We need to faithfully consider the right way to handle the situation, rather than futilely wish for it to be different."

Gillian looked toward the window and folded her arms tightly over her chest while her tears continued to fall. "You're a very wise man, Hugh. I understand what you're saying . . . and I respect it. But I still hate it."

"I would be a hypocrite if I didn't say that I hate it too, but trying to hide from what we know we have to do is like Jonah fleeing from Nineveh. Eventually some metaphorical whale will inevitably appear and swallow any person who tries to run and hide from God's will. I know it, and I know that you know it."

Hugh finally came to his feet, but he did so as if it took great effort to muster the strength. He stood before Gillian and put a finger under her chin, tilting her face to his view. He wiped her tears with his fingers, then took her face in his hands and pressed a lingering kiss to her brow. "I'm here for you, Gillian," he whispered. "No matter what happens, no matter how hard it gets, don't ever stop allowing me to be your friend."

"Never!" she said, not surprised by the sob that rushed out of her on the wake of the word. One sob led to another, and she took hold of his upper arms to steady herself the same moment she pressed her face to his shoulder. He wrapped his arms around her and held her while she cried. The irony of his sustaining embrace only induced more emotion in Gillian, and she cried without restraint for many minutes. She suspected that Hugh might be shedding some tears himself, but he kept them silent and kept his face from her view.

Her crying finally settled, but she kept her head against his shoulder, taking in the strength he gave her while she pondered the truth in all that he'd said and the necessary path that lay before her. It would take much prayer and pondering for her to come to terms with it, and for her to even know where and how to begin to explore these feelings she had for Jamie and to understand them. She felt frightened and wished that she had married Hugh a long time ago. If she'd already been married when Jamie had shown up, none of this would even be an issue. In spite of what Hugh had said about God's hand being in their lives, she couldn't help wishing that Jamie had stayed in Scotland and remained disconnected from them. But time could not go backward, and the present situation could not be altered. She could only move forward and try her best to deal with it as God would have her do. In her heart she hoped that the outcome would be favorable for her and Hugh. She believed that time and some reasonable effort would prove that Jamie was not and never would be good husband material, and she would be able to marry Hugh with a clear conscience and a free heart. But she could not deny that at the moment her heart was *not* free. Her heart *did* feel drawn to Jamie—for reasons she could not begin to comprehend. But she needed to figure it out and deal with it. She could only pray that God would give her the strength to do so, and to do so wisely and with patience and charity. Given the history of her encounters with Jamie, she felt doubtful that she would do well on that account. But she had to try—for all their sakes.

Chapter Eight
Unto the Least of These

Hugh eased back and took hold of Gillian's shoulders. She saw in his eyes that there was something he felt the need to say, but he didn't necessarily want to. She wondered what else could possibly be said.

"Gillian," he said in a gentle voice, "do you have any idea how your father found me?"

"When he was serving his mission . . . in London. He baptized you. Of course I know that."

"That's all true, but I doubt that he'd ever tell you how we met." He leaned closer. "He found me drunk in an alley, almost passed out." She gasped, then she sucked in her breath at the implication in regard to Jamie. He sighed and went on. "He took me back to his hotel room, let me sober up in a place where I wouldn't get robbed or murdered in my sleep, fed me breakfast, and made me listen to what he had to say. It changed my life." He tightened his hold on her shoulders. "Every man deserves that chance. *Every* man." He sighed again. "Even the man who loves the same woman I love. *Especially* him . . . if he's the man who can make you happy."

Gillian felt so deeply stunned that she could hardly breathe. To realize that Hugh saw something of his former self in Jamie made the ironies of the situation almost impossible to bear. Hugh was obviously a much better person than she was. She'd treated Jamie with disdain. Hugh had been viewing the situation entirely through charitable eyes—even while he knew that he and Jamie had feelings for the same woman. And she was that woman! How could this have happened to her? And what was she supposed to do about it? For all that she could appreciate Hugh's theory about her possibly being

the one who could get through to Jamie and teach him things about
life that he'd never been given the opportunity to understand, she
couldn't begin to imagine how she might go about that, especially
while she knew that Hugh's heart was breaking.

Long after Hugh left, Gillian remained sitting in the parlor,
stunned and overcome. Her emotions felt as tightly strung as the
strings of a musical instrument that were close to snapping. She was
startled to hear Jamie say, "Are you all right?"

Given her frame of mind, Gillian wanted to shout at him and tell
him to get out of her house and out of her life. She'd hardly had a
few minutes to accept her conversation with Hugh. Even in knowing
she needed to have a better attitude toward Jamie, at the moment
she could only see and feel how Jamie's presence was breaking Hugh's
heart, and it had put her in a deplorable situation.

"Did you need something?" she asked, evading the question.

"I'm just wondering if you're all right," he said and sat down
across the room, as if she might actually want to talk to him.

Gillian told herself to get up and leave. She felt nothing but
annoyance and irritation and knew that any attempt at conversation
would not go well. But she ignored the impulse to separate herself
from him in such a frame of mind, and instead found herself uttering
the first thought that rushed into her mind. "How is it that you
always look like you haven't shaved," she asked, "but you never
acquire a beard?"

"Did you *want* me to acquire a beard?" he asked in a mildly
mocking tone, as if to imply that her asking such a question was
rude and arrogant. Perhaps it was. He had a way of bringing out the
worst in her. "Given that I've only been here a couple of days, I'm
not certain what you mean by *always* and *never*. Perhaps you could
explain."

Gillian realized how ridiculous this was, but she didn't know how
to reverse the conversation. She made a lame attempt by saying, "I
don't care *what* you do with your facial hair."

He laughed. "You're making a fool of yourself, Gillian. Obviously
you *care* or you wouldn't have asked me such a ridiculous question to
begin with." Gillian looked at him in astonishment, then she heard
her own words come back to her in her mind. He was right. And if

she acknowledged that he was right, she had to wonder why she *did* care. Why did it bother her so much that he continually had a mildly scruffy, unshaven look about him?

"I was simply curious," she said, hoping to retain some dignity.

"Yes, you seem to suffer from that a great deal . . . at least in regard to me. I wonder why that is."

"Can't you just answer a simple question without making it into an ordeal?"

"Making it into an ordeal is much more entertaining."

"I have no desire to get caught up in your idea of entertainment."

"And yet you ask me stupid questions that I cannot resist making into an ordeal."

"Just *answer the question*," she said, trying to sound as insistent as she would with one of the children if they were misbehaving. But he only laughed again. "Oh, never mind," she added and stood up to leave the room, wishing she'd done so when he'd first entered. But he stood just as quickly and grabbed her arm to stop her. Without letting go he took a step closer and looked directly at her, as if he intended to give her an excellent view of the stubble on his face.

"I shave at night," he said. "By morning it's starting to grow back, and by evening I can look downright heathenish." He said that last word as if it were something glorious to aspire to. "Since I also bathe in the evening, it makes sense to shave then as well. I prefer going to bed clean and shaven. I relax better that way."

"And presumably you shave just before you go out to get drunk?"

"Presumably," he said with an edge of spite.

"And it's never occurred to you that shaving in the morning might . . ." Gillian realized what she was about to say and how judgmental it sounded. Why was it that he provoked such thoughts and feelings in her? And why did she allow herself to let those thoughts and feelings actually formulate into words and bad behavior?

"Might what?" he asked when she hesitated.

"Never mind." Hugh's words catapulted into her mind, and she felt ashamed. She swallowed her pride and silently asked God for humility and patience—and an escape from this conversation. Since Jamie was still holding her arm, she felt prone to believe that it would take a miracle to allow her to get away without making an ordeal out of it. "You're right," she admitted then was brought to a new awareness of how close his face was to hers. Her stomach fluttered, and her heart quickened. She forced a steady voice but couldn't force herself to look away. "It was a ridiculous question. Your habits are of no concern to me."

"You're lying again," he said, his voice mildly husky, as if he might be experiencing the same sensations as she. "What is it about me that makes you want to lie to me? Could it be that what you feel makes you so uncomfortable, you have to try to worm your way out of it like a frightened child?"

Gillian felt a sudden jolt, as if the heartbeat immediately following his question had tried to jump out of her chest in response to it. The sensation made her gasp, which spurred Jamie to lift an eyebrow in silent question. There was no way to explain such a reaction without going into territory that already made her deeply uncomfortable. But she was already there. Something in her spirit seemed to whisper the idea as if to make her stop and take in the moment, rather than run away from it. *You're already there,* she heard in her mind. *Look closer. What do you see?* She took a deep breath as she realized she was hearing the voice of an angel. She wondered for a moment who it was that the Lord had sent to minister to her in this moment. A moment later she knew it was her mother.

While Jamie just held her gaze, apparently waiting for her to come to some great realization, Gillian became engaged in one of those moments of feeling suspended between two worlds, or rather hovering at a place where the veil had become especially thin and she could only try to understand the implications. Perhaps her relationship with Jamie *was* more important than she'd been willing to admit. Why else would angelic assistance be present, telling her to look closer? She took a few seconds to convince herself that her place in Jamie's life was simply to guide him to a *better* life, to bring him to the gospel and to the healing that it could offer him. But in that moment it felt impossible to stop at that point. A part of her had to admit that it was more deep and undeniably real. She almost hated him for it; hated him for his smugness, his arrogance, his ability to see through her so efficiently. But at the same time she knew that her own defensiveness and erratic behavior with him surely incited some of that smugness and arrogance. Perhaps that was the only way he knew how to deal with whatever it was that he was feeling. Her anger melted into compassion, and her frustration into some kind of abstract hope. It was as if in that moment she could imagine his potential and feel the truth of his spirit, not the facade of a damaged man who was driven unconsciously by self-destructive choices.

Looking into Jamie's eyes, she wondered what she could possibly say, or how she could possibly undo the damage that had been done in so short a time. She felt emotion overtaking her and knew she needed to leave the room before she burst into tears. She saw his expression soften, as if he sensed that she was near tears. She muttered in a whisper, "I'm sorry, Jamie." She eased out of his grasp and rushed from the room, finding a place where she could be alone long enough to vent her tears and try to think clearly. But she knew this problem would not be easily solved.

* * * * *

Gillian put lunch on the table for her family, then she gracefully left them to eat it, deciding that she needed to fast in order to gain some much-needed spiritual strength and guidance. She knew her family would require no explanation. It wasn't uncommon for any one of them—except for the little ones—to choose to go without a couple of meals. But she wondered what Jamie might think of her absence. She wanted to believe that she didn't care what Jamie might think, but in her mind she heard Hugh telling her that she couldn't lie to herself *or* to him. Was that what she'd been doing? Lying to herself? According to Jamie, she'd been lying to him as well.

While the family ate, Gillian went to the parlor and closed the door, wanting some time alone to try to sort out her thoughts. She needed to pray, and pray a great deal, but at the moment she couldn't even bring herself to do it. She felt confused and even a bit ashamed of her behavior. And she didn't know where to start to make it right, or if such a thing was even possible.

She was surprised by a knock at the door, and turned to see her father peering inside. She was glad at least that she'd not been crying. And she was even more glad that it wasn't Jamie.

"Are you all right?" he asked, closing the door behind him.

"No," she said, certain that Hugh would *not* have said anything to him. It was up to her to tell him where the situation now stood. She just didn't know how to say it; she didn't know where to begin. Recalling their less-than-favorable exchange earlier today, she decided to start there.

"I've been thinking about this morning, and . . . forgive me . . . but I don't understand what you meant when you told me to take breakfast to Jamie. It seemed so senseless. I know it's a simple thing, but obviously you intended it to have some meaning, and I just don't understand."

"Sit down," he said, and she did. He sat across from her and leaned forward. "I want you to understand that I would never allow someone to live under my roof and take advantage of me or my family if I believed they would cause any of us any harm. I've been prayerful about Jamie, and I know that he can benefit greatly from being in our home. Do you understand?"

Gillian nodded but didn't comment. She sensed where this was headed, but was still surprised to hear her father conclude the matter by simply saying, "The answer to your question is that sometimes we just need to do simple things for someone who is struggling because that person is one of the least of these."

"I don't understand," Gillian said, and her father looked astonished.

"He really *has* addled your brain."

"What?" she asked, sounding defensive to the point of nearly sounding rude.

"Your mother told me just last night that I should be patient with you because Jamie being in the house has addled your brain. I think she's right."

"I have no idea how to take that," Gillian said, feeling insulted but still defensive. Given everything else that had happened that her parents didn't know about, she didn't know whether to feel utterly stupid or completely humiliated. Perhaps both.

"Then just consider this: you were raised in a religious home with Christian principles. You should know well enough what it means to do an act of charity to one of the least of these." Gillian sucked in her breath as the words connected in her addled brain and her defensiveness melted into humility—and some degree of shame. There she sat, hearing the same message from her father that she'd heard from Hugh. She'd been so caught up in her own feelings, her own confusion, her own selfish pride, that she'd completely missed what these two good men in her life had been able to see. The fact that her father had sent *her* to give Jamie his breakfast was as good as saying what Hugh had put very plainly. *The pure love of Christ, administered correctly through the guidance of the Spirit, can go a long way to healing a troubled soul. If he feels drawn to you, then you may be the only one who can get through to him.*

Tears trickled down Gillian's face, and her father said, "What else is going on, Gillian? Does this have to do with Hugh? Jamie? Both?"

"Yes," she said, attempting to wipe away the ongoing flow of tears. "Jamie knows how I feel about him, even if it's against my better judgment. And Hugh is not blind; quite the opposite, in truth. He told me earlier that he couldn't go through with the marriage under the circumstances. I've been waiting for him to speak to you to make it official, and all the while I've been breaking his heart without even realizing it." She sniffled and still more tears came. Her father reached into his pocket and handed her a clean handkerchief. "He told me I needed time to make certain I'm doing the right thing for the right reasons." She sniffled again and dabbed at her eyes and nose. "He told me if Jamie has feelings for me, I might be the only one who can get through to him."

"Well, I agree with him," Ian said with no hesitation.

Gillian looked at him in surprise. "I agree with him too," she admitted. "At least I think I do. I can see the wisdom in what he's saying, but . . . I don't understand why *you* agree with him. Why would you want me to become involved with a man who does not share my beliefs? A man who is going out and getting drunk every night?"

"First of all, two nights is not every night."

"He's only been here two nights," she clarified. "It's *every* night!" In her mind she heard Jamie saying, *Given that I've only been here a couple of days, I'm not certain what you mean by* always *and* never. Her shame increased at the evidence of her attempt to categorize Jamie's behavior into something absolute when she was in no position to judge him.

Ian chuckled and shook his head, as if he were exercising great patience. "Gillian, did Hugh tell you how he and I met?"

"Yes, actually," she said. "Just today. I had no idea."

"Clearly it was not up to me to share such details about his past, but if he's told you, then I feel like I can talk about it. Someone believed in him, Gillian. Someone saw past the drinking habit—and the difficulties that had initiated it."

"*You* saw past it; you're the one who believed in him."

"Gillian." He took her hand and looked into her eyes in a way that let her know she was going to hear something difficult; she wondered how much more she could take in one day. "I saw past it because I saw myself."

"I don't understand."

"The Spirit led me down a dark alley and I found Hugh there, drunk and nearly passed out. I remember as if it were this morning, looking down at him and it was as if I saw myself."

"You mean you had a spiritual experience that drew you to him?"

"Yes . . . because the Spirit enhanced my memory and helped me understand. Gillian, it *was* me. Before I married your mother, it was *me* wandering the alleys of London, drinking myself into unconsciousness."

"What?" she gasped.

"I haven't talked about it because I'm not proud of it, but under the circumstances you need to know . . . I was lost and wandering and drowning my issues in liquor—for years."

"I can't believe it," she said, almost wondering if he had made it up to encourage her sympathy toward Jamie. But she knew her father would never do such a thing. He was honest to a fault. And what she was hearing made the way she'd been treating Jamie all the more deplorable.

"Well, it's true. And your mother loved me enough to be there for me when I was ready to put it behind me. She had trouble trusting me because I'd behaved very badly. But she forgave me, and then we found the gospel and our lives were never the same. I'm telling you that love and truth can take away the craving for liquor, Gillian. Your mother never would have put up with me if I'd not been truly penitent and willing to change. But she gave me marvelous incentive to change. And I testify to you, Gillian, that the atoning grace of our Savior is the only way to truly heal *any* pain. How can a man like Jamie understand that? How could I have understood it without having the Book of Mormon put into my hands? How could Hugh have understood it if someone hadn't been willing to give him a chance? As Jesus taught, 'They that be whole need not a physician, but they that are sick.' Jamie needs a family, Gillian. He needs love and compassion and acceptance. He needs the opportunity to learn what we know, and given the way he feels about you, I think you might be the right person to do that. So, yes . . . I agree with Hugh."

"And what if he *doesn't* change? What if—when all is said and done—I still marry Hugh and break Jamie's heart? Will he not just be more hurt and angry? More likely to go out and get drunk?"

"You can provide fertile soil for the seed of truth to grow, Gillian. You can offer charity and compassion and share the truth that you know. And then it's up to him—as for any human being, given the nature of free agency—to choose whether or not he will take it into his life. The Spirit will guide you. If a time comes when there is nothing more you can do, then you will know that God has released you from this obligation. For now, however, I believe you need to recognize what your feelings are telling you and act on them. It's my opinion that you've been trying to avoid what you're *really* feeling because you've been worried about hurting Hugh, and you've been seeing Jamie's problems more than his potential. You're strong enough and wise enough to know how to set boundaries with him and not allow him to hurt you. Truthfully, I don't think he would ever want to hurt you. For all that he's struggling, he was raised by good people, and he's had a lot to overcome."

Ian leaned back. "Of course, I'm just your father, and—"

"*Just* my father? I rely very much on your advice and wisdom. You know that."

"I know, but . . . you're an adult, Gillian. You need to seek the guidance of the Spirit in this and do what *you* know is right. Perhaps you'll get a different answer than I have."

"And yet both you and Hugh have felt inspired to the same end."

"It's still not enough. For you to have the conviction to make a difference in Jamie's life, you need to know for yourself that it's right." He smiled and winked. "Especially given the way he aggravates you."

"Yes, especially for that reason," she said, not seeing the humor in it that her father could apparently see.

"You're fasting?" he asked, given that she'd skipped lunch.

"I am," she said.

"That's good, I think." He stood up and put a hand on her shoulder. "You'll know what to do, Gillian. If you need to talk, you know where to find me, and you know where to find your mother." He looked directly at her and added, "Speaking of which, I want to thank you for all that you do to keep the household running smoothly while she recovers. Neither of us knows what we would do without you."

"You don't have to thank me," she said. "We're family."

"I know that, but I *do* have to thank you, because you need to know how much it means to me. The man you *do* end up marrying is a very lucky man, indeed."

"Indeed," Gillian said with chagrin, wondering how she'd gone from feeling unmarriageable to being a contender's prize in a matter of days.

After her father left the room, Gillian stood at the open window and looked out toward the street, wondering how to go about getting the answers she needed. And once she had those answers, she wondered where she might find the strength and courage to go forward. If this was some kind of testing experience for her faith, she hoped that she might pass it. She remained in the parlor with the door closed for a long while and actually lost track of the time until Sarah came into the room. Then Gillian felt panicked.

"Goodness gracious," she said when she saw her sister, then glanced at the clock. "I've neglected everything. The house must be in a shambles, and it's time we were fixing supper, and—"

"The house is *not* in a shambles," Sarah said as if she resented the implication that she might not be able to entirely take care of Gillian's duties. "Papa told us you weren't feeling well and that we needed to take care of everything for the rest of the day. He sent me to tell you that you should go up to your room and lie down if you want, because everything is under control."

"Oh," Gillian said and resisted the urge to protest when she couldn't deny that she felt extremely tired and she just wanted to be alone and have the time to pray and ponder this overwhelming situation. She gave Sarah a quick hug. "Tell Papa thank you . . . and everyone else, too."

"I will," Sarah said and left the room.

Gillian leaned back on the sofa and exhaled deeply, relishing some time to herself. She realized she'd not slept at all well the last two nights—since Jamie MacBrier had shown up. Since she wasn't eating supper and she didn't have to help clean up the kitchen afterward, she decided that she would go to bed early, and even skip study time and prayer with the family. Her father had given her the perfect excuse to get out of it, and she was determined to take advantage of the time.

* * * * *

Jamie's disappointment at not seeing Gillian during lunch was enhanced when she didn't show up for supper. Ian simply explained, "She's not feeling well."

Jamie nodded in reply, wondering if Ian could read deeper meaning into Jamie's inquiry. Did his uncle know how much Jamie desperately wanted to just be in the same room with Gillian—in spite of how badly their last encounter had gone? A stupid question, he thought, given his conversation with Ian yesterday about the feelings he'd admitted to boldly while too drunk to have any control over the words that came out of his own mouth. He felt startled to realize how out of place he felt at the table without Gillian there. He couldn't think of any reason why it should be that way. The children were all very friendly toward him and had made him feel included without even trying. Ian and Wren—who had been carried down to the kitchen again—were kind and accepting in every possible way. No one had even expressed anything negative or judgmental about the bruise on his face and his cut lip. He'd admitted to getting into the middle of something he shouldn't have been in the middle of, because he'd been somewhere he shouldn't have been. The children had all just shrugged off the explanation when it had come up earlier at lunch. Now Wren simply said to him, "I hope it doesn't too hurt badly."

"I'm fine, thank you," Jamie said, then became preoccupied with Gillian's absence. He wondered if her not feeling well was due to any physical malady, or if it had more to do with his presence in the house—specifically the difficult conversations they'd had earlier.

Jamie helped clean up after supper. Since Ian had declared that everyone needed to pitch in a little extra in light of Gillian's absence, he insisted on scrubbing the dirty pots and pans, while Sarah hovered near him to rinse and dry them. He felt responsible for Gillian's absence, and he wasn't even completely certain why.

When the kitchen was cleaned up, everyone suddenly seemed to have something else to do, and Jamie was left there alone with time to kill until the family gathered to study and pray. Noting that the house felt stuffy in spite of every window being wide open, he wandered outside but didn't get very far. He sat down on the back porch and closed his eyes, wondering how life might be going on without him in Scotland. He wondered if anyone actually missed him. He suspected his friends speculated over him now and then, but they were likely managing fine without his companionship. His aunt might think of him fondly. His uncle probably didn't think of him at all. And his cousins were likely glad for his absence. They'd never gotten along terribly well. The only thing he truly missed about Scotland was his grandmother, and she was dead, so she wouldn't be there anyway. Sometimes he thought of the sweet air of the Highlands and the beautiful landscapes, and he missed that a little. But not as much as he'd thought he would. He looked around himself now. The mountains were magnificent, and they had a strange way of making him feel secure and protected. The beauty of this valley was quickly growing on him for reasons he couldn't quite put a finger on.

He was completely preoccupied with the view of the mountains when he heard a strange sound and looked across the yard to see a man walking with a very strange gait toward the little flower garden at the back of the yard near the fence. He stood up and moved cautiously across the yard, wondering if this was simply a friend of the family that he didn't know, or if it was someone who had an intent to do mischief. As he got closer, Jamie could hear the man mumbling to himself in a kind of baby talk. It only took a minute to realize this man was not mentally sound, but that didn't necessarily mean his being here was a good thing. He was debating whether to go ask a member of the family what he should do when he heard a woman call, "Benny, are you here? Answer your mother!"

Jamie turned to see a woman coming around the fence into the yard. He called to her, "I think he's over here."

The woman hurried closer, stopped when she saw the man who was apparently Benny, and let out a loud sigh of relief. "Oh, that boy!" she muttered. Benny was obliviously looking at the flowers with the fascination of a child. The woman turned to look at Jamie, then her eyes narrowed and her brow furrowed into a scowl. He realized then that this was Mrs. Miller. He recognized the scowl she'd given him when he'd brought her husband home drunk.

"I know who you are," she said as if she'd recognized him in the same moment. Since it had been dark on their previous meeting, they hadn't gotten a very good look at each other. "You're that nephew come from Scotland to make trouble."

Jamie felt his eyes widen. "I *am* the nephew from Scotland, but I must dispute that last part. I can assure you that I have no intention of making trouble."

She looked sourly at the bruise on his face as if it boldly contradicted what he'd just said. "The Brierleys are a wonderful family; the best. They don't need someone like you to taint the family and cause trouble the way my Leland does."

Jamie felt stunned at best, but he had only one truly honest retort. "I heartily agree, Mrs. Miller, but contrary to our opinion, these people seem to like me and have been very kind."

"Well, they would be, now wouldn't they! A lot of good kindness ever did *me* in dealing with my Leland."

Jamie had the good sense to recognize that this conversation was more about her own suffering than it was about *him*. In spite of her accusations, he tried to not take it personally and to look instead at the real problem. He felt tempted to defend himself and point out that the only thing he had in common with her husband was a penchant for drinking. Their commonality stopped there, and Mr. Miller's behavior and personality had *nothing* to do with him. But he knew Mrs. Miller wasn't interested in hearing his theories on the problem. She just needed someone to be angry with, and if his willingness to be a scapegoat might make her feel better, he didn't have a problem with that. He listened to her rant for several minutes about her husband's drinking problem and about his atrocious behavior with her and their son Benny. He wondered if she had any idea how much information about the family she was giving him; things he would actually prefer not to know. But she was talking so fast she didn't give him a chance to jump in and *tell* her that he'd prefer not to know. Apparently there were three adult children who were out on their own, but two of them also had drinking problems *thanks to their father's fine example,* she said with bitter sarcasm. Benny was still at home because he apparently had some kind of mental disorder that would require a parent's constant care for *as long as the good Lord allowed the poor boy to live.* Jamie learned that Mrs. Miller feared every day that her husband would not be allowed to continue his employment at the sawmill because he was so cantankerous there, in spite of being a good employee as far as she knew. Jamie was most astonished to hear her all but admit that Mr. Miller actually hurt her *and* Benny sometimes when he came home drunk. The thought made him want to go break the man's nose. But he just listened, pretending that he hadn't understood the implications and he had no idea what she was talking about.

Mrs. Miller stopped talking abruptly and looked over her shoulder, like a scared rabbit at the appearance of a wild, hungry dog. Jamie felt a chill go down his back to realize that *he* hadn't heard anything, but she was apparently so keenly accustomed to listening for any sign of her husband that she'd heard evidence of his approach seconds before Jamie saw him come around the edge of the fence.

"What are you doin' over here?" Mr. Miller barked at his wife, then he took notice of Jamie and spoke in a completely different tone. "Well, hello there, Mr. MacBrier. Will I be seein' you at our favored establishment this evening?" He laughed as if the question had actually been some kind of very humorous joke. Jamie noted the bruises and cuts on Leland Miller's face, which were more excessive than those on his own. He loathed the evidence he bore on his own face that he had actually been associating with this man. Another chill rushed over him, like some kind of foreboding, as if his inadvertent connection to Mr. Miller would see him undone.

"Well, are you goin' to be there?" Leland growled lightly, startling Jamie from a stupor.

"Not sure," Jamie called back. While he was craving some good, strong whiskey—and the way it would dull his senses—he preferred to do his drinking independently of this man.

Leland turned his attention back to his wife and he repeated, more gruffly, "What are you doin' over here?"

"Benny wandered over here and I've just come to bring him home," she said and turned to go and coax Benny away from his perusal of the flowers.

"I'd think you could keep track of him better than that," Leland growled again with a ferociousness that made Jamie shudder. He would think that this man wouldn't want other people to know how badly he treated his family, but apparently he took some kind of perverse pride in having others see the power and control he had over his wife and son.

Benny went along with his mother dutifully, as if the presence of his father had terrified him into obeying without question. Even poor Benny understood fear and was motivated by it.

After the Millers had departed, Jamie just stood there for more than a few minutes, wondering what to think and what to do with himself. Since his evening routine back in Scotland had usually included drinking with his friends, that was his natural inclination. His weeks of traveling with the wagon company would have driven him mad with boredom except that it had taken so much work to simply travel and eat and sleep. He'd craved liquor every single day, but since it hadn't been available he'd had no choice but to abstain. Now that it *was* available, the craving was difficult to resist. He thought of Ian's confessions about struggling with the same thing in his younger years, but his explanation of the solution felt vague and difficult to grasp. Right now he only knew he wanted a drink, and there was nothing here that might lure him away from that temptation. If he had any hope of spending time with Gillian, he might have felt differently. As it was, he decided that all he had to do was tell one of the children to tell their father that he'd gone into town. He was on his way to the door, hoping to find one of them in the kitchen, when Mont popped out the door to say, "Oh, there you are. Papa says it's study time."

Jamie formed the words in his mind to decline and give his message, but the only thing that came through his lips was, "I'll be there in a minute. Thank you."

He sighed and followed Mont into the house, wondering if Gillian would be there. At least that would make it tolerable. But she *wasn't* there, and all he could do was patiently endure study time and prayer. The problem was that not having Gillian in the room made him feel as agitated as if he had ants crawling all over him. It took all his willpower to sit still through the ritual, when he wanted to be more wiggly than little Gavin, who couldn't sit still for even a moment. When it was finally over, he said good night to everyone, eagerly accepting the hugs he got from the younger children. Wren insisted that he lean over the bed and give her a hug as well, and she told him how glad she was to have him there.

"You're so very kind," he said to her, then glanced around the room. "All of you." She smiled at him, but there was a quiet compassion in her eyes that provoked him to admit, almost against his will, "I'm not sure I deserve it."

"Ye mustn't think that way," Wren said. "It's plain t' see that ye're a good man."

"Is it?" Jamie asked, wondering for a moment if she was being sarcastic, given the bruise and cut lip he was wearing on his face. But her sincerity was evident.

"Of course," Wren said and smiled again, squeezing his hand.

Jamie gave her a smile in return and hurried from the room, quietly saying to Ian, "Could you leave the back door unlocked, please? And don't wait up for me."

He saw Ian wanting to protest or talk him out of leaving, but Jamie hurried out of the room and down the stairs and out the back door, feeling as if some unseen power might catch up and swallow him whole. Twenty minutes later he was sitting gratefully alone at a discreet corner table, glad to have avoided Leland Miller. With the third drink he was finally starting to relax and block out thoughts of Gillian; then he looked up to find Leland grinning down at him.

"I found you, you sly dog," Leland declared.

"So you have," Jamie said. "Although I'm more in the mood to drink alone tonight. I'm certain you can find someone else to bestow your charming personality upon."

Jamie knew this would turn out badly as soon as he saw the way Leland's eyes responded to the comment. He knew very well that *no one* else around here was willing to tolerate Leland's *charming personality.* That's why he'd been so friendly to Jamie when he'd first arrived. He was the newcomer, innocent and naive to Leland's true nature.

"What did you just say, boy?" Leland demanded. Jamie couldn't tolerate having someone angry with him when he'd done nothing wrong, but he *really* couldn't tolerate being called *boy*. He knew that Leland was already fairly drunk, and Jamie himself was getting a little tipsy. He knew that liquor made men do stupid things, but he was still stunned when Leland actually took a swing at him, landing a fist against Jamie's jaw. Thankfully it just missed the bruised area below his eye, or he felt sure that getting hit in a place that was already damaged would have likely made him pass out. He'd never been very tough when it came to such things.

Jamie felt angry for a great many reasons when Leland hit him, but the worst was imagining the moment when he would face Gillian again, sporting a new bruise. The anger urged him to recover quickly from the blow, and before he even thought about what he was doing, he returned the favor and felt a secret delight to see Leland Miller reeling backward, cursing as he went down, as if he'd been innocently assaulted and had no accountability in the situation whatsoever.

Before the fight could get any worse, Jamie and Leland were both escorted, none too gently, out the front door and onto the street. Jamie got up and dusted himself off, then turned toward where he knew he'd left his horse. He turned back when he realized that Leland was *not* getting up. Was he really that drunk? Jamie groaned in response to the nagging of his conscience that told him he could not leave the man there in the street, especially when—for all of his horrid character traits—Leland had made certain that Jamie had gotten home safely when *he* had been that drunk. It crossed his mind that he would not be in this situation if he had stayed at home and minded his manners. But that brought to mind thoughts of Gillian, and he had to conclude that he might actually prefer being in this situation.

Jamie hefted the groaning and mumbling Mr. Miller up off the ground and guided him to his horse. He managed to urge him into the saddle after several tries, then rode at his side to guide him safely home. Once there, he took him to the door and knocked. A perturbed Mrs. Miller answered and let out a disgusted sigh.

"Oh, it's *you*," she said.

"I did get him safely home," he said in his defense.

"How kind of you," she said with sarcasm, as if having him *not* get safely home might be preferable. He wondered if he would have done the woman a favor to leave her husband in the street to possibly get trampled by a passing carriage. But the thought felt terribly wrong and he scolded himself for thinking it, even though he knew Mrs. Miller was probably thinking it too.

She opened the door wider and motioned Jamie toward a couch where he deposited Leland and made certain that he slumped over in a direction that would not catapult him onto the floor. He then walked back out the door, saying over his shoulder, "I'll take care of the horse."

"Mr. MacBrier," she said, and he turned back, prepared to face more scolding words. But she said with a humble sigh and kind eyes, "Thank you."

"Glad to be of assistance," he said, then he turned more toward her and added, "If I can ever be of assistance . . . for any reason . . . please . . ." He nodded instead of finishing the sentence, hoping she knew that he would do anything he could to keep Leland Miller from hurting her or her son. He wasn't sure what he would do exactly, given his own aversion to physical violence—especially putting himself in the middle of it. But he wanted to help, *wished* he could help, and hoped that she knew he meant it.

"Thank you," she said, as if she *did* understand.

He nodded again and left the house. After caring for Mr. Miller's horse, he walked around the fence and cared for his own. When he entered the house, Gillian was *not* there, and he felt more disappointed than relieved. He locked the back door and managed to get to his room without bumping into anything, even though he'd not bothered to light a lamp. He kicked off his boots and laid back on his bed, not certain if he was grateful or angry concerning the way he felt about Gillian Brierley.

* * * * *

Gillian sat quietly in the dark, about halfway up the stairs, leaning her head against the wall. She heard Jamie come in and wondered why she couldn't have been upstairs sound asleep, catching up on her rest, as she had planned. She was deeply tempted to rush down to the kitchen to greet him. A part of her wanted to be angry with him as she had been previously at the evidence that he'd been out drinking. But the events and conversations of the day—combined with all she'd been feeling throughout the evening—made her want to take him in her arms and beg him to change his ways so that they could be together, easing this ache he provoked in her.

She sat there on the stairs and wept silently long after she'd heard the door to Jamie's room close in the distance. Then she crept back to her room, closed the door without making any noise, and crawled into her bed, where she'd already tried in vain to sleep. For what seemed like hours she prayed and pondered, just as she'd been doing *before* she'd felt compelled to go sit on the stairs and wait for Jamie to come home. But now her prayers were reaching deeper, and her pondering was taking her mind and her heart into places within herself that were not easy to look at. She recounted over and over the situation she was in and everything that had led up to this point. In doing her best to face God with a clear conscience and ask for His help and guidance, she had to acknowledge that she had not necessarily handled herself appropriately. She prayed for forgiveness in regard to the way she had treated Jamie, and for perhaps moving forward too quickly in regard to Hugh, or perhaps moving forward for the wrong reasons—which had amplified the problem.

Gillian considered the advice of Hugh *and* her father, and couldn't deny that they had both been inspired. She didn't know why she felt the way she did about Jamie, or if those feelings ever had any hope of turning into something that would have meaning for her future. But she couldn't deny that she had to trust her feelings and follow them. She thought of the story of Joseph Smith, and all that had led up to his prayer in the grove that had resulted in the First Vision. Her parents had taught her that Joseph had experienced many strong feelings in regard to the religious difficulties in the community, and that he had a number of personal concerns. Those feelings had led him to that foreordained moment when he had begun the work that God had sent him to this earth to do. Gillian had heard her parents talk about the feelings they'd both had that had compelled them to come to America and find the Mormons. They had many times related their own experience to that of Joseph Smith in the respect that the Spirit guided mortal men through their thoughts and feelings, and it was important to pay attention and respect such things. Now, in the middle of what felt like an enormous disaster, the one thing that Gillian could not get out of her mind was the way she had felt when she had first seen Jamie MacBrier walk through the door. He was an attractive man, but she could never credit what she'd felt then—or felt now—simply to attraction. It would be impossible for physical attraction to cause such unimaginable stirrings—seemingly all at once—in her heart, mind, body, and spirit. It was a moment she would never forget, and now she knew it was a feeling to which she needed to pay attention.

Gillian finally slept and didn't wake until the room was hot with daylight. A glance at the clock told her that she'd missed breakfast and the rest of the morning routine. Since she was fasting, she wasn't concerned about missing the meal, but she did wonder how the family was managing without her. Probably just fine, she concluded. She didn't hear anyone screaming or crying, and she knew the children were all very capable. Certain that someone would have come to get her if she was needed, she turned over and closed her eyes, immersing herself once again in prayer. She didn't come to any firm conclusions beyond the fact that she needed to approach the situation with more humility and charity, and she needed to offer Jamie MacBrier an apology—which she dreaded immensely. Beyond that, she had no idea what might happen. She could only strive to remain close to the Spirit and pay attention.

Chapter Nine
Paying Attention

Jamie was proud of himself for making it to breakfast—until he realized that Gillian wasn't there; then he wondered why he'd bothered. A warm smile from his uncle made him feel that his efforts were appreciated, but it wasn't the same.

Trying to appear nonchalant, he asked Ian, "Is Gillian still not feeling well?"

"I assume," Ian said, which implied that he hadn't actually spoken to her this morning.

When the meal was finished, Jamie said to Ian, "Is there something I can do to help? Anything? I need something to occupy my time."

"Of course," Ian said, seeming impressed that he'd asked. "If you're up to the heat, the weeds are overtaking the garden. You should wear your hat so you don't get sunburned."

Jamie knew that well enough from his trek across the country. "I'd be happy to," he said. He was up for the heat, and he actually knew *how* to pull weeds.

"Later I could use some help moving some things around in the barn. Alfred and Harry are good and strong, but I don't have the strength I used to."

"I'll plan on it," Jamie said. "Thank you."

"Thank *you*," Ian said and smiled, slapping him lightly on the shoulder before he went upstairs to attend to his wife and the new baby.

Jamie went to his room to retrieve the well-used, dust-absorbed hat he'd brought with him. He went out to the garden and got down on his knees at the point farthest from the house, eagerly pulling up weeds from around the hopeful vegetables. He was still out there when Sarah found him hours later to tell him that it was almost time for lunch. His shirt was soaked with sweat, and he hoped he had time to change it and wash up before the family was seated. He didn't want them waiting for him. He'd thought of nothing but Gillian all morning, but when he walked through the door to see her standing at her familiar spot near the stove, his heart tripped over itself and his brain turned to mush. She turned to see who had come through the door, then she took a second glance and actually smiled at him. He just stood there like a fool, frozen as if a north wind had followed him through the door.

"What *have* you been doing?" she asked, glancing at his clothes.

He looked down to see the dirt on his breeches and hands, along with the sweat-soaked shirt, then he looked at her again. "Weeding," was all he could manage to say before he rushed to the bathing room to wash up, having to share space with the three boys who were all trying to get cleaned up as well.

Over lunch Jamie sensed something different about Gillian, but she wouldn't make eye contact with him long enough for him to be able to even guess what it might be. He wondered again if her not feeling well had had something to do with him. He was surprised to hear Ian speaking to him, especially when he hadn't been paying attention to what he'd said.

"I'm sorry," Jamie said. "What was that?"

"Since you asked if there's anything you could do this afternoon, I'm going to have you drive the wagon out to the Clarkson farm and pick up the pigs I'm buying from him."

Jamie couldn't hold back a little chuckle, certain Ian was teasing. "Pigs?"

"Yes," Ian drawled with a smile. But he *wasn't* teasing. "You can drive a wagon, can't you?"

"Yes, sir."

"Then the rest is easy. They'll be secure in a pen for transporting."

"I can certainly do that," Jamie said, not wanting to be disagreeable but feeling a little intimidated at the prospect of transporting animals. He wanted to remind Ian of his somewhat aristocratic upbringing, but he knew that Ian had been raised the same way in the same home.

They'd not been coddled, and they had a deep respect for hard work. But it had *still* been an aristocratic upbringing. He thought of a glitch and said, "How exactly do I find the Clarkson farm?"

"Gillian can go with you," Ian said. "She knows where it is." Gillian started to choke on her food, and Ian asked her, "Is that a problem?" She shook her head, then ran into the other room, coughing vehemently.

Ian smiled at Jamie. "Food must have gone down wrong. She'll be able to guide you to the farm. You can leave right after we eat."

Jamie nodded, concerned for Gillian, who was still coughing in the distance, and secretly delighted at the prospect of having a good excuse to be alone with her. He felt a little suspicious of Ian's motives, knowing that any one of the children would probably know where to find the Clarkson farm, and Gillian's time would probably be a great deal more effective here at home, especially since she'd taken time off for not feeling well. But Jamie wasn't about to point that out. He just smiled back at Ian and ate his lunch.

Gillian's coughing quieted and she returned to the table, saying nothing beyond, "Sorry. I'm all right now."

When lunch was finished, Gillian stood up and started to clear the table, but her father scooted her out of the way and said, "We can do this. Get yourself ready to go."

Gillian glanced at her father and didn't miss the barely perceptible hint of something conspiratorial in his eyes. She almost wanted to be angry with him, except that she knew very well what his motives were, and she knew he was an inspired man. She'd been praying to know how to smooth over the friction between herself and Jamie. She had to see this as an answer to prayers, rather than a dreadful prospect—which was how it felt at the moment.

Without a word she went upstairs to freshen up and get a bonnet. She peeked in her mother's room to tell her where she was going, but both Wren and the baby were sleeping. She knew her father would explain later.

Gillian said a quick prayer and went out to the yard where Ian had just hooked the team up to the wagon. She made up her mind to go along on this errand and not complain. Jamie appeared to be sincere in his efforts to simply help her father, and he needed her to navigate, since he had no idea where to find the Clarkson farm. Normally she considered a ride to the outskirts of the valley a pleasant endeavor, but the very idea of sitting next to Jamie on a hard wagon seat for a number of miles of possibly awkward silence held no appeal whatsoever. As much as she knew she needed to talk to him, she didn't feel prepared, and this was not how she'd imagined having their conversation take place. She'd brought a pillow along to remedy the hard seat, but they were barely away from the house before the expected quiet settled in, and Gillian hated this already. She focused on the high, floating clouds hovering in the blue sky above them, and the occasional tree they passed as the appearance of any houses gradually became more rare.

Jamie broke the silence so suddenly that it startled her. "Are you going to stay angry with me forever?"

"I'm not angry," she said in an unconvincing tone.

"Just miffed enough to completely ignore me?"

"I'm not ignoring you," she said. "I just . . ."

"Have absolutely nothing to say to me?" he questioned.

Gillian reminded herself to behave like a Christian and opted not to say what she *wanted* to say. Her temptation to point out how disgusted and disappointed she felt by his behavior became smothered by the recent realization that she needed to be forgiving and have compassion. In a kind voice, she said, "If you wish to have a conversation, I'm all ears."

"Really?" He chuckled. "*All ears?* I can say whatever I want and you have to listen because we're miles from home and you have no choice?"

Gillian glanced at him, then looked in the other direction. "It appears that way."

"Don't worry," he said. "I'm not going to talk your ear off, or anything. There's only one thing I really want to say."

"And what's that?" she asked, immediately regretting her impatient tone of voice. His glance told her that he'd not missed it, but his eyes softened as he looked ahead, and she was grateful that he was going to ignore it.

"I would just like to point out that I might not be nearly as horrible a person as you think I am."

"I don't know you well enough to know what kind of person you are," she said. "I can only gauge your character based on what I've seen for myself."

"Which has not been very impressive, I know, but . . ."

"But?" she pressed when he hesitated.

"But I'd be grateful if you'd give me another chance."

Gillian turned to look at him to be certain he was serious. She regretted it when she found him staring at her with an intensity that made her heart quicken. She didn't know how to acknowledge his humble plea for another chance, especially when he didn't know that she knew she needed to do exactly that. And he didn't know what had changed between her and Hugh. At least she knew he'd not been told. But he'd proven to be very perceptive. She couldn't say for certain what he might have sensed from her recent behavior.

Hating the tension of so many facts and feelings that were hanging unspoken between them, she jumped in to clear at least one of them out of the way. "My father manipulated this, you know."

She expected him to be surprised, or perhaps offended. But he said, "I know. He seems to be intent on doing some kind of match making. Although I can't imagine why he'd be trying to match you up with someone like me, when there's a man like Hugh Montgomery wanting to marry his daughter." Gillian couldn't comment for fear of either saying the wrong thing or losing control of her emotions. "Or maybe it's not match making at all. Maybe he just wants you to be nice to me because I'm the new kid in town and I have a drinking problem. Maybe he thinks you could be a good influence on me."

Gillian almost choked again, given the fact that both Hugh and her father had, more or less, said that very thing. She managed to keep her reaction to a gentle cough, but Jamie chuckled, as if he sensed the reason for it.

"Can I?" she asked when he said nothing more. "Be a good influence on you?"

"Maybe," he said and smiled. Gillian couldn't help but smile back. He had a brilliant smile that made his eyes sparkle. Again there was silence until he said, "Tell me something about yourself that I don't know . . . something that most people don't know."

"You make it sound like I have some kind of great secret that's very exciting."

"Don't you?"

"Maybe. What about you?"

"There's nothing. Well . . . I actually like to sing."

"Really?" She couldn't help being pleased. "Are you any good?"

"I'm told that I am," he said.

"Since tomorrow is Sunday, you'll have a chance to show off your voice when we sing hymns."

"Oh," he said, a little unnerved, "hymns. I did promise your father I would go to church."

"It will be good for you."

"Maybe," he said. "You're changing the subject. Tell me something about yourself. Something special."

"You're implying that I trust you enough to share something special."

"And you don't."

"Not really."

"Then there *is* something special," he said firmly.

"Actually, there is . . . but very few people outside of my family know about it."

"I'm part of your family."

"Not really," she said again.

"Does Hugh know?"

"He does, but he's known me since I was a little girl. It would be impossible for him *not* to know."

"You're not going to tell me, are you?"

"Someday, perhaps."

"Well, then . . ." he drawled, "tell me how your family came to a place such as this. I know it all has to do with being with people who share your religious beliefs, but why here?"

"That's not a pretty story," she said. "If you came west with a Mormon company, you should have some idea of the reasons."

"I kept to myself. Tell me."

"All right. I'll give you the brief version."

"I want to hear how it applies to *your* life."

"Well, you know I was born on the ship coming to America. We lived in New York City for a time while my parents were trying to figure out where to find the Mormons. All they knew was that the Book of Mormon had been printed in New York, but they quickly found out the Saints had left New York. They'd also been in Pennsylvania, Ohio, and Missouri, but they were no longer in any of those places."

"Why?"

"Persecution," she said.

"I don't understand."

"There will always be forces of evil fighting against God's work, Jamie. Because this is Christ's true religion, Satan works very hard to destroy it." She saw him narrow his eyes as if to take this in, but he didn't comment. She went on with her story. "We finally found the Saints in Illinois in a beautiful city on the Mississippi River. We were happy there for a time, but then we were driven out . . . in the middle of winter. We had a terrible journey to Winter Quarters, where we stayed for several months before we began the journey to this valley. When we arrived, there was practically nothing here. This community has been built up by our people. Of course you know there are many here who are not Mormons. This is a place where people stop on their way to California, and there are many establishments meant to appeal to them." She didn't comment on how that was the only reason he was able to find liquor amply available in a Mormon community. Instead she said, "We've had some difficult years here, but the community is thriving, and we know that we will be safe here. We will never have to leave this place."

"How can you know that after all of the places you've had to leave?"

"We just know," she said and smiled. "Now tell me about Scotland."

"Surely you've heard all about that from your parents."

"I want to hear your version," she said and enjoyed hearing him talk about the beauty of the Highlands and the magnificent house called Brierley where he'd been raised. She intermittently gave him directions, and he was just winding down on his description of the gardens at Brierley when she pointed ahead and said, "We're almost there. That's it ahead."

Brother Clarkson came out to meet them, having seen the wagon coming up the road. He was kind and friendly and pleased to meet Jamie. He invited them inside where Sister Clarkson was in the kitchen. They were each given cool water to drink and a piece of honey cake. They thanked her, then went outside where Brother Clarkson had five freshly weaned piglets in a wooden pen with a door that was tied shut. Jamie helped him lift the pen onto the bed of the wagon while the little pigs squealed and made them all laugh.

"They'll be all right till you get 'em home," Brother Clarkson said. "They just got fed and had a big drink o' water. And yer pa's got a place all fixed fer 'em, he told me."

"I believe he does," Gillian said. "He told me he's already settled with you . . . that you'd been paid."

"That's right," Brother Clarkson said, and they were quickly off toward home with the new delivery onboard.

"What are you going to name them?" Jamie asked.

"Oh, I don't think we should name them," Gillian declared. "Since they'll eventually be made into ham and bacon, it's probably best not to get attached."

Jamie glanced over his shoulder at the pigpen and mocked an expression of terror on behalf of the pigs. "Yes, probably best."

Gillian was astonished by how dark and ominous the sky had become. She knew they wouldn't make it home without getting assaulted with rain. She could only be glad that with the July heat in the air, it would be a warm rain. Otherwise, it would be even *more* unpleasant. Being alone with Jamie and trying to contend with the tension between them had already left her feeling ill at ease. They'd managed to share some pleasant conversation, but she knew that there was something far more important she needed to say, and she didn't know how to go about it.

"We're going to get wet, aren't we," Jamie said when it became evident that the horses pulling the wagon would not be prodded to increase their speed.

"It looks that way," Gillian said with chagrin.

He laughed as if the prospect were delightful. She glared at him, and he laughed again. A minute later it started to rain, and a few minutes beyond that the rain became hard and heavy, and Gillian was drenched. The pigs didn't seem to mind.

There was no choice but to go along that way for several minutes before a solitary tree appeared in the distance. Jamie guided the horses beneath the massive umbrella of its thick, leafy branches. The tree didn't completely block the rain, but it offered tremendous relief. Then Gillian realized this was the same tree under which she'd been sitting when Hugh had proposed marriage. The irony made her a little unsteady as she stepped down from the wagon. She hadn't waited for Jamie to help her, not wanting him to touch her. But he saw her teeter slightly as he came around the wagon, and he rushed the last few steps to take hold of her arm.

"Are you all right?" he asked with surprising kindness.

"I'm fine, thank you," she said, trying not to be affected by his touch. But she concluded that was impossible.

She steadied herself and moved away from him, closer to the trunk of the tree, hoping for even more improvement in being shielded from the rain. Jamie hovered nearby, making it impossible to ignore that he was watching her while she was watching the rainfall. Unable to tolerate the silence, she said with sarcasm, "This is just great, isn't it?"

"Actually, it is," he said as if he meant it. "Here we are . . . alone . . . with the exception of the pigs, who shall remain nameless. And for some strange reason I get the feeling that there's something you want to say to me. I would think this is the perfect opportunity to say it."

Gillian looked at him, astonished, while her heart began to pound. "How do you *do* that?" she asked, turning her back to him.

"Do what?"

"Practically . . . read my mind."

"I have no idea," he said. "It's never happened before. But . . . you *do* have something you want to say to me, don't you."

"What makes you think so?" she asked.

"You're different . . . toward me. And this after you pretty much disappeared for twenty-four hours. Your father sent us on this little escapade together, and you didn't even protest about having to come with me."

Gillian sighed, figuring now was as good a time as any to get this over with. "Very well." She sighed again, but she still kept her back turned to him. It seemed easier this way. "I need to apologize to you."

"Apologize?" He chuckled. "To what do I owe the pleasure?"

Gillian forged ahead, finally turning to look at him. "I've . . . realized that I've been . . . less than kind to you, and . . . for all that you and I are very different and have many opposing views, my behavior was uncalled for. I'm sorry for that, and . . . I hope that you can forgive me . . . and give me another chance."

"A chance to what?" he asked, and she wondered how he could manage to steer any conversation into such uncomfortable territory.

"To be more kind," she said, hoping that would put an end to it.

"I'm all for another chance at *that*," he said, "but I can't help wondering what brought on this sudden change of heart. It wouldn't have something to do with *Hugh,* would it?"

Gillian turned her back to him again, afraid he'd see the truth in her eyes. And the truth was riddled with guilt and confusion, in spite of her knowing that she needed to take these steps.

"Ah," he said as if the gesture alone had told him all he'd needed to know. "Something's changed between you and Hugh, hasn't it? And I'd wager a great deal that it has to do with me. He noticed, didn't he." It wasn't a question. "He noticed the way you look at me. He realized that . . . how did you put it? That he couldn't hold a candle to me . . . at least not *that* way."

Gillian was determined not to let him rile her, and even more determined to not let him see evidence of it if he did. "He wants to give the matter some time," she said. "That's all. Whether or not that has anything to do with you is simply none of your affair."

"So you say." He took a step closer, but she kept her back turned, trying very hard not to be affected by his closeness. "I think it is very much my affair, and it has everything to do with me." He moved a little closer still, and Gillian closed her eyes, trying to block him out. "I think he knows you're in love with me, and he can't live with it."

"I think your boldness and arrogance are atrocious," Gillian said, but she still didn't open her eyes. She was trying very hard not to feel defensive, which always led her to being unkind to him—without even trying.

"Better to be bold than entirely ignore the truth that is right in front of our faces," he said. "And if stating the truth is something you consider arrogant, so be it." He put a hand on her arm, and she caught her breath. "If what I'm saying isn't true, then look me in the eye and tell me. Tell me to go away, Gillian, and I'll go away. I'll go and live somewhere very far away, and you and Hugh can live happily ever after." His voice lowered. "But not completely happy. How could you be when you would always wonder? That's it, isn't it. He doesn't want you to wonder. Does this mean I have a chance . . . with you?"

Gillian found the ability to look at him now, then wished she hadn't when she realized how close he was. Still, she kept firm eye contact as she said, "Not without some dramatic changes in your lifestyle."

"You're criticizing my lifestyle?"

"Yes."

"And you want me to change who I am in order to be a contender for your hand in marriage?"

Gillian couldn't believe that her apologizing to him had so quickly led the conversation into references of love and marriage. She couldn't deny that everything he'd said was true. But the way it made her feel was difficult to handle. She fought for composure and courage in order to press forward.

"I would never expect a man to change his personality for me," she said, her voice quivering only a little. "If you mean that *who you are* includes your inclination to drinking and your resistance to religion, then you must know that I would simply never even consider marrying a man who holds to such thinking. You have your free agency, Jamie. I can't change you. If that's the life you choose to live, then that's your decision. I have my free agency as well, and I choose to marry a man who does *not* drink—at all. I also choose to marry a man who shows exemplary character traits of kindness and charity and hard work. And I choose to marry a man who shares my religious beliefs."

"You would expect me to become a Mormon for you?"

"I don't expect you to do anything," Gillian said. "And if you think you can make the gospel a part of your life simply to please another person, then you don't understand the nature of the gospel at all. It would make me very happy to see you embrace the gospel, Jamie, but you can't do it for me or for anyone else—except yourself. If you learn more about it and decide that's what you want, then we might have enough in common to consider sharing a life."

She saw surprise in his eyes, then something that made her wonder if he was trying not to cry. "You really mean that. You *are* giving me a chance."

Gillian turned her back to him again, not knowing what to say. He quickly filled the silence, but she didn't necessarily like what he said. "You've been very angry with me."

"Yes, I have," she had to admit.

"And I think that for all your trying to be noble and kind to me, you're *still* angry. I suspect it wouldn't take much to bring it to the surface again."

Gillian said nothing. The temptation she felt to cry was proof of his theory being correct. She *did* feel angry, but she didn't want to talk about it. She'd learned in the very short time she'd known Jamie, however, that he was not one to beat around the bush or put on pretenses, and she wasn't surprised when he pressed forward.

"And I've got a pretty good idea why. You're angry because I came here. If I'd stayed away you could have gone on with your very practical life and you never would have had any regrets because there was no one or nothing better than Hugh Montgomery. Then I showed up, and not only did you feel something you've never felt before, but Hugh figured it out and put a stop to your ridiculous engagement. You think I completely messed up your life and you're angry with me. It's too bad I couldn't have shown up with all of the noble attributes you were looking for in a husband. How unfortunate for you to feel this way about a man who is everything you *don't* want in a man."

Gillian's first impulse was to defend herself, but she knew it would only lead to an argument, and she also knew that she couldn't deny the truth of what he was saying. If she were truly trying to be a better person, and to be more Christlike in her attitude about this situation, she had to humbly admit to the truth and be willing to accept it. She also knew that a soft answer could turn away wrath. Perhaps his wrath was justified. Either way, she could only think of one thing to say, and she *did* say it softly. "Not *everything.*"

She turned to face him as she said it, and she saw him trying to figure out what she meant while it was clear that her tone had disarmed him. "What do you mean?" he finally asked. She felt certain he knew, but he likely wanted some verification.

"I mean that you're not *everything* I don't want in a man. You're actually a tolerably decent human being for the most part, and . . ." Gillian hesitated, wondering if she would regret this. Feeling like she needed to proceed and not worry about the outcome, she said, "And . . . I can't deny how I feel."

She saw his eyebrow go up at her admittance. He pondered her words a long moment, then said, "Tell me the real reason you've had a change of heart, Gillian. I need to know."

She looked down. "This is all happening so fast. I . . . hardly know what to think, or—"

"All the more reason that we need to be completely honest with each other," he said. "Tell me the real reason. Did your father put you up to this?"

"No," she said. "He only told me that I should be more compassionate. And he was right."

"And Hugh?"

"I already told you. He feels like we need to give the matter some time."

"He knows how you feel about me?"

"Yes. You were right. He did see it; he figured it out. I know his heart is breaking, but . . . he's a good man."

"I know he's a good man, but I also know you don't love him." He sighed. "Tell me the real reason."

Gillian wondered how to put it into words, how to be completely honest and not hurt his feelings. She felt some inspiration come to her and said, "You don't know me well enough to know that nothing is more important to me than living my life the way God wants me to live it. No amount of attraction or the lack of it could ever make me live my life any other way." She looked up at him and found a burst of courage along with the words she needed to say shining with clarity in her mind. "I believe God gave us these feelings for a reason, and I believe that He sees something in you that no one else can see. This isn't about Hugh or my father or you, or even myself. I've been praying . . . very hard . . . and I know that God wants me to give this . . . us . . . a fair chance. That's the truth, Jamie. That's the real reason."

She watched his face while she sensed his mind working it out. She wondered if her theories sounded completely foreign to him, or if he would be able to understand. He intensified his gaze as if he could look deeper into her eyes and discover even more than she'd admitted to. She was surprised to realize that he had when he said, "You're relieved, aren't you."

"Relieved?"

"If you believe that God has a reason for you to feel this way, then you can admit to your feelings and not be weighed down with guilt."

Gillian took a deep breath and took in his words. She had to admit, "I'm continually amazed at how well you know me . . . when you don't know me at all."

"I'm rather amazed myself," he said and took her shoulders into his hands.

Gillian looked up at him and became momentarily distracted by how much curlier his hair looked when it was wet. She then found the courage to look into his eyes, instinctively knowing that once she did she would lose herself there. And she did. She both hoped and feared that he would kiss her. The hope came from desperately wanting the experience. She'd recalled—against her will—a thousand times the tender kiss on her brow that he'd given her in the upstairs hall. It had affected her so deeply that she felt certain it had contributed to her intense confusion and overwhelming feelings.

Gillian could hardly breathe when he pressed his hands down her arms, then took both her hands into his. He touched his cheek to hers and she became preoccupied with the feel of his stubbled skin. She'd never experienced any such thing. During her childhood she had many times put her hands on her father's unshaven face, but this was completely different.

"Gillian," he whispered in her ear, then he said nothing more. He eased back just barely enough to look again into her eyes, at the same time easing his arm around her waist.

Gillian felt a momentary panic when it occurred to her that he didn't know or understand the moral boundaries with which she'd been raised. Of course, it was up to her to stand up for what she knew to be right for herself.

"There's something I need to say," she said, surprised at how dreamy her voice sounded.

"Then say it," he said, but his closeness was so distracting that she eased away from him and took a few steps back.

He looked more curious than alarmed, and she just made herself say it. "Trust me when I tell you that no man will ever get anything more than a kiss from me until I am his wife."

"Oh, I trust you!" He took a step toward her. "I never would have believed otherwise."

"Just so we're clear," she said, and he took her hand.

"Oh, we're clear," he said and took a step closer.

"And we must be careful," she insisted, noting the subtle quivering in her own voice.

He stepped even closer. "We'll be careful," he said in little more than a whisper.

"With the way we feel about each other," she said and had to catch her breath as she realized how close his face was to hers, "we must be especially careful."

"Especially careful," he repeated, his voice low and dreamy.

"Do you promise?" she asked, looking up into his eyes, feeling his breath warm her lips, as if to prepare them for what was about to happen.

"I promise," he said and meekly touched his lips to hers.

Gillian held her breath as if that might help her more fully hold on to the experience. The kiss lasted only a long moment, but she felt as if it had somehow created a bridge between the life she had lived up to that moment, and the life that she would live from that moment forward. She slowly opened her eyes to see him looking at her as if he'd never seen anything so beautiful. She was thinking the same about him. He pressed a hand over the side of her face, then over her hair. She followed his lead and did the same, loving the feel of his hair between her fingers. It occurred to her that there had never been any such moment with Hugh; she wondered if there ever would have been, or if their marriage would have remained entirely practical and devoid of any such heart-stopping tenderness. Gillian forced thoughts of Hugh away and focused only on Jamie. It wasn't difficult to do, given the effect he had on her. When he closed his eyes and lowered his head, she felt a jolt in her heart as it perceived the implication that he intended to kiss her again. This kiss was longer, more warm and sweet, but she felt in no way uncomfortable. Quite the opposite, in fact. The entire experience was deeply comforting and soothed something in her that she hadn't known needed soothing.

When he opened his eyes to look at her again, Gillian quietly murmured her most prominent thought. "How can so much have happened in only a few days, when it feels like as many weeks, or even months?"

"I don't know," he murmured. "I feel as if I've known you for all of my life . . . forever."

Gillian looked more deeply into his eyes, considering the possible spiritual implications of what they were feeling. With his ignorance in regard to the gospel plan, he couldn't understand what *she* understood. But she knew that such a thing was possible. Was that the reason for what they'd both felt from the very first moment? Had it been some kind of recognition between their spirits? She was far too practical to believe that any life-impacting decision could be made on such feelings alone. But she also knew that spiritual matters were often very personal and individual, and that the guidance of the Holy Ghost was meant to be the same. It was called personal revelation for a reason. She felt peace and comfort in knowing that she could rely on that guidance. She worked and strove every day to be worthy of having the Lord's Spirit close to her, and she knew that for all of her faults and weaknesses, she would not be deceived as long as she remained humble and receptive. Even her bout of confusion that had provoked some bad behavior in her had been brief, and she'd quickly come to her senses. She knew that God was with her, and she knew that these feelings she had were valid. She simply had to keep paying attention and trust her feelings to guide her, one step at a time—line upon line, precept upon precept. Time. It settled well into her spirit. All they needed was time, and everything would work out as it was meant to. And for this particular moment in time, she felt completely comfortable to just be with Jamie and to explore the experience of what was awakening between them.

Chapter Ten
Time

Not wanting to let this moment go, Gillian impulsively lifted her lips to his, surprised at how easy it was to do such a thing. "Oh, Jamie," she muttered and kissed him again, not surprised by the way he responded and the way he wrapped her in his arms. She looked up at him and whispered, "How is it possible that I can feel this way?"

"I don't know," he said, his voice equally low. "I'm glad that you do, but I almost feel sorry for you on that account."

"Sorry for me?" she asked. "Why?"

"Oh, my dear, sweet Gillian," he said, touching her face again. "It's easy for us to stand here now and believe that our whole lives could feel this way, but we've only known each other a few days, and I've already disappointed and angered you a great deal. As much as I would like to convince you that I will never disappoint or anger you again, I fear it's not likely. You make me want to be a better man, Gillian, but . . . I know my weaknesses . . . and so do you."

"But there must be a way for you to get beyond that," she said, thinking of her father and Hugh. If they had done it, surely Jamie could too. "We cannot discredit the way we feel. There must be a reason, Jamie. There must be."

"If you believe that, then you must believe that God sees something in me that no one else can see."

"Do *you* believe that?"

"I don't know," he admitted. "But you make me *want* to believe it. Do *you* believe it?"

"Yes," she said with no hesitation, and he looked surprised.

"You really *do* believe that," he said, astonished.

"I do. I believe that God loves all of His children . . . more than we could possibly imagine. If you choose to take hold of His love and live your life the way He would have you live it, you could be happier than you have ever believed possible—with or without me. I believe that redemption is truly possible, Jamie, and that any wound can be healed."

He sighed and gazed at her face while he pondered her words, continuing to hold her tightly. "If you believe it's possible, are you willing to teach me *how* it's possible?"

Gillian smiled. "As long as you behave yourself."

"Oh, I'll behave myself," he said and kissed her again. "I have marvelous incentive to behave myself."

As much as Gillian wanted to stay here with him for the rest of the day, she knew it wasn't wise. They needed to get back for a number of reasons. "I do believe it's stopped raining," she said.

Without taking his eyes from her he said, "Has it? I hadn't noticed."

"We should go," she said and eased away from him.

"I suppose we must," he said, taking hold of her hand. He reluctantly led her to the wagon and helped her onto the seat before he sat beside her and took hold of the reins, guiding the horses back to the road. The rain hadn't stopped completely, but it had lessened to a mild drizzle. He took hold of her hand and held it tightly, keeping the reins in the other hand. "Are we supposed to pretend that nothing is going on between us?"

Gillian hadn't thought about it, but she had to admit, "It's probably best . . . for now." She offered her most prominent reason. "It might be confusing for the children. I believe we should give the matter some time."

Jamie didn't comment, which she took as neither an agreement nor a dispute. He remained silent, and she wondered what he was thinking about until she became caught up in her own thoughts. So much had happened today that she could have never foreseen. Pretending that nothing had changed would be much easier said than done. How could she even look at him across the supper table and not betray her feelings? If Hugh had seen it, others would eventually see it as well. And yet, they *did* need time. It hadn't been so many hours since she'd been crying because he'd been out drinking.

After many more minutes of silence, Jamie said, "Before we get back, I want to make something clear between us."

"Very well," Gillian said, turning to look at him.

He squeezed her hand at the same time he met her eyes. "I love you, Gillian." He chuckled and shook his head. "I don't know how this is possible, but I feel like I came halfway around the world just to find you. And I cannot deny what I feel. I know you can't make any promises at this point. I know we need some time, but . . . I'm asking you . . . begging you . . . to give me a fair chance to prove myself."

"I said that I would."

"I know, but . . . I want it to be clear between us exactly what that means. I don't know if I can ever become the man that you deserve, but I'm going to try. I'm new to your ways here in the valley, but I'm willing to learn. Just . . . be patient with me, and . . . if I make a mistake, don't just . . . cut me off. I'm asking you to help me prove myself."

Gillian smiled and nodded. His sincerity was evident, and it gave her the hope that they really could be together eventually. "Of course. I will do everything I can. I *do* want this to work out, you know."

"I'm glad to hear it," he said and smiled, then he lifted her hand to his lips and kissed it. "Now, I have a favor to ask of you."

"What is it?"

"Tonight . . . after study time and prayer . . . will you . . . let me spend some time with you? We can read or talk or make bread or tend the pigs. I don't care what we do. I just . . . don't want to be alone at that time of day when I'm in the habit of . . . going out."

"I would be happy to spend some time with you. Reading and talking are probably the most practical options. You can help me make bread another time, and . . . I think the pigs will be fine on their own once they become accustomed to their new home."

Jamie glanced over his shoulder. "Are you sure we shouldn't name them?"

"I think it's probably best," she said and laughed. She couldn't recall ever feeling quite this happy. She'd never had an *unhappy* life, in spite of the many trials she'd endured along with her family. But what she felt now was completely different. She prayed that it would all turn out the way that she hoped, and she prayed that Hugh would be all right. She couldn't think too much about him, or her happiness would surely be marred. She just asked the Lord to watch out for him, and then focused on the absolute pleasantness of the moment.

Gillian was almost disappointed to arrive at home, knowing her time with Jamie was over. But she reminded herself as he helped her down from the wagon that he was living under the same roof and eating meals at the same table. They would spend time together later this evening. Perhaps it would become a habit. She liked that idea very much.

The children were all excited to see the new pigs. Most of them jumped on the wagon as it went slowly down the drive and around the barn to where the large empty pigpen was located. With the wagon parked close to the pen, Harry helped Jamie lift the pigs down off the wagon. They set the little pen inside the fence, and Harry untied and lifted the door. Five little piglets ran out, and the children laughed to see them scurrying around to explore their new home. They were quickly provided with feed and water, and then everyone had to reluctantly leave them on their own so that chores could be completed and supper prepared.

Gillian was glad for some time to sit with her mother and tell her all that had happened. Wren's pleasure at hearing all that was transpiring between Gillian and Jamie added reassurance that Gillian was on the right path. It seemed her parents had been able to see something that she'd missed. It was evident they both loved and respected Hugh very much, but they both also knew that Gillian didn't love him the way a woman ought to love her husband. When Gillian expressed her concern for Hugh, Wren assured her that he would be fine, and she needed to trust that the Lord would work everything out the way it was meant to be.

Gillian thoroughly enjoyed supper with Jamie there. Having her mother at the table as well made the family feel complete. She found the thought interesting and wondered if it had significance. Hugh's absence was a relief, even though she wondered what he might be doing, and she hated the thought of him being alone. When supper was over, Jamie helped clean the dishes, and she couldn't help noticing how quickly he'd come to feel comfortable working in the kitchen, and how well he interacted with the children.

Gillian enjoyed study time more than she ever had. She always found pleasure in this time with her family, and reading from the scriptures was always uplifting for her. But that, combined with having Jamie in the room—minus the tension that had been between them before—made her feel almost giddy. Knowing she would be able to spend more time with him this evening, she couldn't suppress an occasional fluttering in her stomach. While she was listening to Jamie read from the book of Alma, she noted what a fine, rich voice he had.

He'd told her that he loved her. Given her changed perspective, she could only regard such a thing as a miracle. She wondered if she could say the same to him. As soon as she silently asked herself the question, she knew the answer. She also knew that such feelings were not enough to justify jumping into a lifetime commitment. She was practical and sensible and certainly not naive. She knew that marriage and raising a family were hard work, and that romantic attraction would gradually give way to the need for a more mature and lasting kind of love. But she had grown up seeing both in her parents. For all of the deep commitment and eternal love they shared for each other, they were obviously still very much in love. They wanted to be in the same room with each other, they were always concerned about each other more than anything or anyone else—and they didn't have to *try* to be that way. Gillian knew that was the way marriage should be.

Gillian believed that Hugh would be that kind of husband to her, but she wasn't certain she could be that kind of wife to him. In fact, she knew she couldn't. And perhaps it had been wrong of her to believe that something magical would have changed her feelings. She could see now that for all of her praying to know whether or not she should marry Hugh, she'd not taken the opportunity to fast about it, and she believed that she had allowed her logic and practicality to override her feelings. She hoped that she hadn't hurt Hugh too badly, and that he would forgive her. Of course he would; he was that kind of man. And again, she had to remind herself that she could not be responsible for his feelings or his happiness. She had to put the matter into the Lord's hands, knowing that His grace would ease Hugh's sorrow and make up for her mistakes. In that moment, she was glad for what was evolving between her and Jamie, and she prayed that he would prove himself with time and be the kind of man she needed in her life.

When Jamie finished his turn at reading, he glanced toward her and smiled. Her stomach fluttered again and she imagined what it might be like to see him embrace the gospel and find the peace and healing within its teachings that he so desperately needed. The possibility enhanced her fluttering until she could hardly breathe. She couldn't imagine such joy! Or perhaps she could. And she was going to keep imagining it—and praying for it—until it came to pass. She knew she couldn't force him to take such steps, but she could guide him and teach him and pray for him. And she would do so with all her heart.

Once the children had all gone their different ways to get ready for bed, Gillian made certain her mother had what she needed. She told her parents that she was going to spend some time with Jamie, and they would probably be in the study, or they might be out in the yard. They both seemed pleased. In fact, they seemed *very* pleased, and Gillian felt certain they would very much like to see her and Jamie end up together. She hoped for that too.

Gillian found Jamie in the parlor, his arms up on the back of the sofa, and his legs stretched out in front of him.

"Hello," she said when she entered the room.

"Hello," he said in return, a wide smile spreading across his face. "You're wearing a new hair ribbon."

"You noticed," she said, pleased that her efforts to change the ribbon after study time had been noticed. "What shall we do?"

"Why don't you just sit down next to me and we can talk." She did so, and he added, "I don't know about you, but I very much enjoyed all that talking we did earlier."

"Yes, I *did* enjoy that," she said, but her mind went to their kissing and she resisted adding that she had enjoyed that even more. As if he knew exactly what she was thinking, he tipped his head and pressed a gentle kiss to her lips. "I enjoyed *that,* too," she admitted, and he smiled again.

"Oh, yes," he said and kissed her again.

Gillian eased farther away on the sofa, just out of his reach. "I think it would be wise to talk."

"Very well," he said. "What shall we talk about?"

"I want to tell you about the very most important thing in my life."

He looked a little taken aback but said, "I would love to hear what that is."

"I don't want you to be put off by this, even though you might think it's strange. I want you to seriously consider what it means, and if you don't understand it, you can ask me anything you want."

"Very well," he said again. "I'm listening."

"The most important thing in my life, Jamie, is my knowledge that Jesus is the Christ, and that through Him I have peace in my heart in this life, and the hope of great eternal blessings in the life to come. Nothing is more important than that to me. In fact, it's such a beautiful part of my life that I want to share it with you. I want you to feel the same kind of peace. Such knowledge can heal every wound and compensate for every loss. It's like . . . if I had tasted the most delicious cake that you could ever imagine, and every time I had the opportunity to eat some of that cake, it gave me so much pleasure and joy that the only thing better than eating it myself would be sharing it with those that I love. I would naturally, then, want to share it with you. I would tell you to taste it and have more joy in sharing it together."

Jamie looked at her for a long moment while she let him consider what she'd said. She hoped that he would not feel put off or offended, and that he might be willing to consider learning what she could teach him. "That is a lovely analogy," he said. "I grew up going to church, and I was raised on the Bible—but it was a passive kind of thing. I admit that I cannot comprehend all that your people have sacrificed for the sake of religion. I respect your beliefs, Gillian. And I'm willing to learn and keep an open mind. But I can't make any promises about what I might be able to believe or not believe."

"I understand," she said. "But . . . if you *sincerely* keep an open mind and seek to know whether or not what I share with you is true, you might actually be surprised."

"Maybe I will be," he said. "At this moment, I must admit that there's one thing in particular you just said that intrigues me very much."

"What?" she asked eagerly.

"You said that you would want to share it with those you love. Does that mean what I'm hoping it means?"

Gillian looked down, and he added more softly, "I know what I see in your eyes, Gillian, and I know that you feel what I feel. I just want to know if you can admit to it."

Gillian took a deep breath and lifted her eyes to meet his. It occurred to her that their ability to speak so candidly—and respectfully—with each other was a good indication of his character. She had a great deal of evidence that he was a good man. He was kind and helpful and sincere and humble. For all that he had some difficulties to overcome, she wasn't dealing with a man who was prideful or obnoxious. The idea increased her hope and gave her confidence in being able to say, "I can admit that I've fallen in love with you." He smiled, and she took his hand. "Whether or not we have the kind of love that can see us through a lifetime remains to be seen."

"I think we do," he said with a lift of one eyebrow.

"What makes you think so?" she asked without getting too serious.

"Because what you make me feel far surpasses anything I have ever felt for any woman I've encountered—ever."

Gillian felt a little startled to consider the possibility of other women in his past. Knowing he didn't share the values and teachings that she'd been raised with, she had to accept the possibility that his behavior in that regard might be difficult for her to deal with. She understood the principles of repentance and forgiveness, and that people could not live something that they had never been taught. Nevertheless, the idea was disturbing. But she concluded that it would be more disturbing to have to wonder as opposed to just knowing. Still trying to keep her voice light, she asked, "And how many women have you *encountered*, exactly?"

"I have no idea," he said. She didn't like that answer at all.

"You have no idea?" she echoed, knowing her voice had betrayed her discomfort with the topic.

"Now, don't get all huffy," he said. "By encountered, I mean women I've spoken to or had any association with. I'm not necessarily meaning encountered *romantically.*"

"I'm glad to hear it. How many women *have* you encountered romantically?"

"I have never had any kind of serious relationship with a woman, because I've never *encountered* a woman that made me feel inclined to— until now. I must confess that I've kissed a few women along the way, but I'm not a promiscuous cad, if that's what you're wondering." Gillian didn't comment, and he said with some astonishment, "You *are* wondering."

"Should I not?" she said, trying not to sound as concerned as she felt. "How can a man with a drinking problem be certain *what* he's done when he can't remember?"

"I just *know,*" he said firmly. "I've never awakened with a hangover to find myself somewhere that I shouldn't have been. I can assure you, Gillian, that for all of my shortcomings, I have saved myself for marriage. It was something my grandmother taught me very firmly."

Gillian breathed that in with extreme relief. "I must confess that I'm very glad to hear it."

"Good," he said. "Now that we have *that* out of the way—"

"Don't you wonder the same about me?" she asked.

"No!" he said with an astonished chuckle. "Anyone can look at you and know that you're completely innocent of the ways of the world . . . or any participation in them." He leaned closer and lifted that eyebrow. "And I'm absolutely certain that I'm the first man who has ever kissed you."

"How can you be so certain?" she asked, and he chuckled again.

"I just *know,*" he said exactly as he'd said it a moment ago. He leaned closer and kissed her, as if it might prove his point.

Gillian enjoyed it so completely that she scooted farther away and said with a little laugh, "We're talking."

"So we are," he said.

They talked of many things for a couple of hours, then they both had to admit that they were tired enough to go to sleep. Jamie thanked her for distracting him from his usual habit, and Gillian thanked him for his efforts on her behalf. They parted in the hall with a meek and gentle kiss, then Gillian went up the stairs to her room, feeling as if she were floating on a cloud. She slept better than she had since Jamie had shown up in her life.

The following day being Sunday, the entire routine of the household was different. There were chores that had to be done in order to care for the animals and see that everyone got fed, but there was a different feeling in the house, and Gillian wondered if Jamie would notice it. He was ready to leave for church right on time, wearing a fine suit that he'd purchased earlier in the week. And he'd obviously shaved that morning, since his face was smooth and handsomely respectable. Seeing him dressed that way made her heart respond with more than the usual quickening, but she just smiled at him and looked forward to having him with her throughout the day.

Gillian thoroughly enjoyed having Jamie come along with the family to attend their church meeting. He maneuvered sitting right next to her, which she was pleased about—in spite of the mild awkwardness she felt when Hugh joined the family, as he always did. They exchanged a smile and their usual polite greetings before he sat down among her siblings in order to help keep them under control, which was typical. Gillian did her best to not think about Hugh and to focus on the meeting. But she was keenly aware of Jamie sitting next to her, as if he radiated some kind of warmth that she couldn't ignore. At one point when her hand was planted firmly on the bench at her side, she felt him touch her finger and looked down to see his pinkie finger wrapped around hers while he looked straight ahead as if to imply his complete innocence. Gillian felt thrilled over the gesture, as simple as it was. She concluded that she finally knew what it felt like to be in love—and to be loved—and she couldn't help being grateful for such an experience. She prayed that the end of this path would be a good one for everyone involved.

Sitting next to Jamie through the singing of the hymns proved to Gillian that he'd not made false claims about his singing voice. It was as if he couldn't help but sing loud and clear; he just opened his mouth and a beautiful sound came out without any effort whatsoever. She knew that people around them were discreetly turning to see who was responsible for such a magnificent voice. And she knew that Jamie was aware of their curiosity. But he just pretended not to notice and kept singing. She admired his confidence with it and thoroughly enjoyed sitting close enough to him to bask in the beauty of such a voice singing praises to God. She wondered if he felt the power of the lyrics he was singing, or if they were just words to him. She hoped that in time he would be able to understand the words coming out of his mouth that expressed the glory of the Restoration of the gospel.

Through the remainder of the day Gillian tried to imagine what the previous Sunday had been like—before she had accepted Hugh's proposal, and before Jamie had come into their lives. It felt as if the entire world had flipped upside down in the blink of an eye, and there were moments when she found it difficult to get her bearings.

Later in the day, Ward and Patricia and their children came over for dinner, as they did once a month. Ward had been a friend of the family since before Gillian was born, and he had in fact known her mother very well. He'd met Patricia in Nauvoo, and their families had actually lived under the same roof there. Since Ward was blind and Gillian's father had helped him a great deal to do the things that he couldn't do for himself, it had been a practical arrangement. Ian and Ward had been missionary companions when the Prophet had asked them to go to England. Gillian remembered those years from her very early childhood, and how Patricia had been like a second mother to her, living under the same roof and working with her own mother to see that everything was cared for. Ward and Patricia's oldest daughter, June, had been Gillian's closest friend through their childhood and youth, but June was now married and living about a hundred miles south in one of the many Mormon settlements that were being established in the territory. Ward and Patricia had three other children between the ages of six and sixteen, and both families were as close as two families could be.

Gillian had the pleasure of introducing Jamie to Ward and Patricia and their children while her parents were upstairs dealing with little Deborah having a fussy time. Along with the introductions, she told Jamie a brief version of their history, and they were all pleased to meet each other. Jamie's eyes lit up when Ward told him that he had been to Brierley with Ian and had come to know Jamie's grandmother rather well. While Patricia helped Gillian in the kitchen, Ward insisted that Jamie take him for a walk around the yard so they could chat. Gillian guided Ward's hand to Jamie's shoulder so that he could walk with Jamie's guidance. Jamie seemed momentarily awkward with being put in charge of a blind man, but by the time they got to the back door, he'd seemed to realize it wasn't so difficult. They both came in a while later to wash up for supper, laughing together as if they were the best of friends. Caring for them both as she did, Gillian couldn't help but be pleased.

That evening after their guests had gone home and the children had gone to bed, Gillian and Jamie ended up staying in her parents' bedroom and visiting with them until they were all exhausted. Gillian loved to hear Jamie and her parents talking about Brierley and the people they had all known in Scotland. They all had funny stories to tell about the colorful citizens of the town situated near Brierley where they had all grown up. Gillian wished that she could actually see what it was like there, but she was glad for the vivid descriptions she was hearing and the images they created in her mind.

She and Jamie left her parents' room together, and he gave her a good night kiss in the hall before he whispered, "I love you," in her ear and went down the stairs to go to bed. She felt as gratified by his affection as she was by the evidence that he was safely here beneath the roof and not out indulging in bad behavior.

* * * * *

Jamie had only been in his room for a minute when he heard a soft knock at the door. He opened it hoping to see Gillian, but he was not disappointed to see Ian.

"Sorry to bother you," he said, "but there's something I forgot to ask you."

"Ask away," Jamie said.

"I'll be gone tomorrow, and Harry will be going with me. I wonder if I could count on you to be aware of the children and help out should anything need a man's attention."

"I'd be happy to," Jamie said. "May I ask where you're going?"

"Of course you may ask. It's our designated day to help with the building of the temple."

"Excuse me? What?" Jamie asked.

Ian chuckled. "It's not a foreign language, Jamie. I know you were raised on the Bible, so you've surely heard the word before. We're building a temple, not unlike the temples referred to in the Bible. It will be a grand and beautiful structure where we can worship God more fully and perform ordinances that are necessary for our salvation."

"I see," Jamie said, puzzled over why people would go to so much trouble, but he had no desire to open up a religious conversation. In spite of his desire to please Gillian and his promise to keep an open mind, he felt hesitant to open the floodgates of what these people had sacrificed so much for. He didn't understand and wasn't sure he wanted to.

"Would that be the half-built domed building I've seen in town?" He'd wondered about it but hadn't wanted to exhibit too much curiosity for fear of being offered far too much information.

"No, that's the tabernacle. Its purpose is for meetings and other gatherings. The temple will serve a different purpose. It is currently the very large hole that's next to the half-built domed building."

"I see," Jamie said again, unable to help sounding a little skeptical. "And what exactly does this work entail that you and Harry will be doing?"

"We're harvesting granite from the quarry up the canyon and transporting it to the temple site where we're in the process of rebuilding the foundation."

"Rebuilding?"

"Apparently the foundation we've built isn't strong enough to support the temple, as grand as it will be. So it's being rebuilt." Ian smiled. "Anything of true value needs a good foundation, don't you think?"

"I suppose."

"The prophet has declared that this temple will stand through the Millennium; therefore, its foundation must be strong."

"Did you say the *prophet*?"

"Yes, Jamie." Ian chuckled. "It's also one of those words you can find in the Bible."

Jamie feared this might become the conversation he'd been avoiding. It wasn't that he hadn't heard temples and prophets discussed among the Mormons he'd traveled with. But it felt different to have his seemingly sensible uncle speaking so matter-of-factly of such things. While he didn't want to get into a laborious religious conversation, he couldn't help feeling some curiosity over Ian's motivation in believing such things. He was relieved when Ian offered some clarification.

"What we believe, Jamie, is that the original Church that was on the earth in ancient times became lost and there was a great apostasy. The gospel in its fullness has been restored to the earth. That fullness includes prophets, Apostles, priesthood power, and temples. It's not so terribly complicated."

Jamie expected him to go on, but Ian put his hand on Jamie's shoulder and said, "So, you'll keep an eye on my family for me tomorrow while I'm gone?"

"Of course," Jamie said.

"I appreciate it," Ian said and walked away. He wondered if Ian sensed that giving Jamie *less* information would make him more curious than put off. Whether Ian consciously knew what he was doing or not, it had worked. Jamie wanted to run after him and demand that he tell him more about prophets and temples. But he tabled his curiosity, wondering if it would be better to stick with his original plan to remain aloof from such things. Although, living in the Brierley home—which required study time, prayer, and church attendance—he would surely get all of his questions answered in time. Then he recalled the things that Gillian had said. Her convictions were deep, and she had asked him to at least be willing to listen and learn. He needed to honor her wishes if he had any hope of seeing this relationship evolve, but he would likely find it more enjoyable to get his questions answered if it was Gillian answering them. He smiled at the thought and got ready for bed.

Jamie awoke early, hearing some noises in the house that indicated someone was in the kitchen—even though it was still dark. He heard the back door open and close, and then there was silence. He realized that Ian and Harry had probably just left. Since he didn't go back to sleep, he made certain he was up and dressed when Alfred came down the stairs to go out and do the morning chores. Ian hadn't specifically asked Jamie to take over Harry's role in assisting Alfred, but it seemed the right thing to do. Together they milked the cows, gathered the eggs, and made certain all of the animals had feed and water— including the new little pigs.

"Maybe we should name them," Jamie said to Alfred while they were watching them voraciously eat their breakfast in the early-morning light.

"No, I don't think we should," Alfred said, giving the same argument that Gillian had given. Since Jamie had never been personally involved in the care of the animals that had been raised to feed his family, he'd never had cause to wonder about getting attached to them. He just thought they were rather adorable and felt inclined to give them names. When he told Alfred he thought the pigs were cute, Alfred looked at Jamie as if he were guilty of some kind of insanity and said, "They won't be very cute when they're full grown. Trust me on that." Jamie just shrugged and enjoyed the way Alfred chuckled as he walked away.

The day passed without any unusual incident. Jamie tried to make himself useful, and he believed that he contributed here and there to the work that needed to be done, but overall he felt mostly useless. For all of his efforts, he knew that the family could manage fine without him, and he wished there was a way for him to contribute more actively. He could afford to pay rent for staying in their home, but he knew they didn't need the money. Ian had likely inherited a great deal more than Jamie had, and he knew that was *a lot* of money. Offering Ian money would likely be an insult. Proving himself with active participation in contributing to the needs of the household seemed more appropriate, but he wasn't certain what to do exactly. He spent a considerable amount of time weeding in the garden, but it was starting to look mostly free of weeds, and he knew it wasn't going to fill very many of his hours at this rate.

After supper, Jamie helped clean the dishes, enjoying any work he could do and still be near Gillian. He asked her a question that had occurred to him many times. "Is Hugh not coming to the house because I'm here? I thought he might come for supper, especially since he didn't come by yesterday."

"He told my father that he was having Sunday dinner with another family that invites him over on occasion. Today he is with Harry and my father."

"Working on the temple?" Jamie asked.

"That's right," Gillian said, seeming pleased that he knew. But the conversation ended there.

Jamie helped Alfred with the evening chores, then study time ensued—even though Ian and Harry hadn't returned. Long after the children had gone to bed, Jamie and Gillian sat at the kitchen table, talking and eating way too much of a cake she had baked earlier. They were still sitting there when Ian and Harry came in, very dirty and clearly exhausted. But they were in good spirits, and Ian asked how the day had gone before he went to get cleaned up and get some sleep.

As days passed, Jamie felt more a part of the family. He did his best to work and earn his keep, but he still found that he had far too much time on his hands. Gillian's remedy for that was to have him read the Book of Mormon. He could hardly protest, and he devoted some time to it each day. But he intermixed it with reading from a novel he'd found among the family's books. He could only take reading so much scripture in one day. During their evening conversations, Gillian usually wanted to talk about what he'd been reading, and he tried to be agreeable. He couldn't deny that he was learning a deeper perspective on Christianity than he'd ever known before, but he wasn't certain how he could apply such things to his own life the way that Gillian had apparently applied them to hers. He just kept reading and indulging her in conversation about it, glad for every minute he was able to spend with her, and for the ongoing evidence that she loved him and that there was hope of spending the rest of his life with her.

Hugh came around occasionally and shared a meal with the family. He was very kind to Jamie, and there was no outward indication that he had any problem with Jamie being there, or with Jamie's involvement with Gillian, but Jamie could see the truth in Hugh's eyes, and he knew Gillian could see it too. Jamie was kind to him in return, and they even engaged in some trivial conversation occasionally. But Jamie could see that Gillian was less relaxed with Hugh around, and he suspected that Hugh could see it as well. He suspected that Hugh was determined not to let the situation change his habits with the family, for his sake as well as theirs. And Jamie respected him for it, especially when he knew it had to be difficult. More than once he'd considered how he might behave if he were in Hugh's position, and he couldn't imagine being quite so noble; he also wondered if he would be so kind and gracious. He would have been more likely to never show his face again. All in all, Jamie couldn't deny that Hugh was a fine man. But he believed firmly that Hugh was *not* the man for Gillian, and he was willing to do whatever it took to prove it.

Living in the Brierley household, Jamie couldn't help but regularly encounter their friends and neighbors. He had more opportunities to visit with Ward, and he truly liked the man and enjoyed his company. Many of the people who lived on the same street, and those who attended church together, were kind and warm toward Jamie. He couldn't deny that overall the Mormons were some of the best people he'd ever known—with few exceptions. He encountered the Millers on occasion and sought to just avoid the cantankerous Mr. Miller. He'd seen Mrs. Miller and Benny at church, but she'd seemed to want to avoid him, even though she did so politely. The neighbors on the other side of the Brierley property left Jamie quite aghast. He wasn't certain what to think of the younger Mr. Skimpole when he first met him, but after the man had come over a few times, clearly annoying everyone in the family while he seemed oblivious to his own social obnoxiousness, Jamie realized that Mr. Skimpole was quite taken with Gillian. When Jamie pointed it out to her, she eagerly told him of her disdain for the man.

"I can put a stop to this," Jamie said.

"How?" Gillian asked, sounding suspicious.

He refused to tell her, but a few days later when Mr. Skimpole wandered into the yard while Jamie and Gillian were in the garden, he pretended not to notice the man's approach before he drew Gillian fully into his arms and kissed her.

"What was that for?" she asked, pleasantly surprised.

Without taking his eyes from hers, he said, "I don't think Mr. Skimpole will be bothering you any further."

They both heard an astonished gasp and turned to see their pesky neighbor looking disgusted as he hurried back around the fence into his own yard. Gillian laughed and kissed Jamie again, then she insisted that they get back to work and not let the children see such behavior. Jamie agreed, but he felt sure her siblings were already well aware of the romantic feelings between him and Gillian.

Given the spare time that Jamie had to kill, he asked Ian if it would be all right for him to go along next time that he and Harry worked on the temple. "If you need me here," Jamie said, "then I'm happy to stay and do whatever needs to be done, but—"

"I would love to have you come along," Ian said, "if you think you're up to it."

"I'll never know if I don't try it," Jamie said, wondering what he was in for.

When the day came, Ian had Harry stay at home, and he took Jamie instead. Jamie didn't ask if there was a reason for that. He just rode at Ian's side through the still-dark streets until they came to the temple site at the center of town. Having heard Ian say something about harvesting granite from the canyon, he'd wondered if they'd be going there. But they spent the day mostly shoveling dirt and putting the heavy granite blocks into place. The work was overwhelming and exhausting, and Jamie wondered again why it would be so important to these people. Hearing them talk about the intended size and magnificence of the completed temple, he wondered how many decades it might be until it *was* completed. But the workers were all cheerful and pleasant, as if such grueling labor in this wretched heat was some kind of honor and privilege. Jamie just looked at it as a willingness to make a fair contribution to the family who had opened their home to him. If this was important to them, then he was willing to do it. Hugh was there as well, and Jamie could see that he was a hard worker, and his enthusiasm for the project rivaled that of any man there.

The following week Jamie went again with Ian, and Harry came along as well. Alfred had insisted that he could manage all the manly chores on his own; he considered it his own contribution to the building of the temple. Jamie didn't mind the hard work. In fact, it felt good to him to be doing something worthwhile—even if he didn't fully understand what that was. Gillian seemed pleased, and so did her parents. Given that they were good people that he'd grown to respect and love dearly, he was fine with that.

Jamie was surprised to realize after a few weeks that he'd actually come to enjoy study time—not only for being with the family, but for what he was learning. He became more engaged in his own personal reading of the Book of Mormon, and he began to look forward to church meetings, wondering what he might learn. He couldn't quite figure *why* he felt that way, when he could see no logical reason for it. He didn't feel consciously interested, but he was drawn to it with a strange kind of pull that he didn't understand. He could only compare it to the feelings that drew him to Gillian. It was like some kind of deep-rooted instinct inside of him that was bigger than himself and completely out of his control. If that was what Gillian referred to as the Light of Christ or the guidance of the Holy Spirit, then he couldn't deny that it was real. He just wasn't certain what to do with it. He didn't admit his feelings to Gillian— not yet, at least. He wanted to better understand them himself before he started trying to talk about them. While he was wondering how to better understand what was happening, Gillian asked him if he'd ever prayed about the things he was learning. He admitted that he'd never prayed at all—not formally, anyway. She suggested that he do so, and gave him an impressive tutorial on proper prayer. He felt decidedly nervous the first time he was alone in his room and knelt down to address his Maker. But once he got started, it went more smoothly than he'd expected. He didn't feel any immediate change or enlightenment, but he hadn't expected to. He figured that God would require a great deal more effort than that before He would be forthcoming with any answers.

Chapter Eleven
The Misunderstanding

More time passed while the summer heat became even more unbearable. Jamie *always* felt sticky with sweat, except when he was drenched with it while working outdoors in the middle of the day. But he knew that everyone around him was the same, and it just seemed a way of life here. He was surprised to learn that the winters here in the valley were very cold and produced a great deal of snow.

"You'll be wishing for some of this heat come January," Ian had said to him lightly while they'd been working at the temple site.

Occasionally in his comings and goings, Jamie encountered the neighbors. He was amused by the way the younger Mr. Skimpole seemed to be miffed at him. Now and then he saw Mr. Miller, who tried to joke with him about things that Jamie didn't think were funny. He always asked why he hadn't seen Jamie at their favored drinking establishment. Jamie just told him that he'd given up that kind of thing, and Mr. Miller accused him of being softened by those cursed Mormons, as if that were a bad thing.

Since Jamie had seen Mrs. Miller and Benny at church meetings, he knew that the marriage had many reasons for division in it. He learned to call her *Sister* Miller, as all people who involved themselves with the Church went by *brother* or *sister*. He wasn't sure how he felt about being called *Brother* MacBrier, but since he was attending church and participating in many of the family's religious practices—including his efforts to help build the temple—he could hardly protest.

Now and then Benny wandered into the Brierley yard, and it would be a few minutes before Mrs. Miller would find him. Jamie became rather fond of Benny and found his behavior to be similar to that of little Gavin, while he was more the size of Harry—and very strong, as Jamie learned when they'd engaged in a childish wrestling match on the lawn. Sister Miller softened somewhat toward Jamie when she saw his kindness to Benny. The fact that her husband had grumbled to her about how Jamie was no longer one of his drinking buddies added to his favor in her eyes.

One of the greatest benefits of time passing was the evidence that Wren was getting stronger. When she was able to actually walk down the stairs on her own, it was a great moment for the entire family. She began spending her days on the main floor of the house, even though that meant resting on the sofa in the parlor or just sitting at the table, where she was able to do some tasks to help with meal preparation. Jamie enjoyed seeing a more accurate picture of the relationship that Gillian shared with her mother. He found it ironic that Gillian's real mother was actually Wren's sister. But no one would ever guess that they weren't related by blood. While their coloring was different, their features had a strong resemblance. And the relationship they shared was as close as any mother and daughter could be.

Jamie became more and more attached to all of Gillian's siblings. He even earned some favor with little Gavin, and he became brave enough to hold the baby. He couldn't imagine ever leaving this place, and prayed that Gillian would be convinced of his worthiness to have her heart.

As summer began to ease toward autumn, the opportunity for work increased in the harvesting and preserving of the food that had been grown. Jamie had helped on multiple occasions to guide the irrigation water into the yard and the garden at the designated times for the Brierley water turn, but he fully appreciated its value when the fruits and vegetables that were being grown reached their fruition. He began to realize how hard the people in the valley had worked to be able to sustain themselves, with very few provisions coming in from other places. If they didn't grow and preserve their own food, they would have nothing to eat. It was as simple as that.

On a pleasant September evening, following a hot day when they had been busy transporting vegetables into the root cellars, Gillian and Jamie walked into the yard after the children had gone to bed. The fact that it was already dark evidenced the shortening of the amount of time the sun was spending in the sky, which meant that winter was inevitably approaching at a slow and steady pace. But for now, the evening air was the perfect temperature, and the moonlight was lovely. Or rather, Jamie thought, Gillian looked lovely in the moonlight's effect. They sat down in the center of the lawn, then Gillian laid back on the grass to look up at the sky. Jamie sighed and enjoyed admiring her from a comfortable distance. He also knew that her parents had a perfect view of the back lawn from their bedroom window. Not that it would have made any difference. He knew well enough the strictness of Gillian's boundaries, and he would never be tempted to cross them, mostly because he would never want to offend her.

Gillian loved the feel of the cool grass beneath her in contrast to the arduous heat of the day. She looked up toward the stars and wondered how different heaven might be from the beauty of the world they lived in. She imagined it to be very much the same, except that heaven would be perfectly peaceful and free of sorrow and pain. She looked at Jamie sitting close by and found it easy to include him in such thoughts.

"What are you thinking about?" Jamie asked.

"Heaven," she said.

"Do you see me there?"

"No, I see you right here . . . on earth . . . with me. However, if you and I go about getting married the right way—should we decide to get married—we can be together forever."

"The right way?"

"Surely you've heard eternal families being discussed at church."

"Maybe. I've heard a lot that doesn't quite fit together or make sense."

"You should ask me to explain if you hear something that doesn't make sense."

"I wouldn't know where to begin. But what do you mean by . . . getting married the right way?"

"You found a place to begin," she said and smiled. "Because the fullness of the gospel has been restored, along with all of the proper priesthood keys, it is possible for a man and woman to be sealed for eternity, which means that marriage will not end at death if they both live worthy of those blessings."

Jamie liked the sound of that very much, but he knew there was a catch. "And what is required to get married in such a way?"

"We must both be worthy members of the Church so that we can be married in the Endowment House."

"What is that?"

"It is the place where we can make eternal covenants with God, and be married for eternity. Once the temple is finished, such work will be done there."

"The Endowment House could be in use for a long time," he said lightly, and she chuckled.

"Have you been praying?" she asked.

"I have," he said.

"And?"

"And what? I'm assuming that eventually I'm supposed to feel something that will let me know all of this is true—as you have pointed out on numerous occasions. But so far, I'm just . . . praying."

"That's good, though."

"I hope so."

"You're happy here," she stated as a fact.

"I'm very happy here," he said. "But I'd be happier if you were my wife."

"Perhaps . . . all in good time."

"And what if I don't get these answers from God that you think I'll get?"

"I don't know. If God wants me to marry you, I'm sure He'll let me know."

"I'm counting on it," he said. "As long as God is talking to one of us, then I guess we'll be all right."

"I guess," she said with another chuckle. More seriously she asked, "Do you still have the desire to drink?"

"Yes," he admitted truthfully. "Every day."

"What is it that makes you want to drink?" she asked. He looked startled and she said, "You don't have to get offended; just answer the question."

"I'm not offended. I just thought you already knew."

"Should I?"

"My first day here . . . I told you how I discovered the truth about my parents."

"Yes," she said, not making the connection.

"Well, that's when I started drinking. Or I should say . . . that's when my drinking became a problem. I can't say there's any logic to that. I only know that I felt like a completely different person when I learned the truth, and I didn't know how to *be* that person. So I started trying to just block it out, and the easiest way to do that was to dull my senses."

"But if you recognize there's no logic to your drinking, why keep drinking?"

"I guess you could say I developed a craving for it. Sometimes I just want it so badly that it's all I can think about, and . . . as much as I might want to resist that temptation, I usually haven't been able to think of any good reason *not* to drink."

"Do you have a good reason now?"

"You know the answer to that. I've not had a drink in weeks."

"But . . . if something changed between us . . . would you go back to your old habits?"

"If you're trying to ask me if you are the only reason I stopped drinking, the answer is yes. I'm trying to be a better man, because beyond any logic, you seem to *want* me to be a better man. Spending time with you makes it easier to ignore the craving. Knowing I would disappoint you doesn't hurt."

"But if you're only doing it for me, what happens if I disappoint you or make you angry?"

"I can't answer that."

"Yes, you can. You just don't want to. You would probably go out and get drunk, and I can't be responsible for that."

"I would never *expect* you to be responsible for that," he insisted. "You have to do what you feel is best for you, but I can't help hoping you'll choose to make me a permanent part of your life."

"And if I did, would you be willing to never drink again? Never! Not a drop!"

"You just said I shouldn't do it for you."

"And you shouldn't. I'm just wondering."

"I would like to think I could do that, but sometimes I think I'm just a damaged soul, and such damage has a way of haunting a person."

"If you mean that learning you're illegitimate has damaged you, surely you must realize that such wounds can be healed. You can't use it as an excuse to behave badly or indulge in a temptation or vice. You have a wonderful example in your grandfather, of course. *He* never allowed his situation to make him indulge in bad behavior."

Jamie's confusion was as evident as his astonishment. "I have no idea what you're talking about. My grandfather? Apparently you know something I don't know. If we're talking about your father's father, I don't even remember the man."

"Anya's husband, Gavin."

"Yes," Jamie said. "I know *who* he is, but I don't know what you're talking about."

Gillian let out a chuckle of disbelief. "I can't believe that no one would have told you . . . given the commonality of the situation."

"*What* commonality?" he demanded, becoming impatient.

"That he was born illegitimate, of course."

Jamie couldn't even make a sound. He felt sure she had her stories mixed up, or that there was some kind of mistake. Gavin MacBrier had died when Jamie was a baby, but Jamie had grown up hearing of his exemplary character and amazing accomplishments. He was a legend in the realms of Brierley. But one fact stood out strongly, and he finally found his voice enough to convince her that she was wrong. "He was the Earl of Brierley. Such a position would never be given to an heir that was not legitimate."

Gillian laughed softly. "I cannot believe you haven't heard this story. He *was* actually the legitimate heir. He had the MacBrier birthmark, which confused him because he had evidence that the earl had never been unfaithful. He was raised by a servant woman, *believing* he was illegitimate. It turned out that as a baby he'd been switched with the child of this servant."

Jamie felt utterly dumbfounded for more reasons than he could count. When Gillian just stared at him expectantly, he said the first thing that came to his mind, "You're making this up."

"I'm *not*. You can ask my father."

"I can't believe my grandmother never told me this."

"Perhaps, since she knew you were illegitimate, she feared it would hit too close to the truth that she was trying to avoid. Perhaps she was saving it for the time when she planned to tell you the truth."

"And then she died," he said with dismay. He was thoughtful for a few minutes and was glad that Gillian allowed him the silence to think. He turned to find her staring at him, as if she could know what he was thinking simply by doing so. "Does your father have the MacBrier birthmark?" he asked. "It *is* hereditary, you know."

"No. He said that both of his brothers had it, but he doesn't." She gasped. "Your father?"

"Apparently. He *is* one of your father's brothers."

"You?" Gillian asked, and her eyes widened when he unfastened two buttons of his shirt to reveal the front of his shoulder. "That's incredible," she said, her eyes widening farther.

"All through my childhood," he said, refastening the buttons, "my family talked about the birthmark and how I'd inherited it from my father. I knew my grandfather and my uncle had it as well. What they *didn't* tell me was that it had let the family know beyond any doubt that I was actually my father's son, since I was the result of an affair."

"But the family resemblance is undeniable."

"There's that too, but the birthmark was the clincher. I always felt proud of the mark, but now I'm not sure I do."

"Why wouldn't you? It's rather amazing, don't you think? That such a thing could be hereditary? For all that your father made some poor choices, I've heard he was a very good man. And again I must say that the choices of your parents are no reflection on you—no matter what the stuffy people of the Highlands might think. And I would also like to point out once again that if your grandfather grew up believing he was illegitimate and was such a fine man in spite of it, surely you can see the same in yourself."

"The same?"

"You *are* a fine man, Jamie. You just don't believe that you are."

"I suppose I do have my doubts on that account." He looked at her intently. "More than anything, Gillian, I pray every day that I can be a fine enough man to be worthy of you."

"That's very sweet," she said and took his hand.

Jamie put her hand to his lips, hoping he wasn't engaged in some kind of massive delusion in believing that such a thing could be possible, when all was said and done.

* * * * *

For days Jamie pondered what Gillian had told him about his grandfather. He went to Ian and asked to hear the story straight from him. He verified that it was true and added some fascinating details that Gillian had omitted. Jamie said to his uncle, "It would seem that if Gavin MacBrier could live with something like *that* in his life, I ought to be able to live with my parents' poor choices."

"I would think so," Ian said and put a fatherly hand on Jamie's shoulder. "You're a fine young man, Jamie. I'm proud to call you mine, and I hope that you will always want to stay here and be a part of the family."

"I would like that more than anything," Jamie said, then took the opportunity to say what he felt certain Ian already knew. "It's my deepest hope that Gillian will want to make me a part of the family . . . officially."

"I hope for that too," Ian said and smiled. "I'm sure it's only a matter of time."

Ian didn't bring up that it was also a matter of Jamie coming to share their religious beliefs. He wondered if it simply went without saying that this would be a requirement. Did he believe it was only a matter of time until Jamie came around? Or only a matter of time before Gillian decided she could live with their differences? Either way, Jamie kept reading and praying, longing for something to happen that could help him understand why this was all so important to the Brierley family.

Thinking more about what he'd learned from the examples of his grandfather and his uncle, Jamie decided that he didn't have to give in to this ridiculous desire to block out his difficult thoughts with liquor. It *wasn't* his fault that his parents had made poor choices, or that his existence had been what some people believed a mistake. And it wasn't his fault that his grandmother—for all her good intentions— had kept the truth from him and left him vulnerable to the ridicule and disdain of the community. He had to take accountability for his choice to manage the situation by getting drunk on a regular basis, but he could also choose to never do it again. He truly believed that he'd reached a point where he could embrace abstinence from liquor as a new way of life—whether or not Gillian chose to make him a part of her life. He felt so good about the decision that he wondered if that was an answer to his prayers. Perhaps at least it was a beginning of the answer. He looked forward to sharing his thoughts and feelings with Gillian, and he anticipated more than usual their habitual time together later in the evening.

Jamie went to his room to change his shirt before supper, aware of the noise of the family gathering in the kitchen to put the meal on the table. He heard a soft knock at the front door and realized he was the only who *had* heard it. He answered it, surprised to see a very upset Sister Miller.

"Oh, thank heaven it's you, Brother MacBrier," she said. "I do need your help, and I don't want to bother Brother Brierley or anyone else."

"What is it?" he asked, certain it had something to do with Benny. He was usually at her side, but right now he wasn't.

"That wretched husband of mine has run off and taken Benny with him, and they've not come back and I'm sick with worry, and I wonder if you could help me, but . . . I'd rather that no one else know. He's already the cause of so much grief among the neighbors and—"

"I'm glad to help," Jamie said. "Wait here just a moment." She nodded, and he stepped back inside, closing the door in order to protect her privacy, if that was the way she wanted it.

He saw Mont approaching in the hall, who said to Jamie, "Was there a knock at the door?"

"Yes, I've got it. Will you tell Gillian and your parents that I've gone to help find Mr. Miller. I'm not certain when I'll be back."

"I'll tell them," Mont said and turned back toward the kitchen.

Jamie stepped back outside, and Sister Miller walked at his side around the side of the house where they would not draw any attention from the family, according to her request. As they went to the barn so that Jamie could saddle his horse, she explained to him, "My Leland lost his job at the mill, you see. And he's been ever so upset. He's been drinking almost nonstop, which leaves me to wonder how we're going to make ends meet on top of having to keep him from banging Benny about."

"I'm sorry to hear that, Sister Miller," he said, trying to be compassionate and wondering—as he did each time he talked to her—if he would prefer to not have quite so much information. He wasn't certain what he'd done to become her confidant, but he simply listened, wanting to be helpful.

"He got ever so upset with Benny this afternoon. I try to keep the boy out of his way, but sometimes I just can't do it with everything else I've got to be doing."

"I understand," Jamie said, wondering if he should offer to look out for Benny now and then so that Sister Miller would not have that burden on her shoulders every minute of the day.

"He started bullying the boy," Sister Miller said, and Jamie wanted to give Leland Miller a black eye. Or worse. He felt sure that his family wouldn't be impressed with his less-than-Christian attitude, but that's how he felt. "Then he started saying that he was going to teach him to behave like a man." Sister Miller made a disgusted noise that expressed Jamie's feelings perfectly. They entered the barn where he set to work saddling his horse while she finished her explanation. "Can you imagine such a thing? For all that his body is grown up, anyone who knows Benny knows that he could never understand such a thing. His own father more than anyone ought to understand that."

"I would think so," Jamie said, trying not to betray his growing anger.

"And that's when Leland told me he was taking Benny out with him. Benny didn't want to go, but Leland hit him hard when he protested, and Benny went along, scared not to. And I didn't dare argue, certain he'd do worse harm to Benny—or to me. I've been praying and wearing out the floor with my pacing, certain they wouldn't be gone long because Leland can't hardly stand to be in charge of the boy for more than a minute. But it's been hours, and I just don't know what to think."

"Where do you think they might have gone?" Jamie asked, stepping into the saddle.

"I hate to think it, but I wonder if he took Benny to that awful place where he goes to drink and—"

"You want me to go and see."

"Would you? It's not proper for a respectable woman to go in there, and . . ."

"I understand," he said. "I'll check back with you as soon as I can get there and back."

"Oh, thank you, Brother MacBrier."

"I'm glad to help," he said, wondering how he was going to explain this to Gillian. With all the smoking and drinking that went on in that place, he knew he couldn't even walk in there without coming away stinking with evidence of where he'd been. Perhaps Sister Miller would explain on his behalf. He wondered as he rode out if he should ignore Sister Miller's request to keep this a private matter and ask for Ian's help, but he figured he would get to that step if he gave the matter some fair effort and still couldn't find Benny and his odious father.

Jamie felt a little sick to his stomach when he walked into the place where he'd once felt so comfortable. He was surprised at how he had no desire to order a drink. Rather, he felt a desire to just get out of there as quickly as possible. He wondered if that was any indication of some change taking place within himself. Perhaps his prayers were being heard after all.

A quick perusal of the place made it clear that Leland and his son were not there. He asked the bartender and a few of the regulars ,who adamantly declared they hadn't seen Leland Miller. They were well acquainted with his atrocious behavior, and they would have noticed if he'd been there in the last few hours. He was glad to get out of there and know that Leland hadn't brought Benny to such a place, but he was dismayed wondering where they might have gone. He felt worried for Benny, and knew that Sister Miller would be too when he gave her his report. He hurried back to her house and tethered his horse to her front fence where he knew it wouldn't be sighted by anyone in the Brierley household, given the obstruction of the view by the fence between the two yards.

Sister Miller rushed out the front door to meet him. "They weren't there," he reported. "They haven't been there."

"Oh, no!" she said and put both hands to her face.

"Where else could they have gone?" Jamie asked.

Sister Miller thought for a moment and said, "Sometimes Leland takes him for a walk in the woods, but . . ." She became emotional and put her hand over her mouth.

"But what?" Jamie asked, taking a step closer.

"He used to take him out there to give him a . . . beating . . . when he misbehaved." Jamie felt sick to his stomach. "But that's not happened for years. Not since Benny got too big for him to control."

"Perhaps we should ask for my uncle's help in searching for them, and—"

"Oh, no!" she said emphatically. "No, no, no! I'd so prefer this remain a private matter."

Jamie hesitated, then nodded, knowing that to keep Sister Miller's confidence, he would probably have to allow the family to believe that he'd been where he wasn't supposed to be, doing what he shouldn't have been doing. He concluded that he could confide in Gillian and trust her to keep his confidence. And he would contend with that later. Right now, Benny needed to be found. He could care less whether Leland Miller was *ever* found.

"Can you tell me where to look?" he asked.

Sister Miller walked with him around the house and into a wooded area. The two of them searched and called until it started to get dark, then they went back to the house to get some lanterns. Jamie insisted that Sister Miller stay at the house in case they came back, while he would continue to search for Benny. He was determined that if he couldn't find the boy in another hour, he would call out a massive search party—whether Sister Miller wanted him to or not. He felt sure that his uncle would know how to go about that.

Jamie set out again into the woods, walking farther than he had before, already knowing which areas he had searched. When he'd wandered a long while, calling Benny's name over and over, he began to feel an ominous dread. He started to pray in a way he never had before. He needed help, and he needed it now. He felt sure that Sister Miller was praying too, and if he could be the person to help answer those prayers, he was glad to do it. He just needed some help. He had no idea if he was even on the right course. What if Leland hadn't even taken Benny into the woods? What if there was some other option that a drunk man might have thought of that no one in his right mind would have considered?

Jamie stopped when he heard a strange sound. He held very still, listening intently, silently uttering another prayer. He distinctly heard whimpering and moved toward the sound, holding the lantern high. A minute later he found Benny, kneeling on the ground, rocking back and forth and whimpering with a helpless fear that tore at Jamie's heart. He looked around but couldn't see Leland, and he wondered if the man had actually abandoned his son out here in the woods in the dark. The thought made Jamie's blood boil. Or maybe the man had passed out somewhere and Benny was just lost. Highly likely. It still made Jamie's blood boil. He approached Benny to offer some help and comfort, but apparently he approached too quickly and startled him. Benny jumped to his feet and threw a punch that hit Jamie square in the jaw and landed him flat on his back. The only thing he could think of as he hit the ground was how he not only had to explain the way he smelled, but now he had to explain why he would inevitably have a bruise on his face. And he had to do it all in a way that would not make Sister Miller feel that her privacy had been violated. This was definitely not turning out to be the evening he'd anticipated.

* * * * *

As soon as everyone was seated at the table for supper, it became startlingly evident that Jamie was missing.

"Where's Jamie?" Gillian asked.

"Oh," Mont said as if he'd just remembered something, "he said to tell you that he went somewhere."

"Where?" Ian asked.

"I think he said he was going somewhere with Mr. Miller," Mont said.

Gillian's heart dropped like a rock to the chair where she was sitting. She shot a panicked look at her father, who said, "I'm certain there's some logical explanation."

"I'm certain there is," Gillian said, but she could only think of how heartbroken she'd felt that first night he'd chosen to go out and get drunk, instead of being here so that she could clarify what she'd been feeling. What could have enticed him to do this now after all the progress he had made? It just didn't make sense. But it *did* break her heart. She hurried from the table and up the stairs before anyone had a chance to see the tears that were threatening to burst out of her. Alone in her room, she cried for several minutes, glad that she was left undisturbed to do so. Once she'd vented her sadness and disappointment, anger quickly came in to replace those feelings. How could he do this? How *could* he? Had she been a fool all along to believe that he could become the man she wanted him to be? Had it been nothing but a ridiculous notion to believe that he would change for her? Apparently so. And she didn't know whether to be more angry with him for doing such a stupid thing, or with herself for being so gullible. In her mind she imagined slapping Jamie good and hard when she saw him again, and then she imagined going humbly to Hugh and telling him that she'd had all the time she needed. She was ready to accept his proposal of marriage.

* * * * *

Jamie wasn't sure how he managed to calm Benny down and convince him that he was not being threatened. Perhaps that too was an answer to prayers. Benny soon recognized Jamie as someone he'd felt safe with, but then he began to cry in his childish way, and there was no reasoning with him, and there was certainly no hope of getting information out of him. Jamie urged him to let him take him home, and he was able to guide him through the woods back to the house. By the time they got there, Benny had finally stopped his crying, but when Jamie asked him if he knew where his father had gone, he began to get upset again, so Jamie let the matter drop.

Sister Miller was so relieved and happy to see Benny that she wept openly and thanked Jamie profusely while Benny clung to his mother and whimpered.

"I'm glad I could help," Jamie said. "He's pretty upset. I'm not sure what happened, but I'm sure you'll be able to calm him down."

"And you didn't see Leland?"

"Not a sign of him, but I'll go back and look again, if you like."

"No, I don't want you to trouble yourself any further, Brother MacBrier. You've been so kind. I'm certain he's just passed out drunk somewhere. He'll sleep it off and come crawling back here some time tomorrow. The weather is fair tonight. I'm sure he'll be fine."

"I'm sure he will be," Jamie said, and Sister Miller closed the door.

Jamie wondered for a moment if he should go looking for Leland in spite of what she'd said, but he didn't feel inclined to do that. He even followed Gillian's advice to pray over anything at any time. He asked God if he should go and look for Leland, even though he didn't want to. He still didn't feel inclined to, so he got his horse and walked it around the fence and into the barn, knowing the family would have long since gone to bed. He wondered if Gillian had waited up for him, and he wondered how to go about telling her what had happened. He determined that with the relationship they shared, he had to be completely honest with her. He knew she would keep Sister Miller's confidence in the matter; he knew she would understand. He looked forward to kissing her good night and getting some sleep. It had been a long day.

* * * * *

As soon as the house had become quiet, with the children all in bed, Gillian began pacing the kitchen, waiting for Jamie to come back, wondering when he would. She still could not believe he would do this. Not now. Not after all the progress they'd made.

When he finally came through the door, she could see from the glow of the lamp burning on the table that he was severely disheveled, and even worse, there was a definite bruise on his jaw. And even from where she stood, she could smell the distinct aroma of that place. She had worked herself into such a frenzy that it took great self-discipline not to hurl herself at him like a rabid cat. She struggled to swallow her anger while she took a deep breath and faced him squarely. When his eyes met hers, they seemed to reach past whatever amount of liquor might be distorting his thinking. In fact, they looked surprisingly lucid. She immediately saw his recognition that she was upset with him. But she wondered if he felt any regret over what he'd done, or whether he simply regretted her finding out about it. Their eyes exchanged a silent battle of wills while Gillian thought of all the awful things she wanted to say, then dismissed each one of them as inappropriate, even with as justified as she felt in her anger. She was both disappointed and relieved when Jamie spoke first. "Please let me explain, before you—"

"Did you think we wouldn't notice that you were gone?" she interrupted, not wanting to hear his excuses. "Did you think we wouldn't figure out where you were?"

"I certainly expected you to notice I was gone, which is why I told Mont to tell you that I was leaving."

"With Mr. Miller?"

"I told him I was going to *find* Mr. Miller. There's a difference."

"Is there?" she asked, and Jamie couldn't believe what he was hearing. She had assumed the very worst, and didn't seem intent on hearing what he might have to say.

"You have no idea what you're talking about," Jamie said and moved past her as if he might be able to dismiss the conversation before it got started.

"Oh, yes I do!" she said, then quickly added, "Don't you dare walk out on me. You owe me an explanation, Jamie MacBrier."

Jamie turned on his heel and faced her with such immediate fury that she took a step back, actually feeling momentarily afraid. "I don't owe you *anything*! What makes you think you have a right to speak to me that way? You don't know nearly as much as you think you do, *Miss Brierley*. Before you start staring me down and trying to put me in my place, you should try to get your facts straight."

"Oh," she said with the same sarcasm he'd used when speaking her name, "facts like the amount of liquor you're capable of consuming in an average evening? Facts like your ability to get yourself in the middle of a fight while you claim absolute innocence? Are those the facts you're talking about?"

"I am many things," Jamie thundered, "but I am *not* a hypocrite. I don't have a problem admitting to my weaknesses, my dear, sweet cousin." His sarcasm intensified. "I'm well aware of the kind of man I am. But that doesn't mean that what happened this evening is what you *think* happened this evening. Things are not always what they appear to be."

"You're just trying to avoid the truth because you don't want to admit that you made a mistake."

"You know what?" he said, so angry that it took great effort not to shout at her. "It's obvious that you're already convinced of what happened tonight. If you're so quick to condemn me without even bothering to ask me, then I have nothing to say. What point is there in defending myself when you've already judged me as guilty? After all this time, you still can't see me for who I really am. Ironic, isn't it. You're the one who has been trying to convince me that I'm actually a good person, and yet you're the one who believes that—for no apparent reason—I would run out on an impulse and go back on everything I've promised you. So be it. Consider me guilty as charged. I have nothing to say to you."

He moved past her to go to his room, leaving Gillian even more confused. The words he'd just thrown at her swirled around in her head until they threatened to explode. She could do nothing but go to her room and futilely try to sleep, knowing that all of her hopes and dreams that were tied into Jamie MacBrier had just been shattered.

Chapter Twelve
The Judgment

Jamie felt so utterly furious that he paced his room for more than an hour. He finally slumped onto the edge of his bed, deeply exhausted. The fury then melted into the heartbreak beneath it, and he hung his head and cried like he hadn't since long before he'd put his past behind him and had come to America. It wasn't that he didn't believe the misunderstanding couldn't be cleared up. But Gillian's lack of faith in him had cut him to the core. He felt sick to his stomach and completely abashed. He allowed his head to fall to his pillow and lifted his booted feet off the floor, curling up on his bed like a frightened child. He wondered what tomorrow would bring. If Gillian didn't believe in him, then it was destined to be a horrible day. He wondered if he should just leave here, but he knew that wagon companies would not be heading east this late in the season. He wondered if he ever should have come here, and felt so desperate that all he could think to do was pray. But he had intelligence enough to know that even God couldn't force Gillian to see past her bitter judgments. Even God couldn't solve this problem if Gillian was too stubborn to be willing to look at the truth. He loved her so much that he couldn't help but feel that he hated her for doing this to him.

Jamie's next awareness was of being dragged out of bed abruptly and harshly. In the long moment it took him to orient himself to the situation, he realized that two officers of the law were in his bedroom, treating him none too kindly. He was glad that he'd fallen asleep in his clothes—and his boots—which helped him maintain some kind of dignity. He looked in question at these two men, then he saw Ian in the room and silently pleaded for an explanation. With all the possibilities of how he'd considered today might go, this was not one of them.

"I'm sorry, Jamie," Ian said. "They were very insistent."

"I don't understand," Jamie said when he realized his wrists were being put into handcuffs behind his back. His wish that he'd never come here deepened immensely.

"You're under arrest," said one of the men who was holding his arm.

"For *what?*" Jamie demanded, glad that he'd not been drinking, which would have made it necessary to endure this with a hangover.

"For the murder of Leland Miller," the other officer said.

"What?" Jamie retorted, understandably astonished. "I have no idea what you're talking about." Ian's expression made it clear that he too had had no idea that Leland was even dead. *Dead?* Was that why Jamie had been unable to find him?

"We've already established that you were gone last night," one of the officers said, "and that you were looking for Mr. Miller. We also know that the two of you have had reason to disagree in the past. Given that bruise on your face, I would assume you got into it again last night, and it didn't turn out so well."

"I did *not* see Leland Miller last night," Jamie said, then he realized that Gillian was standing just outside the door to his room, looking horrified—and condemning. She believed he was guilty. Murder? He wanted to shout at her. She really believed he would be guilty of murder? He felt certain he would have a chance to explain himself, but he wasn't going to do it now. Not with her standing there assuming that his guilt had already been decided. As he was escorted from the room, he said to his uncle, "I think you should have a talk with Mrs. Miller."

"I will," Ian said, then quickly added, "We'll work this out, Jamie. You mustn't worry. I know you're innocent."

Too bad your daughter doesn't think so, Jamie thought while he tried to be assuaged by the fact that at least *someone* believed in him. He glared at Gillian as he was forced to walk past her. She looked away, and he wondered if she felt any guilt over her tendency to be so atrociously judgmental. He might not have a clear understanding of all of the elements of her religion, but he was familiar enough with the Bible to know that Jesus didn't condone being judgmental. He wanted to tell her that, but he didn't want her to accept him because he talked her into it. He wanted her to accept him simply because she loved him and believed in him.

* * * * *

Jamie sat alone in a cell for what seemed like hours before he heard footsteps and voices. Hearing his name, he knew that *someone* was coming to get him. Most likely to hang him, he thought. Did they have trials in this out-of-the-way place? Or had he already been judged as guilty the way Gillian had judged him? Jamie came to his feet, startled at who he saw standing there with the officer.

"Hugh?" he said. "What are you doing here?"

"He's come to take you home," the officer said as if he resented it. "Turns out we don't have enough evidence to hold you."

"How comforting," Jamie said with sarcasm, wondering if that meant his innocence was still in jeopardy.

"Come along," Hugh said to Jamie. "We'll talk on the way home." He said it with a discreet glance at the officer, as if he wanted to talk privately. Jamie was fine with that.

Once outside, Jamie got into a trap harnessed to one horse, and Hugh sat beside him and took the reins without saying a word.

"Thank you for coming to get me," Jamie said.

"I'm glad to do it," Hugh said.

"Why?" Jamie asked.

Hugh looked surprised. "What do you mean *why?*"

"I would think you'd prefer for me to be guilty and out of the way, although I think Gillian is done with me, so you don't have to worry about that anymore."

"I don't think we should talk about Gillian right now," Hugh said. "The marshal and one of his deputies spoke to Mrs. Miller. She told them everything . . . about how you'd helped her, and how she'd asked you not to tell anyone. Apparently Mr. Miller was found in the woods early this morning by someone out for a walk. It looked like he'd been in a pretty bad fight and that he'd fallen and hit his head on a rock. Mrs. Miller is convinced that Benny is responsible, although he could hardly be held to blame. The boy has some bruises that imply his father was hurting him. It all makes sense, but . . ."

"But it's Mrs. Miller's word against the belief that I was surely out drinking last night, and that I've had disputes with Mr. Miller before. And the bruise on *my* face implies that I must have been fighting with him."

"That seems to be the belief of some, yes."

"Including Gillian," Jamie said.

"We're back to her again?" Hugh asked.

"She thinks I'm guilty without even asking me what happened."

"She can be very stubborn when she wants to be," Hugh said. "She'll come around."

"I'm not sure she will . . . or if I want her to. I think she's better off with you. You're obviously a much better man than I am, Hugh. I say that with sincerity. I'm not sure it's in me to be what Gillian wants—or needs."

"I heartily disagree," Hugh said.

"Why would you say that?" Jamie asked, looking directly at Hugh.

"I want Gillian to be happy. I believe you're the man who can make that happen."

"Yesterday I might have believed that," Jamie said.

"This will blow over," Hugh said.

"Will it?" Jamie asked.

"You've obviously had a very difficult day . . . and last night must have been an ordeal as well. I think you need to get some rest and look at this through fresh eyes tomorrow."

Jamie sighed. "I appreciate your kindness, Hugh—and your advice. I really do. I'm just not so sure that this problem can be solved that easily."

They continued on in silence while Jamie's thoughts slipped away from his own horrific dilemma to the unfathomable attitude of the man sitting beside him. He wondered how Hugh could be so completely selfless in regard to Gillian—and to him. What reason did Hugh have to believe that Jamie had that much potential, to truly make Gillian happy? Ironically, Hugh's example made Jamie want even more to be a better man, whether Gillian wanted him or not. Given the present situation, however, he wasn't certain that any effort he made to become a better man would ever be enough. Would he now be tainted in the community over this event? Whether or not there was evidence enough to legally convict him, he'd been arrested and taken to jail, and surely gossip was spreading. He thought of all of the people he'd gotten to know around town and at church, and he was surprised at how much it hurt to think of them believing badly of him. And then he thought of Gillian, and his heart cracked in half. How could he ever undo what had been done? If she was so quick to believe the worst of him, could he live his life with her, never knowing when she would jump to conclusions and judge him harshly?

As Hugh turned the trap off the road onto the long drive next to the house, he broke the silence between them by saying, "It's going to be all right, Jamie. You just need to trust in the Lord. He'll see you through this."

"And how do I go about that?" Jamie asked, hearing a hint of cynicism laced into his humility.

Hugh pulled the trap to a halt near the barn and turned to look at him. "You do your part, and you ask the Lord to do His. Your part is to do your best to replace your fears and concerns with faith that the Lord *will* help you, after all you can do to make this right. If you're doing your best to make the right choices and handle your life with Christian principles, you are worthy of the Lord's blessings, and I can tell you that He is eager to bless you."

"Me?" Jamie asked, more humble than cynical.

"Yes, you, Jamie. I am living proof that God sees in us what we cannot see in ourselves, and with some faith and effort on our part, He reaches down and lifts us out of the mire, whether it be of our own making or simply matters of the world that are beyond our control."

The conversation ended when five of the Brierley children ran out the door to eagerly greet Jamie as if he'd come home from war as a celebrated hero. He accepted their greetings with laughter and hugs and behaved as if everything was all right, even though his stomach was churning at the thought of facing Gillian. Ian and Wren stepped out onto the porch, smiling over the reunion. Jamie went up the steps with Rachel on his back and Sarah's arms wrapped around his waist. Ian gave Jamie a hearty embrace and repeated exactly what Hugh had said, "It's going to be all right."

Jamie smiled at him, then welcomed an embrace from Wren. "This silly misunderstanding will all get cleared up," she said. "Ye'll see."

"I hope so," Jamie said and was escorted into the house where Gillian was standing at the stove, her back turned to him, her aura bristly. He found it ironic that, of all the family, she supposedly loved him the most, but she was the only one who couldn't even give him a proper greeting.

Jamie was surprised to find Ian right beside him, whispering in his ear, "She'll come around. Don't let her attitude sway what you know in your heart."

"And what is that?" Jamie asked him, equally quiet.

"Your innocence and your intentions," Ian said and then turned his attention to herding the children to where they needed to be. He wondered if Ian had done that on purpose when Jamie found himself alone in the kitchen with Gillian. He wasn't sure where Hugh had gone, but he suddenly wished for his camaraderie. He wondered if Hugh could talk some sense into Gillian.

Jamie felt tempted to just leave the room and save this confrontation for later, then he decided that he would like to have it over with.

"Hello, Gillian," he said.

"Hello," she said in a prickly tone without looking at him.

Jamie refused to ignore this. For all that he was an imperfect man, he deserved better than this from her. "I would think you could give me more than a terse hello. Everyone else was actually happy to see me." He lightened his voice a bit, hoping some sarcasm might ease the tension. "I've had a very trying day, you know. Handcuffs. Jail. Some very *unfriendly* officers."

Gillian glanced over her shoulder for only a second. "You don't look any worse for wear." She took a quick second glance and added, "Although that bruise on your face looks pretty nasty." *Her* sarcasm had no hint of humor; in fact, it was downright biting.

"Your concern and compassion are very touching," he said with the same sarcastic bite.

She let out a huffy sigh, then said, "I assume you were *entirely* innocent in all of this."

"Entirely," he said with a seriousness that caught her attention, and she finally turned to look at him.

"Well?" she said when he didn't say anything more.

"Well what?"

"You're not going to tell me what happened?"

"I was prepared to tell you what happened last night," he said.

"And now?"

"Well . . . as the story goes, I impulsively decided to skip supper and go out and get drunk for some unknown and illogical reason. And since I've been known to have cause for disagreement with Mr. Miller in the past, I apparently followed him home, lured him into the woods, and initiated a terrible fist fight. I obviously got the better of him since I only came away with one blow and he was beaten up rather badly. I didn't intend to kill him, but since he fell and hit his head against a rock, he's dead anyway. And apparently it's all my fault. I should have just minded my own business and not been out doing something I wasn't supposed to be doing."

Gillian could acknowledge the ridiculousness of what he was saying—some of it, at least. She still felt angry with him for putting himself in this situation at all. If he *hadn't* been out doing something he wasn't supposed to, none of this would have happened. But she didn't know how to say that without sounding critical and rude. And she didn't know how to address *any* of it without acknowledging how deeply he'd hurt her. She tried not to let his sarcasm or his anger get to her, but it wasn't easy. When he said nothing more, she tried to bring herself to a point where she could listen to his side of the story with an open mind—even though she didn't want to. She finally said, "But that's *not* what happened? Is that what you're trying to tell me?"

"If I thought that you really wanted to understand what happened, as opposed to judging me as guilty based on your own assumptions, I might feel inclined to tell you what really happened. As it is, I don't think I'm in the mood to have that conversation."

"Well, fine, then," she said, sounding bitterly angry, and surprised at how out of control she felt over her own behavior. "Just keep it to yourself."

"I will," he said and left the room, more angry than she had ever seen him. She figured that gave them something in common.

Days passed with nothing changing and nothing out of the ordinary happening except for the pervasive silence between Gillian and Jamie. Gillian hated it but didn't know what to do about it. She figured that he owed her an apology, and he should be humbly admitting to her that he'd made a mistake. Until that happened, she couldn't see what *she* might do about it. Her siblings had all questioned her about her reasons for being angry with Jamie. She had simply told them all that they were too young to understand, and it was complicated. She almost resented the way they all seemed to favor Jamie's company over her own, but she couldn't deny that she was in a foul mood and she wasn't likely very pleasant to be around.

Gillian's mother had encouraged her to talk about the situation. Wren listened and said little except that Gillian should keep her mind open and not be too hard on Jamie. Gillian felt sure that her mother was so taken in by Jamie's charm that she simply couldn't see the whole truth. Ian too seemed to be under the same illusion that Jamie was completely innocent in this. She pointed out to both of them that where there was smoke there was fire, and his history implied that he surely must have done something to bring on this horrible event of Mr. Miller's death. Each time Gillian tried to imagine what could have happened, she felt so sick inside that she simply couldn't think about it.

The family all attended the funeral service for Mr. Miller. Jamie came as well, and she wondered how he could show his face. She was aware—as she knew he had to be—of some people looking at him askance and whispering. She noticed how both of her parents stayed near Jamie and showed visible approval and acceptance. Of course, that was the Christian thing to do, and she felt sure that she could take a lesson from them in being more Christlike. But she still felt certain they were a little too optimistic in regard to Jamie's character. Gillian was surprised to see Hugh standing at Jamie's side and even putting a hand on his shoulder. She saw them talking quietly and wondered what on earth they might be talking about. Then Hugh actually gave Jamie a brotherly embrace and smiled at him. Had they become friends or something? Based on what? Since Hugh had volunteered to go and get Jamie out of jail, he had been spending more time with the family, and things had seemed more the way they had been before he'd proposed marriage to her. He seemed happy and content and she wondered why. But it wasn't a conversation she felt prepared to open with him. She was *anything* but happy and content. And she almost resented the fact that Hugh might feel that way.

The evening after the funeral, Gillian helped her mother put some baked goods and vegetables into a basket to take over to Sister Miller. While Gillian was trying to arrange them to have a somewhat aesthetic appearance, she said to Wren, "What will they do without Mr. Miller to provide for them?"

"As I see it," Wren said, mildly indignant, "they're better off without him. His death is likely the greatest blessing that could have come t' Benny and his mother."

Gillian gasped. "Are you saying that Jamie was justified in doing what he did?"

Wren gasped more loudly and looked at Gillian as if she'd broken out with purple spots. "Ye really believe that Jamie was responsible for his death?"

"Not intentionally, but . . . don't you?"

Wren took a deep breath, as if Gillian were a three-year-old that required exercised patience. "Whatever I believe is irrelevant. What *ye* believe is breaking Jamie's heart."

"Maybe he deserves a broken heart," Gillian said curtly, and Wren looked even more astonished.

"Maybe ye should go back and reread some specific passages in the Book of Mormon; start with King Benjamin's address, my darling."

"Are you telling me that I shouldn't feel the way I feel?"

"What ye feel is what ye feel," Wren said. "What ye do with what ye feel is another matter." Wren followed her statement with a firm, motherly gaze, then she turned her attention to adding more food to the basket. "As for the Miller family, Mr. Miller had lost his job at the mill due t' his drunkenness and bad manners. He was not providing for their needs, as it was. The Saints will rally around her, as they always do in helping support the widows and orphans. They'll not go without. She's a resourceful woman. I'm certain with time she'll find a way t' meet their needs." She handed the basket to Gillian for delivery. "They have good neighbors, if I say so myself. We'll not let them go without."

"Of course," Gillian said, still stuck on her mother's comment about reading King Benjamin's address. She'd read it. Many times. And she felt insulted to think that her own mother would believe she was out of line, when the situation seemed so obvious.

Gillian delivered the basket to Sister Miller, and stayed a short while to visit. Sister Miller seemed in surprisingly good spirits. At first Gillian felt confused, then she considered what her mother had said about Mr. Miller's death being a blessing. Given what Gillian knew from her own encounters with this family, she realized it was probably true. It seemed callous to consider someone's death a blessing, but there was no disputing the fact that Mr. Miller had caused grief for everyone with whom he came in contact—most especially his wife and his son.

When Gillian was on her way out the door, Sister Miller put a hand on her arm and said, "And tell your sweet cousin hello for me. What a fine man he is! I shudder to think what my poor Benny would have gone through that night if not for Brother MacBrier finding him when he did."

Gillian wanted to demand to know what she was talking about, but given the fact that she lived under the same roof with Jamie, she would have looked like an utter fool to admit that she *didn't* know what Sister Miller meant. Gillian simply nodded and made a gracious departure. Once at home she fled to her room, wondering if her mother was right. If her father was right. If Sister Miller was right. And if they were all seeing something she couldn't see, then she'd made a complete and utter fool of herself already. Her indignant belief that Jamie owed her an apology started to make her feel sick to her stomach. Knowing there was work to be done, she tabled her thoughts and emotions and went downstairs to help put supper on as usual. But afterward she pleaded a headache—which had become completely legitimate—and went to her room, avoiding study time with the family. Instead she courageously opened her Book of Mormon to reread the address of King Benjamin. Struggling through certain phrases, *her soul began to be harrowed up under a consciousness of her own guilt*—just as it was stated in the book of Alma. How could she read the words of this great man in light of the present situation and not wonder what kind of madness had taken hold of her?

The first verse that caught her attention led her to believe that, through her anger and selfishness, she had cut herself off from the guidance of the Spirit, which had left her vulnerable to a distorted way of thinking. It was right there in black and white. *And now, I say unto you, my brethren, that after ye have known and have been taught all these things, if ye should transgress and go contrary to that which has been spoken, that ye do withdraw yourselves from the Spirit of the Lord, that it may have no place in you to guide you in wisdom's paths that ye may be blessed, prospered, and preserved.*

Gillian felt deeply humbled—perhaps humiliated—as she read on, further into the book. *Perhaps thou shalt say: The man has brought upon himself his misery; therefore I will stay my hand, and will not give unto him of my food, nor impart unto him of my substance that he may not suffer, for his punishments are just— But I say unto you, O man, whosoever doeth this the same hath great cause to repent; and except he repenteth of that which he hath done he perisheth forever, and hath no interest in the kingdom of God. For behold, are we not all beggars? Do we not all depend upon the same Being, even God, for all the substance which we have, for both food and raiment, and for gold, and for silver, and for all the riches which we have of every kind?*

Gillian considered the implications. For her, this was not about offering Jamie the actual substance needed for physical survival. It was about how she had withheld her mercy and compassion from him. He was right. She *had* refused to hear his side of the story and had assumed the very worst. She closed her eyes and prayed for forgiveness and understanding and courage, and then she read on.

And behold, even at this time, ye have been calling on his name, and begging for a remission of your sins. And has he suffered that ye have begged in vain? Nay; he has poured out his Spirit upon you, and has caused that your hearts should be filled with joy, and has caused that your mouths should be stopped that ye could not find utterance, so exceedingly great was your joy. And now, if God, who has created you, on whom you are dependent for your lives and for all that ye have and are, doth grant unto you whatsoever ye ask that is right, in faith, believing that ye shall receive, O then, how ye ought to impart of the substance that ye have one to another. And if ye judge the man who putteth up his petition to you for your substance that he perish not, and condemn him, how much more just will be your condemnation for withholding your substance, which doth not belong to you but to God, to whom also your life belongeth; and yet ye put up no petition, nor repent of the thing which thou hast done.

"Oh, what have I done?" Gillian muttered and hung her head while tears slid shamefully down her cheeks. She thought of how her parents—and even Hugh—had given Jamie the love and support that he needed during a difficult time. And she—of all people—had shut him out and behaved so unkindly toward him. She prayed ardently for forgiveness and the courage to make this right. Even while she prayed, she felt compelled to look more closely at another principle that was taught boldly by King Benjamin. His words entered her heart with strength, giving her a deep, abiding hope that she could make this right and make peace with it. *And moreover, I say unto you, that there shall be no other name given nor any other way nor means whereby salvation can come unto the children of men, only in and through the name of Christ, the Lord Omnipotent.* Above all else, Gillian knew in her heart that Jesus was the Christ, and that He had suffered all things for *all* people. But His sacrifice felt deeply personal when she knew she had behaved so contrary to His teachings, and she had surely caused a great deal of pain for Jamie. She didn't know where to begin to make it right, but she did have the good sense to get on her knees and pray with all the energy of her soul.

Throughout the night, Gillian slept only intermittently while she pondered and prayed and shed many tears. By morning she knew that she simply had to start by humbly apologizing to Jamie. Depending on how he responded to that, she would prayerfully decide what to do next. Whether she should marry Jamie and spend her life with him remained to be seen, and it would need to be a matter of serious prayer—even more so than it had already been. For now, she simply needed to ask his forgiveness and try to heal the wounds festering in this current situation. She gathered all her courage before going down to the kitchen to begin her day. If Jamie wasn't already there, he soon would be. And the sooner she could speak to him, the better.

Nearing the bottom of the stairs, Gillian could hear Jamie in the kitchen talking with Alfred and Harry. They had apparently just come in with fresh milk and eggs. She stepped into the kitchen to see Harry go out the back door while Alfred was pouring milk into the pitchers that would be used for breakfast. Jamie turned to see her, while Alfred remained oblivious. Then something happened that froze Gillian solid while her mind became completely consumed. Only then did she realize that it had been many weeks since she had felt or heard any evidence of her mother's spirit close by. The gift she possessed that gave her such great strength had been recently absent. She wondered if that had at least partly been due to her own behavior. Whatever the reason for its absence, it was clearly back. Standing at Jamie's right shoulder, she could see her mother's spirit. She'd rarely actually *seen* anything since her childhood, when her mother had—more than once—guided her away from danger. She was vaguely aware of Jamie staring at her, but her mind was completely focused on the vision before her. She didn't see her mother's lips move, but in her mind, Gillian clearly heard her say, "He was guided here for you, my precious daughter. The posterity you share will be great."

Gillian barely heard the words before the vision faded and she heard Jamie ask, "What's wrong?" She felt startled as she focused on his face, trying to take in what she'd just seen and heard—and what it meant. The warmth in her chest and the tingling of her limbs only verified—in a way that she knew as tried and true—that the Spirit was witnessing the truth of what she'd just experienced. It was not some kind of hallucination or fantasy. It had been an experience of the ministering of angels in its most miraculous form. She felt humbled, awed, and completely overcome.

"Gillian?" Jamie asked, not sounding angry with her at all. He only sounded concerned, and she wondered how he could be so kind when she had been just the opposite. She felt tears burn into her eyes and fall at the same time she heard him say, "You look as if you've just seen a ghost."

Gillian let out a nervous chuckle at the irony of such a comment, then she looked away.

Jamie watched Gillian closely, attempting to understand what had just happened. He felt as if he'd been praying constantly—either on his knees or in his heart—since he'd argued with her days ago. He wanted only to have her forgiveness and understanding. He wondered if something had just occurred in answer to that prayer. She seemed more humble and open, and more like herself than she had since this horrible misunderstanding had occurred. She also had that telltale red spot below her left eye that let him know she'd been crying even before she'd entered the room. But something else had just happened, and he couldn't begin to imagine what.

Even though Gillian wasn't looking at him, Jamie felt intrigued and concerned by the way her eyes had widened at his comment. He tried to figure it out, and wondered what on earth he could say after days of silence between them. Then Alfred walked past him to leave the room and said lightly, "She probably did."

Gillian looked up abruptly, showing visible alarm as a result of what her brother had just said. Jamie realized that he was alone with Gillian at the same moment she seemed to realize it too. He looked hard at her and asked, "What does he mean?"

Gillian had not come down the stairs planning to tell him about this strange gift she possessed. In her heart she had known it was inevitable if their relationship was to continue, but this was not how she'd imagined having it come up. But it *had* come up. She wondered if she should make excuses and put the conversation off until later. Breakfast needed to be made and there was work to be done.

"After breakfast," she muttered and moved past him, setting herself to work.

"Does this mean you'll actually *talk* to me after breakfast?" he asked.

She glanced at him, hoping that he could at least sense some of the humility she felt. "Yes," she said.

"Promise?"

"I promise," she said, and a moment later her mother entered the room, ready to help.

"Is everything all right?" Wren asked.

"Fine," Gillian said, trying to imagine how she might tell Jamie what needed to be said in order to explain what had just happened. She just needed to tell him; simple as that. And if he believed it was crazy, then they could both get on with their separate lives, and her dilemma would be solved. Except that with what she'd just seen, she had to believe that her dilemma was over. She just wasn't sure how to go about accepting it, or exactly what to do now.

By the time breakfast was finished, Gillian felt so bottled up with all she needed to say to Jamie that she wondered whether she might start sobbing simply to vent some of the pressure. She whispered to her mother, "I need to talk to Jamie. Will you be all right with having the girls help you clean up?"

"Of course," Wren said, looking both concerned and hopeful. Gillian knew she had cause for both.

Gillian stood from the table and said to Jamie, who was still sitting, "I believe we need to talk. Will you join me in the parlor?"

"Of course," Jamie said, springing to his feet. His eagerness made her hopeful that this would go well. Had he simply been defensive during these days past few days while she'd been believing he was full of pride and arrogance? Probably. The thought made her stomach churn, but she had to go into this with humility and the faith that her Savior would make up the difference in all the ways she felt short.

Gillian hurried to the parlor, hearing the step of his boots close behind her. She felt an unexpected flutter in her stomach to think of being in the same room with him, and possibly having all of these negative feelings gone between them. She knew she needed to explain to him what had happened earlier, but it seemed more important that she needed to apologize first and get it out of the way. Perhaps his response would determine if she felt comfortable telling him about her gift and sharing what she'd seen.

Gillian walked into the parlor and heard him enter right behind her. He closed the door and said, "Are you all right?"

"I think so," she said. "Or at least . . . I think I will be."

"What did Alfred mean?" Jamie asked.

Gillian turned to look at him. "Let's sit down," she said. "Before I answer that question, there's something else I need to say."

Jamie nodded and took a seat at one end of the sofa. She took the other end. He turned to look at her, and she looked straight ahead to avoid eye contact. "I hope you'll hear me out," she said, "because this isn't easy."

"Did you really think I wouldn't . . . hear you out?" he asked. She glanced at him, then looked straight ahead again. "As long as you're not here to lecture me, I will listen for as long as you want to talk."

Gillian squeezed her eyes closed and said humbly, "No, I'm not here to lecture you. In fact, I'm here to promise that I will never lecture you again. And I will never assume that I know what's going on when I don't, and I need to say that I have no right to judge you or the things you do or the reasons why you do them. I have been entirely inappropriate over this entire situation." Tears began to fall and she wiped at her face. "I don't know what came over me. Perhaps I was just afraid. I don't know. It doesn't matter. I allowed my emotions to get out of hand and completely distort the situation. I don't know what happened or why. I don't know why you did what you did, or what exactly you did, but I sincerely apologize for my judgmental attitude and my bad behavior. I hope that you will find it in your heart to forgive me."

"Who told you what happened?"

Gillian felt surprised but still couldn't look at him. "No one told me. Sister Miller told me she was grateful that you'd found Benny. That's all I've heard. I don't know *what* happened."

"You're asking me to forgive you . . . when you don't know what happened?"

"Yes," she said, afraid that he would be upset with her. And he had a right to be. She just needed to press forward with the hope that time would heal this chasm between them.

"I forgive you," she heard him say with a tremor in his voice. She turned to see tears falling down his face. She felt alarmed over the evidence of his emotion, but he smiled and said, "It seems that God hears my prayers after all. I love you, Gillian. All I need is for you to accept me and believe in me, and I can become the man you need me to become. I know I can."

"Oh, Jamie," she muttered and moved closer, throwing her arms around his neck. "I'm so sorry," she cried and felt such relief to be in his arms that her tears increased and she cried without restraint, her face pressed to his throat. He held her close and pressed a kiss into her hair, making her believe that everything would be all right.

Chapter Thirteen
No Greater Love

"Do you remember," Gillian asked, keeping her head against Jamie's shoulder, "when you asked me to tell you something special about myself, and I told you that I would someday?"

"I remember," he said, a hand on the back of her head.

"I need to tell you," she said, and Jamie drew back, taking her shoulders into his hands so that he could see her face.

"Why now?"

"Because . . . of what happened earlier. And . . . the way it happened. I know by the way your attention was drawn to it . . . and the way I felt . . . that I need to tell you."

Jamie gave an encouraging nod. "Then apparently you need to tell me." She nodded in return but hesitated. "Does this have some connection to what happened when you came down the stairs earlier?"

Gillian nodded again and took a deep breath. "When I was a little girl, my mother—the mother who raised me . . ."

"Wren."

"That's right. She became worried that I had inherited my real mother's illness."

"What illness?" Jamie asked, wondering if Gillian might have some dreadful disease that would cripple her or cut her life short.

"Her mind was ill," Gillian said, and Jamie felt a different kind of concern. "She believed that there were people around her, talking to her, telling her to do things; people who didn't really exist. She died because she threw herself into the ocean. Apparently she did it because she believed that one of these imaginary people had told her to."

"I had no idea," Jamie said.

"It's not discussed much, as you can imagine," Gillian said. "The thing is, when I was a little girl, I started seeing people . . . and talking to them . . . and my mother—Wren—became very concerned. Her sister's illness was very trying for her, so you can imagine her fear."

"Yes, I think I can," he said.

Gillian smiled at him as if she could read his thoughts and said, "There's no need to worry, Jamie. I did *not* inherit my mother's illness. There's nothing wrong with my mind."

"I didn't think so, but I'm not certain where your explanation is leading."

"Just give me a minute. One day I got lost in the woods, and—"

"The day that Hugh found you?" he asked.

"That's right. The thing is . . . I saw a woman who led me away from the river, and she stayed with me until Hugh found me. She told me that she was my real mother, and I went home and told my *other* mother things about my mother's death, and about Hugh, that I had never known. My mother had some spiritual experiences that let her know for certain I was *not* ill. I had been given a very special gift. I've learned over the years that this is true, and I cannot deny it."

Jamie turned his head slightly, as if looking at her from a different angle might make this easier to understand. "What are you saying, exactly?"

"I have what is referred to in the Book of Mormon as the gift of the discerning of angels and ministering spirits." She inhaled, then exhaled, then said, "I can hear angels speak to me, and sometimes I see them."

Jamie leaned back and tried to get his mind to absorb such a concept. He was surprised at how comfortably it settled. He was surprised to hear Gillian say, "You think I'm crazy, don't you."

"Making assumptions again?"

"Sorry," she said, looking down.

"No, I don't think you're crazy. I think it's remarkable."

She looked up again. "You do?"

"I do," he said. "So, what happened today?"

"I'd been praying for the courage to apologize to you . . . and I've been praying for weeks about . . . well, about us. When I came down the stairs and saw you there, my mother was standing beside you." Gillian felt hesitant to tell him exactly what her mother had said, but she did say, "I believe she helped guide you here, Jamie."

She saw a glimmer of moisture in his eyes and heard a subtle tremor in his voice as he said, "That's truly exceptional."

Gillian smiled and asked, "What did you just feel?"

"I don't know. I just . . . felt like it's true."

"That's the witness of the Spirit, Jamie. That's what it feels like. That's how you can know that all the things I've shared with you about the gospel are true."

Jamie absorbed her words and their implication, feeling a deep hope that he might yet be able to come to understand all of the things that were most important to her.

"Are you sure?" she asked.

"About what?"

"That you don't think I'm crazy?"

"I'm sure," he said.

"I know you'll keep this in confidence."

"Of course."

"Beyond my family, practically no one knows this about me."

"Hugh knows."

"That's right. He's spent a great deal of time with the family since I was a child. It was impossible for my family *not* to know what was going on when I was too young to know that talking to people that no one else could see might draw attention to myself."

"That must have been very entertaining," Jamie said and smiled.

Gillian smiled back and said, "Is everything all right between us now?"

"I hope so," Jamie said, but an awkward silence fell between them. "I need to tell you what happened the night Mr. Miller died."

"You don't have to," she said. "If you tell me you're not responsible, I'll believe you."

"You're the most important person in my life, Gillian. I need to tell you what happened. There shouldn't be any secrets between us."

Gillian nodded, secretly relieved to have him tell her, even though she'd felt strongly that her terms of forgiveness could not require any expectations or explanations.

"Sister Miller came to the door, asking for my help to find her husband, who had taken Benny away from the house hours earlier. I told Mont to tell you and your parents that I had gone to find Mr. Miller. Apparently the message didn't come across quite right. I *did* go to the place where I've gone before to drink, but only to look for them. They weren't there, and I left."

Gillian sucked in her breath and had trouble letting it out. Realizing how thoroughly she had misunderstood what he'd done—and his intentions—deepened her regret. She reminded herself that she had already apologized, and he had already forgiven her, but she couldn't prevent the tears from showing in her eyes as she bit her quivering lip. He noticed them and smiled, as if he understood her remorse.

"I went searching in the woods for Benny. It took some time, but I eventually found him. I'm certain that my prayers were answered, or I never would have found him until morning. I looked for Mr. Miller but didn't see him. It was Benny who hit me. He was frightened when I found him, and I approached him too quickly. It startled him, and he swung at me. Apparently it was Benny who hurt his father."

Gillian put a hand over her mouth and whimpered, both from feeling the horror of how frightening the situation must have been for Benny, and also for her own regret at how she'd misjudged the situation.

Jamie went on. "Sister Miller said her husband had been drinking more since he'd lost his job. He'd been especially unkind to Benny and had taken him out, but she didn't know where they had gone, and she was frightened. It would seem Benny's a lot stronger than his father realized, and Benny had no idea what he was doing. He was just trying to defend himself."

Gillian sniffled and said, "Again, I'm so sorry. I was so wrong."

"No more apologies. It's over. Hopefully the people of this community won't think too badly of me. I'd like to be able to find acceptance here. But I don't know how much people will know about the situation. I would rather have them think badly of me than of poor, sweet Benny. What really matters most to me is that *you* don't think badly of me. If I know that you and your family can accept me and not care what others are thinking, then I don't care either."

"Apparently my family has been much more wise and perceptive than I've been."

"It doesn't matter anymore," he said and took hold of her chin to kiss her. "I love you, Gillian."

"Oh, I love you too," she said, and he kissed her again.

"Do you think we could go somewhere together tomorrow?" she asked. "A picnic perhaps."

"I would love to," he said, "but we're going to work on the temple tomorrow. We volunteered for extra shifts since a few men have been ill."

"Of course," she said. "The day after, then."

"We'll plan on it," he said with a smile, and Gillian felt as if the world had turned from dark to light. She knew in her heart that it was only a matter of time before she could give her heart to Jamie, freely and completely.

Through the remainder of the day, Gillian felt better about her life than she had in days—or perhaps ever. That evening between supper and study time, she and Jamie walked around the yard, holding hands, enjoying the cool evening of early autumn. After study time the men went right to bed since they had to be up very early to get to work on the temple site. Gillian slept well that night and didn't wake until daylight, and she knew that Jamie would have left the house by then with Harry and her father. She thought of the irony of a man who had very little understanding of the beliefs of the Saints who had settled in this valley, and yet he was willing to work hard on the construction of a temple—the value of which he had no comprehension at this point. But Gillian understood its value, and it was her deepest wish that Jamie *would* come to understand, and that they could be together forever.

* * * * *

Jamie found as the day wore on that it was an especially pleasant day. The cooler temperatures made the work less miserable, and he could see some progress in the growing foundation of the temple in the weeks since he'd been helping. A very slight progress, but progress just the same. He and the men around him—including Ian, Harry, and Hugh—had actually become quite proficient at lowering the heavy granite blocks into place, which was no small feat considering how weighty and cumbersome they were. But most pleasant of all for Jamie was knowing that everything was right again between him and Gillian. On top of that, he'd had a glimmer of what he could recognize as spiritual feelings, which gave him hope that he was on the right path with his life. He devoted a great deal of thought to what Gillian had shared with him about her special gift and what she'd seen yesterday. He wondered if she had only *seen* her mother standing beside him, or if she'd heard something as well. He wanted to ask when he saw her again, which wouldn't be until very late this evening. He knew they wouldn't be quitting until it was no longer light enough to see what they were doing.

Jamie had no idea that anything was wrong until he heard someone shout indiscernible words of warning the same moment that he was literally shoved from where he was standing, landing him on the ground, mostly on his face. His hands only managed to ward off a portion of the blow, and he felt painfully disoriented—a feeling that was enhanced by the dirt in his mouth and the bite of the ground on his hands and face. The sounds he heard somewhere on the edge of his consciousness were hideous, and what they told him was unthinkable. His heart was pounding with fear before he found the presence of mind to sit up and turn around and assess what had happened. There were so many men gathered in a huddle that he couldn't see *anything*. The words being passed between them incited knots in Jamie's stomach. He finally scrambled to his feet and forced his way through the throng, horrified by what he saw, and what it meant.

"What were you thinking?" Jamie demanded, dropping to his knees beside Hugh. Ian was holding Hugh's head in his lap.

"I . . . wasn't thinking," Hugh said and groaned. The sound combined with the writhing grimace on his face were both evidence that he was enduring pain that was unendurable. "I just . . . did what I was told to do."

"Told?" Ian asked Hugh, but he didn't seem to hear.

Jamie knew that someone had gone for medical assistance, and he'd heard Ian order Harry to go home for Wren and Gillian and bring them here. But the minutes felt eternal while they waited. Jamie could only hold Hugh's hand, feeling his painfully tight grip, and wondering how he was ever going to be able to live with what had just happened.

* * * * *

Gillian and her mother were working together to clean up lunch when they were both startled by the way Harry ran through the door. The fact that he shouldn't have been home at all, along with his panicked expression, let them know something was terribly wrong.

"There's been a dreadful accident," he said. Gillian and Wren both gasped, having no idea *who* had been hurt. "Father wants you both to come . . . now!"

"Who?" Wren muttered with a trembling voice.

"It's Hugh," Harry said. "I'll harness the trap. Hurry."

Gillian and Wren grabbed their bonnets and shawls and instructed the older children to watch out for the little ones, who were both napping. By the time they stepped outside, Harry had harnessed the trap in record speed. He drove at an almost frightening pace toward the center of town where the temple was being built. Gillian's heart was pounding, and her palms were cold with sweat. She wanted to ask what had happened, and how badly Hugh was hurt. But her mouth was so dry she couldn't even open it. The silence that prevailed implied that her mother was suffering from the same ailment. Finally, she heard Wren ask in a trembling voice, "What happened, Harry? Ye must tell us."

By the way *his* voice also trembled when he spoke, Harry had obviously been deeply traumatized. "One of the blocks of granite slipped when it was being unloaded. Hugh was the only one who saw what was happening. I just turned around in time to see him push Jamie out of the way . . . or it would have been Jamie that got hit with it."

Gillian clutched her shawl in her quivering fists in response to the images in her mind and the feelings clutching at her heart. *It could have been Jamie?* The irony put her stomach in knots for more reasons than one. She wanted to ask how badly Hugh was hurt, but Harry's urgency in taking them to him seemed to answer that question. *Hit with a block of granite?* Gillian had taken food to the workers many times. She had seen with her own eyes what they were doing. How could a man survive such an accident? Her instincts told her he couldn't.

"How bad is it?" Wren asked after minutes of silence.

Harry hesitated and cleared his throat. "I think it's real bad. I hope he hangs on till the doctor gets there."

Hangs on? Gillian wanted to scream. They were talking about Hugh! This couldn't be happening! What if he didn't *hang on* until *she* got there? She'd struggled over her complicated feelings for him, but she knew well enough how *he* felt about *her*.

The moment Harry halted the trap, Gillian jumped down and ran toward the huddle of men. She knew Harry would help her mother. While she was scrambling to get to Hugh, she came face-to-face with her father, who seemed to be blocking her view with his body.

"Look at me," he said in a quiet, firm voice. And she did. Her heart pounded into her throat. "The doctor just said that from the appearance of his abdomen, he's bleeding internally and very badly. He won't last much longer." Gillian gasped and put a hand over her mouth. "He also said that his back is obviously broken, and even if he *did* live, he would never walk again. But he *won't* live, Gillian. We've given him a blessing, and I know he won't live. Do you hear what I'm telling you?"

"Yes," Gillian said with forced courage.

"He's in a great deal of pain, but he's asked for you. He needs you to say the right things. Do you understand?" She nodded. "Don't lie to him, but tell him what he needs to hear."

"I understand," she said and tried to draw a deep breath, but she couldn't do it.

Her father turned to guide her through the small crowd, saying loudly, "Let's give them some privacy, shall we?" The concerned men moved back to form a larger circle. Gillian saw Jamie kneeling on the ground, holding tightly to Hugh's hand. The pain on Hugh's face was enhanced by his pallor and the white-knuckled grip with which he held on to Jamie. As she eased toward the two men, she was vaguely aware of hearing her father telling her mother what he'd just told her.

Gillian knelt on the ground next to Hugh, on the opposite side from where Jamie was kneeling. Their eyes met for a long, grueling moment while Hugh was still oblivious to Gillian being there.

"He's been asking for you," Jamie whispered, and she realized he'd been crying. "He's losing strength."

Gillian nodded, then put a hand on Hugh's face. He opened his eyes, but the evidence of pain in his expression was not lessened by the faint smile he gave her. "You came," he muttered, his voice weak and strained.

"I'm here," she said and managed a smile, but she couldn't hold back her tears. She saw tears leak out of the corners of Hugh's eyes, and she had to use great willpower not to sob.

"Don't cry for me," he said. "It's . . . better . . . this way."

Gillian wanted to protest but she could barely speak, and the ironies between them made it difficult to know what to say. Her father's advice came back to her and she said what she knew needed to be said. "I love you, Hugh," she muttered. "You know I do."

"I know . . . you do," he whispered. "You have . . . given me . . . such joy."

Gillian nodded, and her tears increased. Jamie observed the exchange between Hugh and Gillian, and he wanted to unleash what little emotional self-restraint he was holding on to. He felt completely responsible, even if he didn't know how he could have done anything differently. He wanted to die himself, and wished that this situation could be somehow reversed. He felt certain it would be appropriate, somehow.

He became distracted when Gillian looked up, away from Hugh, as if she'd seen something, but nothing had moved in that direction. He thought he was the only one who'd noticed it, but Hugh asked, "Who is here? Someone . . . to get me?"

Fresh tears trickled down Gillian's face as she said, "Many people, Hugh." She laughed softly, a sound that seemed completely out of place for the situation. She looked back at Hugh's face and said with a peaceful voice, "Felicity is here." Hugh's expression softened, and his pain seemed to lessen. Then he smiled when Gillian added, "I think she's glad that the waiting is over."

"I think . . . I'm glad too," Hugh whispered, then his eyes shifted, as if he too could see something that wasn't there.

Ian put a hand on Gillian's shoulder and said, "Give your mother a moment."

Gillian eased back only a little as Wren knelt on the ground and put both her hands to Hugh's face. "We love ye so," she said tearfully. "Ye must know how ye've blessed our lives."

"You've been . . . my family," he said. "I'm . . . very . . . grateful."

Again Hugh's eyes shifted away from Wren, then he lifted his face heavenward, took a ragged breath, and he was gone. Gillian pressed her face to Hugh's shoulder and sobbed uncontrollably. Jamie managed to keep his tears silent, but he couldn't keep them from flowing. Even though Hugh's grip had relaxed into death, Jamie kept a tight hold on his hand, wondering how he was ever going to make peace with this.

* * * * *

It seemed hours before Jamie arrived at the house, even though it had only been minutes. He'd excused himself abruptly, run to where his horse had been tethered, and had ridden home as quickly as he could manage. He rode directly behind the barn, dismounted, and sank to his knees where he knew no one would see him and where he hoped he wouldn't be found. He wrapped his arms around his middle and curled around them, sobbing like a lost child. He heaved painfully until it felt as if his chest would burst open. He rocked back and forth, asking God over and over why this had to happen. He was startled to feel a hand on his shoulder and looked up to see Ian standing at his side. His initial temptation to feel ashamed of his tears seemed pointless. He just looked away and tried to gather some composure.

Ian knelt beside him and tightened his hand on Jamie's shoulder. "You've grown to care for Hugh . . . in spite of the circumstances."

"The circumstances?" Jamie let out a bitter laugh. "You mean that we both love the same woman, and he was by far the better man? *Those* circumstances?"

"Hugh was a good man," Ian said, "but not necessarily a *better* one."

"I'm not certain I agree," Jamie said. He looked at Ian's face. "Why are you not crying like a baby?"

"It will come," Ian said with a quavering voice that implied his grief was close to the surface. "I mostly feel in shock at the moment. I think we're all in shock."

"I would agree with that," Jamie said and groaned. "This is my fault, Ian. It should have been me."

Ian sounded astonished. "How can it possibly be your fault when there is no way you could have possibly prevented it? You didn't even know what happened."

"If I hadn't been there. If I had—"

"How ridiculous is that?" Ian said. "If you hadn't been standing in that spot, someone else would have been."

"But it *wasn't* someone else," Jamie said. "It was *me*. Wasn't it enough that he gave up Gillian for me? Was it really necessary that he give up his *life?*"

"Only God can answer that question, Jamie. Hugh was a good man. If it had not been his time to go, surely God would have provided a way for the accident to be avoided."

Jamie looked hard at his uncle. "You really believe that?"

"I really do," Ian said, but Jamie shook his head.

"I don't know what I believe."

"You're in shock and you're grieving," Ian said. "Now is not the time to try to figure out what you believe. It will come in its own time." Ian took hold of Jamie's arm and urged him to his feet as he stood himself. "Come into the house and be with the rest of us, so we can all be in shock together."

Jamie went along, feeling the shock settle in and numbing his desire to cry. But perhaps that was best. He and Ian cared for the horses and were on their way out of the barn when Jamie said, "What if Gillian blames me for this . . . the way she blamed me for Mr. Miller's death?"

Ian stopped walking and stared at him, aghast. "Do you really think she would do that?"

"I don't know," Jamie said.

"I thought that was all taken care of."

"I thought so too, but obviously we have a new complication to contend with, and I—"

"You're getting yourself worked up when you don't even know if there's a problem." Ian took hold of Jamie's arm again and guided him toward the house. "You'll only know how she feels when you talk to her. I suspect she needs you."

"I hope you're right," Jamie said, because he certainly needed *her.*

Jamie found Gillian sitting in the parlor, as unmoving as stone, gazing ahead at nothing. He figured if she'd wanted to be alone, she would have gone to her room. She apparently didn't hear him come into the room, but when he closed the door she looked up at him, startled. With a great lack of grace, she sprang to her feet and bolted into his arms, holding to him as if he could save her. He wasn't sure that he could. But he held to her just as tightly, glad that they were at least in this together. Her shock melted into mournful tears and he guided her back to the sofa where they sat together and cried in each other's arms. The irony was horrible. The loss felt unbearable. Jamie didn't know how to come to terms with it, and he certainly didn't know how he might possibly help Gillian through this when he couldn't imagine getting through it himself. All he could do was hold her and pray that she could forgive him for taking Hugh away from her and from her family.

* * * * *

Attending Hugh's funeral was likely the most difficult thing Jamie had ever done. Losing his grandmother had been very hard on him. But it hadn't been like this. He couldn't stop feeling that it should have been *him* in the casket, and it might have been better if it *had* been. The service was beautiful, and Jamie heard many words of peace and comfort being spoken. He knew that he should be able to take them into his heart, but they just wouldn't penetrate. At the cemetery, Jamie considered it a privilege to be one of the men who was allowed to help carry Hugh's casket to its final resting place, along with Ian, Harry, Alfred, and even Ward. They were aided by a few men Jamie hardly knew who were friends of Hugh's. Since Ian and Ward had been the missionaries who had found Hugh in London, they had remained his closest friends ever since. Jamie had felt hesitant to take on this duty when Ian had asked him, but it seemed only fitting that he be allowed to help escort Hugh to the grave, when Hugh had given his life so that Jamie could live.

Later that day, Jamie sat in the study, staring toward the window. He could hear a great deal of commotion in the kitchen and knew that supper was being put on the table. But he didn't feel like eating, and he certainly didn't feel like socializing. Ward and Patricia and their children were here and would be joining the family for supper. He barely felt comfortable exposing any evidence of his grief to the family. He certainly wouldn't be exposing it with anyone else around. So, he preferred to remain in here and hope that no one noticed—or cared about—his absence.

While his thoughts wandered through sporadic memories of his interactions with Hugh, Jamie was surprised to find himself staring at the Bible that was lying innocently on a little table next to the chair where he sat. He felt constrained to pick it up even while he consciously thought that he was far too distracted to read. The book was way too cumbersome for him to hope to be able to find anything in particular that might offer him comfort. He set the spine of the book on his lap and allowed it to fall open in his hands. At the very same moment, Jamie felt as if someone were in the room with him, but when he turned to look, he saw no one there. He glanced down at the book on his lap, then he could have sworn that he heard a woman say his name. Again he turned, but no one was there. A gentle chill rushed over him, and he wondered for a moment if he might be sensing the presence of an angel, the way that Gillian did. When the feeling subsided he dismissed the thought as silly and turned his attention back to the book in front of him. He scanned the page that the Bible had fallen open to, stunned by the phrase he was reading. It was as if the words had been illuminated by light. *Greater love hath no man than this, that a man lay down his life for his friends.*

Jamie gasped and felt his heart tighten in his chest. He couldn't believe what he was reading. Of the millions of words in the Bible, he was reading *that*? And what did it mean? "I don't understand," he said aloud, as if someone might hear him and explain. He closed his eyes and made his plea more specifically prayerful. "Please, God. Help me understand!"

A light knock at the open door startled him, and he looked up to see Ian.

"Are you all right?" his uncle asked.

"Not really."

Ian stepped into the room and closed the door. "Is there anything I can do?"

Jamie wondered if the timing of his appearing and asking such a question could possibly be a coincidence. He trusted Ian more than any man he knew. He figured it couldn't hurt to ask. "Maybe," he said. "Perhaps you could explain to me why the Bible fell open to *this* page, and why I could see only *these* words, and *what exactly* it's supposed to mean."

Ian leaned over Jamie and read the phrase that Jamie was pointing to. "You've obviously been guided," he said.

"Have I?" Jamie asked, looking up at him.

"The Spirit often answers our prayers by guiding us to specific passages of scripture. My experience has been that what I read, combined with what I feel, gives me an answer I've been seeking. This has obvious significance to the present situation."

"I suppose it does," Jamie said. "But . . . I can't . . ." his voice trembled, ". . . comprehend that Hugh would. . . ." He couldn't finish.

Ian scooted a chair closer and sat on it so that he could look directly at Jamie. "As I see it, Jamie, there's only one thing that you need to truly understand here. If you can take this *one* concept into your heart, everything else will fall into place, and you will find peace."

Jamie looked at him eagerly, desperately hoping there was some such concept that could solve all of this confusion and eradicate all of this pain. "I'm listening," Jamie said, noting that Ian's expression became more intense.

With a hand on Jamie's shoulder, Ian said with quiet strength, "You need to realize, Jamie, that what Hugh did for you physically, the Savior has done for you spiritually. Hugh is gone. That cannot be changed, and wallowing in regret over what can't be changed is completely fruitless and will only lead you to anguish and despair. Rather than seeing this as something unfair and difficult to accept, try seeing it as a gift. If you believe that Hugh gave his life for you, then what are you going to do with that life?"

Jamie sucked in his breath as the question struck him deeply. He became fully absorbed in Ian's words as he went on. "He's given you a precious gift, Jamie. So live your life to its fullest; live it the way that Hugh would want you to live it."

Make Gillian happy, Jamie heard in his head, as if it had been spoken by a voice that existed inside of his mind, and yet the thought hadn't come from him.

Ian continued. "You also need to understand, Jamie, that our Savior already suffered all of this for us. He not only took upon himself all of our sins and mistakes, but he took upon himself our sorrow, our pain, our grief. When you can accept *that* into your heart, and give your burdens to Him, you will understand *why* Hugh gave his life for you, and you will understand everything else, too."

"Everything else?" Jamie echoed.

"You'll understand why we came here, why we live the way we do, why Gillian wants so desperately for you to share her beliefs. She wants you to be happy. We *all* want you to be happy. That's what Hugh wanted too. I believe that's probably what was going through his mind when he did what he did."

"He wants *Gillian* to be happy."

"You don't believe that her happiness and yours go hand in hand?" Ian asked, and Jamie couldn't answer. With what they felt for each other, he knew it was true.

"There is *no* other source of true happiness, Jamie. You've spent enough time in our home, sharing study and prayer with us, and going to church with us, to put the pieces together. It's the only right answer to every question that matters."

Jamie felt stunned and overwhelmed as Ian's words seemed to fly around his head, attempting to find a comfortable place to settle. As if Ian sensed his need to have some time to himself, he stood up and said, "I'm available any time, day or night, if you need to talk."

"Thank you," Jamie said.

"Are you coming to supper?"

"I . . . uh . . . no, thank you. I need to be alone."

"I understand," Ian said and left the room, closing the door behind him. Jamie looked down again at the Bible on his lap, and the words illuminated there. *Greater love hath no man than this, that a man lay down his life for his friends.* Ian was right. It had double meaning. Hugh had spared him physically, but the spiritual meaning in regard to the Savior was something more difficult for him to grasp. He slammed the book closed and set it aside, then he hurried to his bedroom, closed the door, and sank to his knees beside the bed, crying before he could even begin his prayer.

The room grew dark and the house became quiet before Jamie moved with difficulty off his knees and onto the bed, where he curled up and tried to assess and understand all he was feeling. And that's when it happened. He hadn't known exactly what he'd been searching for all this time, or how it would feel when he found it. Even while it was happening, he wondered how he would try to describe it, and he could find no words. He only knew that he felt a warm swelling in his chest at the same moment his mind felt enlightened with an enormous amount of understanding. Everything that Ian had said to him earlier made perfect sense, and he knew it was true. It was all true! The peace and comfort that filled him were so complete and intense that he never would have imagined such feelings to be possible. Everything made sense! Everything felt right! Everything!

Jamie sprang from his bed, wondering if he could find Gillian and talk with her. He wasn't even certain how late it was, but he had to try. How could he possibly hold all of this inside? He lit a lamp and opened the door of his room to find her standing there, about to knock. They were both startled and both let out a gasp at the same time, then they both laughed.

"What are you doing?" they both said at the same time and laughed again. But they were laughing. It seemed the only emotion he could express. Given the circumstances, and the way he'd been feeling since Hugh's death, it seemed undeniable evidence of the miracle that had taken place inside of him.

"I just had the most amazing thing happen," Gillian said, "and I couldn't wait to tell you."

Jamie smiled and felt gratified to see that she noticed, and she smiled too. "I don't think it could be any more amazing than what *I* was coming to tell *you.*"

Gillian's eyes widened and sparkled in the lamp light. "You go first."

"No, you go first," he said and guided her across the hall to the parlor where he set the lamp down. They sat on the sofa, turning toward each other. "Tell me," he insisted. "I can't bear the suspense."

Gillian didn't speak. She was looking into his eyes as if she were searching for something, then she smiled as if she'd found it. "Something's changed," she said. "You're different."

Jamie laughed again, feeling such perfect joy. "Am I?" he asked. "Is it so obvious?"

"To me it is," she said. "You go first."

"No," he insisted. "You go first. If you want to know why I feel different, you're going to have to hurry."

"Very well," she said. "I was just about to get changed for bed when I felt a presence in the room with me."

Jamie drew in a deep breath as he realized what she meant, and he was surprised to also realize that he already knew who it had been. But he waited for her to tell him.

"Jamie," she took both his hands into hers, "it was your grandmother."

He smiled, gratified with his own inspiration. He *was* different! Something had changed inside of him, as if some kind of floodgate had opened, allowing him to feel and see life from a completely different perspective.

"She wanted me to tell you that she has been with you, that she led you here, and that she guided you to the passage in the Bible."

For all that Jamie had been feeling the truth of her words, he felt startled. "Did you speak with your father this evening?"

"About you, you mean? No. He told everyone that you were skipping supper and needed some time. That's all. Why?"

"Nothing," he said, overcome again with that swelling sensation in his chest. "Go on."

"I also realized something else," she said. "When I heard her voice, I knew it was familiar. She was with me in the garden, Jamie, several days before you came here. I know now that it was her."

"Remarkable," Jamie whispered, in awe.

"This part doesn't make sense to me, but I think it will make sense to you. She said to tell you that she has gone to the place where there are rainbows without rain."

Jamie suddenly found it impossible to breathe. He'd not doubted the verity of Gillian's gift. But what she'd just said made it completely impossible to ever doubt that she had this miraculous ability to hear and see angels. He had to force himself to breathe when his chest began to burn for want of air. Hot tears stung his eyes, then trickled down his face.

"What's wrong?" Gillian asked, tightening her hold on his hands. "Have I upset you?"

"No," he muttered, forcing himself to take another breath. "I'm fine. Just . . . give me a moment." While he was gathering his ability to think clearly, the entire circumference of what had occurred— to both of them—settled more fully into his spirit. He pulled her into his arms and held her close, crying into her hair. She held him close and whispered of her love for him along with reassurances that everything would be all right. He took her shoulders into his hands and whispered, "Everything *will* be all right, Gillian. I know it will."

She smiled and asked, "What does it mean? Rainbows without rain?"

Jamie laughed softly. "It was something my grandmother used to say about where she imagined my grandfather to be. A place where there would be rainbows without rain. She told me many times that it was a secret between us, that she'd never shared the thought with anyone else. You couldn't have possibly known." He touched her face. "It's a miracle."

"Yes, it is," she said and sighed. "Now it's your turn. Tell me what you were coming to tell me."

"Where do I begin?" he asked and laughed again. "I've never imagined I could be this happy, Gillian." He saw tears pool in her eyes and said, "You already know *what's* changed in me."

"I can guess," she said. "In theory, at least. But tell me. Tell me everything."

Jamie kissed her first, then he took her hand and told her every detail of how his life had completely changed in the hours since he'd realized that Hugh had given him the gift of being alive. He could see now, as he verbalized the experience, that it had been coming on slowly, that he'd been working toward it for many weeks. But the miracle was too enormous to hold, and too undeniable to ever question. He knew now why the Saints had sacrificed so much to come to this valley, and he knew why Gillian had been holding out with the hope that he would come to know these things for himself. Now, as he looked into her eyes, his entire future—in this world and in the world to come—spread out before him with perfect clarity. He had come to this place hoping for a fresh start. He had never expected to discover the truth of who he really was. But he had. He'd found it through Gillian's love, through the acceptance of this beautiful family, and through the sacrifice of a dear friend. And mostly he had found it through the grace of his Savior. With so many miracles, Jamie felt sure that Hugh would be pleased to know that the gift he'd given him would be put to good use.

Epilogue

Jamie sat on the back porch, glad to have been given the job of holding the baby while she slept. It was one of his favorite things to do. Through the open door he could hear a great deal of commotion in the kitchen as Sunday dinner was being put on the table for the entire family and some close friends. He wasn't certain where they were all going to sit, but he knew from vast experience that the Brierley family always found a way to manage.

Jamie heard footsteps and looked up to see Ian. "Mind if I join you?" he asked.

"Not at all . . . Grandpa." He chuckled. "I love calling you that."

"I love being called that," Ian said, then he smiled at Jamie. "You gave a beautiful blessing earlier for your daughter. I confess it moved me to tears."

Jamie looked down at his new little girl and admitted, "It was one of the greatest privileges life has afforded me."

"Yes, I know what you mean."

"I'm certain you do."

"And I must confess that it thrills me to hear that her surname is Brierley."

"As I've told you before, it only seemed right that we all share the same name, since we all belong to the same family."

"Yes, I know," Ian said. "But it still thrills me."

"I'm glad to hear it," Jamie said.

"And it thrills me to know that this child has been born into an eternal marriage."

"That thrills *me* as well."

"There's something I've been meaning to tell you," Ian said.

"Something good, I hope."

"I think so," Ian said. "Do you remember the first morning you woke up in my home?"

"With a hangover, you mean?" Jamie chuckled. "I remember."

"I told you then that we needed each other. Do you remember *that*?"

"Come to think of it, I do." Jamie turned more toward his father-in-law. "You told me I needed a family—which was absolutely true. But you never *did* tell me why you needed *me*."

"I've thought about telling you, many times, but it never seemed like the right moment."

"And now is the right moment?"

"I believe so," Ian said and turned toward the noise coming from inside the house. "It's the first big social event in your new home. I'm certain there will be many more."

"I'm certain of it. That's why Gillian insisted we build such a large kitchen." A burst of noise from the children erupted from inside, making both men chuckle. "Good thing we did."

"She has excellent insight, your wife," Ian said.

"She does, but you've changed the subject. I'm waiting to hear how you needed me."

The conversation was interrupted when Gillian stepped outside and carefully took the baby out of Jamie's arms. "Hey, what are you doing?" he demanded in a quiet voice.

"I need you to get the extra chairs from the parlor," she said and put the baby in her father's arms. "Besides, Grandpa's been waiting all day to hold her."

"I have, yes," Ian said, looking down at his beautiful grand-daughter.

Gillian turned back to Jamie and kissed him. "Thank you, my darling. We'll be ready to eat in just a few minutes."

"A pleasure," Jamie said, squeezing her hand before she went into the house, smiling at him over her shoulder as she did.

"There's your answer," Ian said, gazing at the baby.

"What answer?" Jamie asked.

"You see that smile on Gillian's face?"

"I see a smile on *your* face right now," Jamie said as he stood up.

"And why wouldn't I smile?" Ian asked. "You've made Gillian a very happy woman, and you've made Wren and me very happy as a result. That's why I needed you."

Jamie sat back down. "Are you telling me that's what you were thinking that first morning, when I had a hangover?"

"That's what I was thinking," Ian said, smiling at him. Then he smiled down at the baby. "Go get the chairs, Jamie. As you can see, I'm very busy."

Jamie chuckled and went into the house, stopping on his way to the parlor to grab Gillian by the arm and drag her into the hall, away from the crowd.

"What are you doing?" she laughed.

Jamie kissed her and whispered, "Thank you."

"For what?" she asked, surprised.

"Everything," he said and kissed her again until she shooed him away to get the chairs.

About the Author

Anita Stansfield began writing at the age of sixteen, and her first novel was published sixteen years later. Her novels range from historical to contemporary and cover a wide gamut of social and emotional issues that explore the human experience through memorable characters and unpredictable plots. She has received many awards, including a special award for pioneering new ground in LDS fiction, and the Lifetime Achievement Award from the Whitney Academy for LDS Literature. Anita is the mother of five and has two adorable grandsons. Her husband, Vince, is her greatest hero.

To receive regular updates from Anita, go to anitastansfield.com and subscribe.